The outstanding mind and personality of his time

François Marie Arouet de VOLTAIRE was a center of controversy throughout his life.

Born in 1694 to an influential family, he had easy access to the nobility and the highest society. But his prodigious talent, his passionate hatred for injustice and oppression, his unparalleled courage and daring in expressing his beliefs—all served to win him as many enemies as friends, numerous exiles and even two terms in the Bastille.

Voltaire's more than fifty plays, many of them spectacular successes, established him as the greatest dramatist of his age. He also wrote essays, verse and history.

But he is best remembered as one of the world's immortal satirists, the man who with his clear, direct style became the spokesman for the anticlerical and rationalist ideas of the entire Age of Enlightenment.

Luther—work for god

Voltaire—work selfish for yourself

CANDIDE
& ZADIG

—◆—

VOLTAIRE

Translated by
TOBIAS GEORGE SMOLLETT

Edited and with
an Introduction by
LESTER G. CROCKER

WASHINGTON SQUARE PRESS
POCKET BOOKS • NEW YORK

CANDIDE & ZADIG

WASHINGTON SQUARE PRESS edition published October, 1962
5th printing.....................October, 1976

A new edition of a distinguished
literary work now made available in
an inexpensive, well-designed format

Published by
POCKET BOOKS, a division of Simon & Schuster, Inc.,
A GULF+WESTERN COMPANY
630 Fifth Avenue, New York, N.Y. 10020.

WASHINGTON SQUARE PRESS editions are distrib-
uted in the U.S. by Simon & Schuster, Inc., 630 Fifth
Avenue, New York, N.Y. 10020, and in Canada by Simon
& Schuster of Canada, Ltd., Markham, Ontario, Canada.

Candide or the Optimist

CONTENTS

CONTENTS

Chapter		Page

Zadig or Fate an Oriental History

INTRODUCTION

In 1758, Voltaire had lost his high zest for life. He was in a trough of despondency. At sixty-four, not many illusions are left—not, at least, when one has the corrosive realism of a mind like Voltaire's.

It had not always been that way. Once, as a brash and cynical youth, he had soared, a new star, into the glittering heavens of the aristocratic salons. The young François Marie Arouet (that was his real name), gifted with coruscating wit and a genius for verse, had pushed hard for fame and worldly recognition. Reckless with the *hubris* of youthful success, he had daringly tweaked the noses of the great, until his insolence sent him to a cell in the Bastille, and from there to England, where he discovered that men could be free. When he returned, in 1729, chastened and resolved on prudence, he dedicated himself to building a fortune and exiled himself to safely located country estates near Switzerland—with an interval in Paris and, later, at the court of Frederick the Great, where he spent three years that started in sweetness and ended in bitterness. World fame came quickly. He was the greatest dramatist of the age and its outstanding neoclassical poet. His philosophical tales and his histories were unmatched in conception and execution. After a few minor, youthful love affairs, he formed a *liaison*, destined to last sixteen years, with one of France's most brilliant women, Mme. de Châtelet, mathematician, scientist, philosopher—and passionate mistress.

Life was good. Voltaire sang his optimism in poetry and expounded it in prose. He mocked the primitivists' regrets for a golden age—"Oh, what a good time is this century of iron!" Happiness was available, in any social rank, he said, for the man who knew how to live wisely and love wisely. And all over Europe, among intellectuals, the doctrine misnamed "optimism," spread by Leibnitz and by Voltaire's favorite poet, Alexander Pope, acted like an opiate: "Everything is for the best in the best of all possible worlds."

Then the tide ran out. As the middle years of the century approached and youth ebbed to a distant, lost shore, Voltaire's horizon became tinged with more somber hues. Always fragile, he now worried constantly about his health. Mme. du Châtelet, perhaps seeking a more vigorous lover, perhaps looking for revenge after Voltaire had succumbed to the charms of his young widowed niece, had taken on the dashing Marquis de Lambert. She died, in 1749, in giving birth to her new lover's child.

It was an end, now, to Voltaire's tight little autonomous world at Cirey. Off to Berlin, then, and to a still unhappier experience. But it was not only what was happening to him. It was his view of man and the world that was changing. He had been unable to hold on to his cherished belief in free will. God exists, he was still sure of that, but what help is He to man? Voltaire pondered, wondered, doubted. The doctrine of optimism began to seem absurd, antihumanistic, antiprogressive. As he delved into the annals of the past, he found the same tale of human cruelty, meanness, selfishness and folly, written in the same letters, wherever he turned. And it was little better in his own century, the "century of philosophy." Were not he and his comrades constantly persecuted by an intolerant church, by an archaic regime unswervingly hostile to dissent, freedom and new ideas? The world was run, not by reason, but by folly and ambition; the quarrel between the Church and the Parlements, and especially the Seven Years' War (1756–1763) were ample testimonials to the charge.

Slowly, the lights grew dimmer. In 1738 he had already admitted that evil is in equilibrium with good: "Unhappiness is everywhere, but happiness, too." In his tales and poems we can follow the course of encroaching gloom. *Zadig* (1747) is a first crisis. The story is a parable, in which Voltaire seems to be doing his best to convince himself that, in the total scheme, all *is* well, and that we are presumptuous in trying to judge what is beyond our ken. That he is not successful is apparent in the climactic scene in which Zadig, overpowered by the angel but unconvinced, keeps repeating a "but" pregnant with human protest, and to which no answer is forthcoming. It is akin to Job's intellectual refusal, even as he bows to the fact that God is God. The angel is triumphant, in the sense that all does work out according to right and justice—something that Voltaire knew did not always happen in life. But Zadig's protest does not lose its significance. It anticipates, without going so far, the rebellion of Ivan Karamazov's "even if." Even if he were wrong, even if Father Zossima's way were the way of salvation, Ivan would not accept salvation at the price of evil, of suffering and wrong done to the innocent and in exchange for the implied acceptance of such a world of God.

Voltaire finally had to choose (to use Camus' phrase) between the realm of grace and the realm of justice. As a humanist, his decision, despite his agony, could not be in doubt. But it was complicated and obscured by his desire to retain the sacred (a moral world of God) as a support and guarantee for the human. Thus Zadig both accepts the divine plan and protests against it. Why should it have to be done this way? Why should good and justice have to be brought about through evil and injustice? These agonizing questions are the implications of Zadig's "but," to which Voltaire knew there could never be an answer.

It is typical of Voltaire's spirit and method that the underlying anguish never shows. *Zadig* is a swift-moving tale of adventures, with a succession of ups and downs that never allows an instant's relaxation in our enthrallment with the trials of its virtuous hero. Voltaire merely makes us see that virtue and the world are at odds and not meant for each other. He does so with endless and delightful humor, taking every opportunity, *en route*, to puncture the foibles of men, women, customs and institutions with the dazzling rapier thrusts of his incomparable irony. Yes, all does work out well; but we cannot avoid the impression that it is because of a *deus ex machina* ending—like Victoria's messenger at the conclusion of *The Threepenny Opera*, snatching an incredible pardon from the grinding wheels of the unpardoning mill of life.

Another tale, *Memnon*, written in 1750, shows Voltaire to be further shaken. The world is *not* exactly an insane asylum, "but it is close to being one." The following year, we find him portraying God as a capricious being, always looking for something to keep himself from boredom, constantly disarranging his little system. "He puts fever in our climates and the remedy in America." Voltaire, who had read (if not admired) Shakespeare, may well have recalled the famous line from King Lear, "As flies to wanton boys, are we to the gods."

Although Voltaire was already cutting loose from optimism before the great Lisbon earthquake of 1755, that event had a compelling and dramatic effect on him, as it did on countless other consciences, provoking his most emotional work, the important *Poème sur le désastre de Lisbonne* (1756). Its central theme is that providence may well exist, but it certainly ignores the well-being of man on earth. What has happened in Lisbon is not just. "Will you say, It is the effect of eternal laws that necessitate the choice of a free and good God?" The Leibnizian optimist not only insults human pain, but condemns us to a despairing philosophy of necessity. "We are then only wheels that make the great machine run; we are no more precious in God's eyes than the animals that devour us." And an indifferent God seemed to Voltaire like none at all, so far as our living and our values are concerned. Such a God, he later said, results in each man being "a god to himself," ready to sacrifice the whole world to his fancies. Here Voltaire borders on a profound tragic perception—man is a stranger in a world not made for his categories.

We do not know what impelled Voltaire, in 1758–59, to write *Candide*. We do know that this slender work stands out, in the fifty large volumes of his collected writings, as his one immortal masterpiece. After two centuries its freshness has not even begun to fade. It is a masterpiece because it reaches down into the deepest problems of human existence and transmutes our dilemmas and uncertainties into the graphic representation of art.

On the surface a simple, even a superficial work, even one of improvisation, *Candide* was actually the result of long months of labor, and it is both complex and profound. Like many great classics, it starts out to be one thing, and ends by being many more. Voltaire wrote *Candide* to demolish a pretentious and false philosophy of the day, mistakenly labeled "optimism." But if this were its ultimate range, *Candide* would have a very limited audience today. Even when it was written, optimism was already a waning philosophy. It is not without significance that in the same year as *Candide* appeared, Samuel Johnson published his *Rasselas*, a work with remarkable similarities to it, but heavy-handed, narrow in scope and lacking the spark of genius. The failure of optimism to account for evil in terms satisfactory to human realities was becoming apparent. The devout were uneasy about its contradiction of Christian doctrine, and the progressive *philosophes* rejected it as a formula for paralysis and pessimism. The rise of scientific materialism was even more fatal to it; evil, for materialists like Diderot and La Mettrie, who conceived a world without values, was merely a subjective reaction. But Voltaire was enraged by the "insulting" absurdity of optimism, and disgusted with the spiderwebs of metaphysics—which he could never understand very well, anyhow.

Candide has remained alive as a great work because of the richness of its meanings and the perfection of its art. It evolves on a series of levels. Beyond the question of optimism, beyond the local satire of contemporary society, it offers us a general view of man. The portrait, a profoundly pessimistic one, stems from Voltaire's contemplation of the human present and the human past. Beneath the optimism that surged forth in the eighteenth century with the rise of science, the faith in education and in the rational reconstruction of society, lay a deep pessimism about man himself. It is best seen in the psychology that reduced motivation to pleasure and self-interest. Voltaire reflects this ambivalence in his efforts for reform and enlightenment, and in his portrait of man.

In *Candide* we see that men find relish in evil. They are cruel, stupid, intolerant, greedy, savage, selfish, rapacious, unjust; not to mention many other equally unflattering epithets listed by Candide in the last paragraph of Chapter XXI. We see the cruelty and corruption of men reflected in their institutions: the courts of "justice," the Church, slavery, wars, monarchy and aristocracy. The past and the present are unchangeable signposts to the future, because men will no more improve their nature than sparrow hawks. Only in El Dorado are men happy. And El Dorado is a kingdom they cannot get to, and where they would not stay if they could; for man is an ever restless, unsatisfied being, devoured by the rage to excel and to dominate others, by the drive for prestige and power.

But Voltaire's pessimism is even more radical: just as it surpasses the local conditions of a particular culture, so also does it extend beyond human nature itself. Its final reach embraces a universe that is indifferent to human fate and without recognizable moral value or plan. In *Candide*, as he does at several other moments of his career, Voltaire reveals a tragic view of human destiny. "You see," says Candide to Martin, "that crime is sometimes punished; that scoundrel of a Dutch shipowner has had the fate he deserved." "Yes," says Martin, "but did the passengers who were on the ship have to perish too?" The good Jacques' reward is to be drowned, while the sailor who is evil, but strong, is saved, so that he may work further evil. Voltaire finally compares us to the rats in a ship, whose comfort is of no concern to the shipowner.

Though the meanings of *Candide* are multiple, there is a basic unity, necessary to a great work of art. The unity lies in the ultimate question posed by the story. What basis for action is there, what justification or direction, in a world such as this satire exposes? Through *Candide*, Voltaire comes to know the blackness of nihilism. Its challenge and the response are the questions with which he finds himself grappling. They were not the original subject, to be sure—Voltaire did not intend to write about these matters. But in refuting optimism he was compelled to, because he was compelled to paint a picture of the world as it is—and it turns out to be the *worst* of all possible worlds. The problem is constantly brought out by his method, which is to oppose the *candid* attitude to life's realities. The candid attitude would be fine if this were, not the best of all possible worlds (a phrase that is meaningless in terms of the good), but a *decent* world, one that corresponded in some degree to human needs, as well as to moral notions. But from the beginning, the candid attitude is defeated by the realities of existence, both natural and human. The clash is symbolized ironically and humorously by Candide's search for an ideal, in the form of Cunegund, and its outcome. Candide, at the end of his long road of suffering, comes to realize the harsh truth.

The essential element in the Voltairean response to these realities is his belief that, everything considered, reason is man's best (and his distinctive) weapon in fending off the trials of life and in dealing with its problems. That is why Voltaire is the archfoe of all the mystic and antirational philosophies of his time and of ours. By "reason" he clearly does not mean ratiocination, an arid and abstract philosophizing. His "reason" is, first of all, common sense, and then the pragmatic. It is philosophy in action. Over and above these, it is that supreme play of the intellect for setting things in their true perspective and restoring balance, that cleanser and objectifier: irony.

In the light of this ironic rationalism, the ultimate implications of Voltaire's attack on optimism become clear. The discovery of universal evil is not, for him, the surrender to despair. He has wrestled with the angel of darkness; he has known real anguish in his struggle with what we, in the twentieth century, would call "the absurd." His determination is to reject both extremes, that of the mystic, that of the nihilist. He refuses to choose between the sacred and destructive revolt, between all or nothing. He accepts God as a defense against nihilism, but refuses to justify God. While he does not submit to despair, he has no neat refutation to offer, no vista of unlimited hope. What is left, then? A human way: to avoid Pascal's absolutes and infinities, to accept the pragmatic and the utilitarian—a circumscribed view and field of action.

There is, then, resignation to the inevitability of evil in *Candide*, but no total surrender, no cynical feeling of "What's the use? Let's do like the others." The rational attitude seeks a balance, based on the real and the possible. The rejection of Pangloss through Candide's experiences is the revenge of common sense against quixotism of all kinds, whether in philosophy or in life. In order to cure some evil, we must first reject the notion that all is good, and, paradoxically, accept the notion that evil is an ineradicable, incurable reality. Only then can we know man's nature, his place and his best course on earth. This is Voltaire's constructive revolt, against the world, against man, against history. We must give up aiming for the stars, but refuse, too, to join the wolves: we must cultivate our garden. Our garden is the limited realm of virtue, justice and honest labor that is within the compass of our creative powers. We must start at home, in our own little worlds. Many will feel that the philosophy of *Candide* has never been more needed than today.

Voltaire was the master of the "philosophical tale," a genre designed for the popularizing of ideas. His genius raised it from the level of propaganda to that of literature.

The essential value of the philosophic tale lay in its effective presentation of a point of view, and that effectiveness depended on two elements: action and style. First of all, the interest of the reader had to be captured and fixed. This implies "story value." The "philosophy" of the *conte philosophique* had to be in action more than in words; yet it also called for a judicious mixture of palatable, unmistakably clear moralizing, to drive the points home. It is just this *mélange* that Voltaire succeeds in creating almost to perfection in *Candide*. Two of the episodic characters, Martin and Pococurante, formulate the conclusions, which are obvious and clear in the case of the former, novel and provocative in the mouth of the latter. In both situations, Candide acts (to use the jargon of our own day) as "stooge," or sounding-board, for their views; and always their ideas are drawn from specific events or situations that give their words a veneer of reality and the concrete.

However, it is the story itself that carries us along and Voltaire's narrative art is seen here at its best. His secret is in the rapidity with which events succeed each other: just as a situation seems settled, a new circumstance unexpectedly arises, creating a new turn and twist that carries the reader forward with unabated curiosity. The situation is always an unhappy one, for Voltaire is writing a satire of optimism. The new turn often promises a better fortune, a hope that is inevitably belied, as the concatenation of circumstances, in this "best of all possible worlds," leads always to misfortune. The events themselves are utterly fantastic, but this fantasy is ambivalent. Voltaire exploits the most outrageously romantic inclinations in his readers at the same time as he is creating a delightful burlesque of all novels of adventure, of his day and of ours. All the time-worn devices are utilized: fantastic reunions and recognitions, pirates, kidnapings, sudden flight. The chapter headings summarize the story in traditional style. The stock characters—prostitutes, corrupt monks, innocent heroines, swindlers and the like—are all present, and are frequently given the stock adjectival attributes ("the faithful Cacambo," "the prudent Cacambo"). The reader is aware of the tongue-in-cheek, but is carried on with all the greater interest, as he both yields to the naive romanticism that is in us all and simultaneously contemplates it with amused objectivity.

Each episode, with its reversals, terminates in sudden flight. The narrative thus acquires one of its most notable characteristics: the sensation of movement and the feeling of space. There is no settling down until the very end, when the philosophical search is over, its resolution attained. We are transported on a magic carpet to the four corners of Europe, to the New World and the Levant. We journey with the hero, learning with him, by dint of accumulated experiences, that nowhere on earth—except in the unattainable El Dorado—does Pangloss' philosophy of optimism correspond with reality. The geographical diversity imparts a universal value to the lesson.

From the aesthetic viewpoint, it is regrettable that Chapters XXII and XXV break up the rhythm and movement. The satire in these two chapters, though often amusing in its revelations of the foibles of contemporary Paris, is too long, and in places too topical to be of lasting interest.

The *philosophical tale* is a genre of restricted scope and

value. Its limits are inherent in its definition, and their viola-
tion would betray its purpose. It does not aspire to the quali-
ties of a great novel: the creation of individual character and
of present reality in the whole, or the relating of substan-
tially complete characters to their living environment. In the
philosophical tale, the scope is narrowed, the perspective
foreshortened. The author, it is true, is not so tightly bound
as in the modern short story. Nonetheless, psychology must
yield to propaganda and ideas; the human element is sub-
servient to the story itself, though it may ultimately receive
illumination from the ideas. The characters are all on the surface, restricted to several pertinent characteristics to which
are added a few conventional or caricatural effects. They are
the author's puppets, no more. We cannot say that Voltaire
has surpassed the limits of the genre. He did not, in any case,
possess the ability to create character; but in this instance his
weakness does no disservice to his form, for working within
its confines he succeeds in giving his figures a maximum of
life. They are fresh and humorous, react vigorously and capture our imagination. Candide and Pangloss, and to a lesser
degree the minor characters, remain as sharply etched in our
memories as those heroes of novels whom we know more
deeply and more in the round. Candide, most of all, charms
us with his candor, as he reacts with disarming naiveté to the
wickedness of men and tries desperately to remain loyal to
his beloved master's philosophy.

Voltaire's overall method of ideological propaganda em-
ploys a variety of technical devices, but principally a devas-
tating ridicule. He refutes ideas not by logic but by a *reductio
ad absurdum*. This *reductio* has two aspects, the episodic and
the stylistic.

Voltaire is above all operating on concrete materials. He is
demolishing an abstract philosophy, a metaphysic that denied the existence of evil and turned its back to the realities of
life. His method is precisely to accumulate the "realities of

life" in concrete form: the adventures and experiences of all the characters. These are inevitably fashioned by the cruelty, stupidity and vices of the human species. The story grows into a catalogue of horrors, each one of which pricks the balloon of a pompous and empty philosophy with an explosive effect that no logical disputation could ever have. *Candide* may be called, then, a burlesque with a serious purpose; an apparently lighthearted tale with undertones of pessimism and bitter satire. The serious and the burlesque are constantly intermingled, with the latter predominant. The names are burlesque. The characters are divided between the straightforward (Martin, Jacques), the burlesque (Pangloss, the Baron) and those who are a mixture. Voltaire never lets the action or conversation remain serious for too long; he knows the right moment to shade it into the humorous, or to break it up with the brusque intrusion of the adventurous or the comic.

Voltaire's style is the other aspect of his offensive technique. It is at its exquisite best in *Candide,* lucid, limpid and graceful, a keen-edged instrument for the play of ideas. It is above all gay and festive, imparting to the whole work the tonalities of a lampoon. It is impudent and disrespectful, picturesque, incisive and at times a bit too "gallic" for a puritanical taste. Poor in emotional or lyrical values, it abounds in wit and irony.

Wit is a purely intellectual play of words or ideas that hits upon incongruous relations or analogies. Thus the old woman urges Cunegund to marry the Spanish governor, Don Fernando d'Ibaraa y Figueora y Mascarenas y Lampourdos y Souza, the greatest lord of South America, "who has a very handsome moustache." The natives declare with relish, "We shall eat well, let us eat Jesuit." Irony is a unique weapon of the intellect, combining subtlety and depth. Irony is a way of destroying: it annihilates false values or illusions. It works by an affirmation of the false value that simultaneously and patently involves its negation. Irony is also frequently verbal, as when Pococurante's pretentiousness and dogmatism are pricked by Candide's naive remarks, "Oh, what a superior man! . . . Nothing pleases him!" But irony, unlike wit, does not have to depend entirely on word play. It may be equally implicit and effective in action and in situation. While the world lies in ruins, covered with a bleeding, crippled, slaughtered humanity, the Churches sing *Te Deums* for a glorious victory. At the *auto-da-fé*, the ladies are served refreshments between the mass and the execution. Candide, expecting to find the best of all possible worlds, encounters everywhere the worst of all possible worlds. The rationalist is universally belied by absurdity. Honesty meets only deceit, and good impulses are repaid by cruelty and rapacity. Happiness, which all men seek, exists only in a realm men cannot get to, and where they would not stay. Candide roams the world and faces death a dozen times in dogged pursuit of the beautiful Cunegund, only to win her at the end in the form of a repulsive and shrewish hag. Such are the victories of men!

—LESTER G. CROCKER

Western Reserve University

CANDIDE

OR

THE OPTIMIST

Translated from the German of DOCTOR RALPH*

With the additions that were found in the Doctor's pocket
when he died at Minden, in the year of grace 1759.

---

* James Ralph, a minor English poet and dramatist
(1705–1762), satirized by Pope in *The Dunciad*.

CHAPTER I

HOW CANDIDE WAS BROUGHT UP IN A MAGNIFI-CENT CASTLE, AND HOW HE WAS DRIVEN FROM THENCE

In the country of Westphalia, in the castle of the most noble Baron of Thunder-ten-tronckh, lived a youth whom nature had endowed with a most sweet disposition. His face was the true index of his mind. He had a solid judgment joined to the most unaffected simplicity, and hence, I presume, he had his name of Candide. The old servants of the house suspected him to have been the son of the Baron's sister, by a mighty good sort of a gentleman of the neighborhood, whom that young lady refused to marry because he could produce no more than threescore and eleven quarterings in his arms; the rest of the genealogical tree belonging to the family having been lost through the injuries of time.

The Baron was one of the most powerful lords in West-phalia, for his castle had not only a gate but even windows,* and his great hall was hung with tapestry. He used to hunt with his mastiffs and spaniels instead of greyhounds; his groom served him for huntsman, and the parson of the parish officiated as grand almoner. He was called "My Lord" by all his people, and he never told a story but everyone laughed at it.

My lady Baroness weighed three hundred and fifty pounds,

---

* An ironical reference to wealth, since taxes were laid on doors and windows. Voltaire had been struck by the poverty and backwardness of Westphalia.

consequently was a person of no small consideration; and then she did the honors of the house with a dignity that commanded universal respect. Her daughter Cunegund was about seventeen years of age, fresh colored, comely, plump, and desirable. The Baron's son seemed to be a youth in every respect worthy of his father. Pangloss* the preceptor was the oracle of the family, and little Candide listened to his instructions with all the simplicity natural to his age and disposition.

Master Pangloss taught metaphysico-theologo-cosmolo-nigology.** He could prove admirably that there is no effect without a cause, and that, in this best of all possible worlds, the Baron's castle was the most magnificent of all castles and my lady the best of all possible baronesses.

"It is demonstrable," said he, "that things cannot be otherwise than they are; for as all things have been created for some end, they must necessarily be created for the best end. Observe, for instance, the nose is formed for spectacles, therefore we wear spectacles. The legs are visibly designed for stockings, accordingly we wear stockings. Stones were made to be hewn, and to construct castles, therefore my lord has a magnificent castle; for the greatest baron in the province ought to be the best lodged. Swine were intended to be eaten; therefore we eat pork all the year round. And they who assert that everything is good do not express themselves correctly; they should say that everything is for the best."

Candide listened attentively, and believed implicitly; for he thought Miss Cunegund excessively handsome, though he never had the courage to tell her so. He concluded that next to the happiness of being Baron of Thunder-ten-tronckh, the next was that of being Miss Cunegund, the next that of seeing her every day, and the last that of hearing the doctrine

---

* "Pangloss," from the Greek words for "all" and "tongue," or "windbag."
** "Nigology," from the French word for "booby."

of Master Pangloss, the greatest philosopher of the whole province, and consequently of the whole world.

One day, when Miss Cunegund went to take a walk in a little neighboring wood, which was called a park, she saw, through the bushes, the sage Doctor Pangloss giving a lecture in experimental physics to her mother's chambermaid, a little brown wench, very pretty, and very tractable. As Miss Cunegund had a great disposition for the sciences, she observed with the utmost attention the experiments which were repeated before her eyes; she perfectly well understood the force of the doctor's reasoning upon causes and effects. She retired greatly flurried, quite pensive, and filled with the desire of knowledge, imagining that she might be young Candide's sufficient reason and he hers.*

On her way back she happened to meet Candide; she blushed, he blushed also. She wished him a good morning in a faltering tone; he returned the salute, without knowing what he said. The next day, as they were rising from dinner, Cunegund and Candide slipped behind the screen. She dropped her handkerchief; the young man picked it up. She innocently took hold of his hand, and he as innocently kissed hers with a warmth, a sensibility, a grace—all very extraordinary—their lips met, their eyes sparkled, their knees trembled, their hands strayed. The Baron of Thunder-ten-tronckh chanced to come by; he beheld the cause and effect, and, without hesitation, saluted Candide with some notable kicks on the breech and drove him out of doors. Miss Cunegund fainted away, and, as soon as she came to herself, the Baroness boxed her ears. Thus a general consternation was spread over this most magnificent and most agreeable of all possible castles.

---

* A satire of Leibniz's famous "principle of sufficient reason," which Voltaire found incomprehensible, and so a model of metaphysical obfuscation and futility.

CHAPTER II

WHAT BEFELL CANDIDE AMONG THE BULGARIANS

CANDIDE, thus driven out of this terrestrial paradise, wandered a long time, without knowing where he went; sometimes he raised his eyes, all bedewed with tears, toward Heaven, and sometimes he cast a melancholy look toward the magnificent castle where dwelt the fairest of young baronesses. He laid himself down to sleep in a furrow, heartbroken and supperless. The snow fell in great flakes, and, in the morning when he awoke, he was almost frozen to death; however, he made shift to crawl to the next town, which was called Waldberghoff-trarbk-dikdorff, without a penny in his pocket, and half dead with hunger and fatigue. He took up his stand at the door of an inn. He had not been long there before two men dressed in blue fixed their eyes steadfastly upon him.

"Faith, comrade," said one of them to the other, "yonder is a well-made young fellow, and of the right size."

Thereupon they went up to Candide, and with the greatest civility and politeness invited him to dine with them.

"Gentlemen," replied Candide, with a most engaging modesty, "you do me much honor, but, upon my word, I have no money."

"Money, sir!" said one of the men in blue to him. "Young persons of your appearance and merit never pay anything. Why, are not you five feet five inches high?"

"Yes, gentlemen, that is really my size," replied he with a low bow.

"Come then, sir, sit down along with us. We will not only pay your reckoning, but will never suffer such a clever young fellow as you to want money. Mankind were born to assist one another."

"You are perfectly right, gentlemen," said Candide; "that is precisely the doctrine of Master Pangloss; and I am convinced that everything is for the best."

His generous companions next entreated him to accept a few crowns, which he readily complied with, at the same time offering them his note for the payment, which they refused, and sat down to table.

"Have you not a great affection for—"

"Oh, yes!" he replied. "I have a great affection for the lovely Miss Cunegund."

"Maybe so," replied one of the men, "but that is not the question! We are asking you whether you have not a great affection for the King of the Bulgarians?" *

"For the King of the Bulgarians?" said Candide. "Not at all. Why, I never saw him in my life."

"Is it possible! Oh, he is a most charming king! Come, we must drink his health."

"With all my heart, gentlemen," Candide said, and he tossed off his glass.

"Bravo!" cried the blues. "You are now the support, the defender, the hero of the Bulgarians; your fortune is made; you are on the high road to glory."

So saying, they put him in irons and carried him away to the regiment. There he was made to wheel about to the right, to the left, to draw his ramrod, to return his ramrod, to present, to fire, to march, and they gave him thirty blows with a cane. The next day he performed his exercise a little better, and they gave him but twenty. The day following he came

---

* I.e., Prussians.

off with ten and was looked upon as a young fellow of surprising genius by all his comrades.

Candide was struck with amazement and could not for the soul of him conceive how he came to be a hero. One fine spring morning, he took it into his head to take a walk, and he marched straight forward, conceiving it to be a privilege of the human species, as well as of the brute creation, to make use of their legs how and when they pleased. He had not gone above two leagues when he was overtaken by four other heroes, six feet high, who bound him neck and heels, and carried him to a dungeon. A court-martial sat upon him, and he was asked which he liked best, either to run the gauntlet six and thirty times through the whole regiment, or to have his brains blown out with a dozen musket balls. In vain did he remonstrate to them that the human will is free, and that he chose neither. They obliged him to make a choice, and he determined, in virtue of that divine gift called free will, to run the gauntlet six and thirty times. He had gone through his discipline twice, and the regiment being composed of two thousand men, they composed for him exactly four thousand strokes, which laid bare all his muscles and nerves, from the nape of his neck to his rump. As they were preparing to make him set out the third time, our young hero, unable to support it any longer, begged as a favor they would be so obliging as to shoot him through the head. The favor being granted, a bandage was tied over his eyes, and he was made to kneel down. At that very instant, his Bulgarian Majesty, happening to pass by, inquired into the delinquent's crime, and being a prince of great penetration, he found, from what he heard of Candide, that he was a young metaphysician, entirely ignorant of the world. And, therefore, out of his great clemency, he condescended to pardon him, for which his name will be celebrated in every journal, and in every age. A skillful surgeon made a cure of Candide in three weeks by means of emollient unguents prescribed by Dioscorides. His sores were now skinned over, and he was able to march when the King of the Bulgarians gave battle to the King of the Abares.*

CHAPTER III

HOW CANDIDE ESCAPED FROM THE BULGARIANS, AND WHAT BEFELL HIM AFTERWARDS

NEVER was anything so gallant, so well accoutered, so brilliant, and so finely disposed as the two armies. The trumpets, fifes, oboes, drums, and cannon, made such harmony as never was heard in hell itself. The entertainment began by a discharge of cannon, which, in the twinkling of an eye, laid flat about six thousand men on each side. The musket bullets swept away, out of the best of all possible worlds, nine or ten thousand scoundrels that infested its surface. The bayonet was next the sufficient reason for the deaths of several thousands. The whole might amount to thirty thousand souls. Candide trembled like a philosopher and concealed himself as well as he could during this heroic butchery.

At length, while the two kings were causing *Te Deum* to be sung in each of their camps, Candide took a resolution to go and reason somewhere else upon causes and effects. After passing over heaps of dead or dying men, the first place he came to was a neighboring village, in the Abarian territories, which had been burned to the ground by the Bulgarians in accordance with international law. Here lay a number of old

---

* I.e., French. The Seven Years' War had begun in 1756.

men covered with wounds, who beheld their wives dying with their throats cut, and hugging their children to their breasts all stained with blood. There several young virgins, whose bellies had been ripped open after they had satisfied the natural necessities of the Bulgarian heroes, breathed their last; while others, half burned in the flames, begged to be dispatched out of the world. The ground about them was covered with the brains, arms, and legs of dead men.

Candide made all the haste he could to another village, which belonged to the Bulgarians, and there he found that the heroic Abares had treated it in the same fashion.* From thence continuing to walk over palpitating limbs or through ruined buildings, at length he arrived beyond the theater of war, with a little provision in his pouch, and Miss Cunegund's image in his heart. When he arrived in Holland his provisions failed him; but having heard that the inhabitants of that country were all rich and Christians, he made himself sure of being treated by them in the same manner as at the Baron's castle before he had been driven from thence through the power of Miss Cunegund's bright eyes.

He asked charity of several grave-looking people, who one and all answered him that if he continued to follow this trade, they would have him sent to the house of correction, where he should be taught to earn his bread.

He next addressed himself to a person who had just been haranguing a numerous assembly for a whole hour on the subject of charity. The orator, squinting at him under his broad-brimmed hat, asked him sternly what brought him thither and whether he was for the good cause.

"Sir," said Candide, in a submissive manner, "I conceive there can be no effect without a cause; everything is necessarily concatenated and arranged for the best. It was necessary

---

* Voltaire was not noted for his patriotism. His detachment enables him to flay both sides.

that I should be banished from the presence of Miss Cunegund, that I should afterward run the gauntlet, and it is
necessary I should beg my bread till I am able to earn it: all
this could not have been otherwise."

"Hark you, friend," said the orator, "do you hold the Pope
to be Antichrist?"

"Truly, I never heard anything about it," said Candide,
"but whether he is or not, I am in want of something to eat."

"You deserve not to eat or to drink," replied the orator,
"wretch, monster that you are! Hence! Avoid my sight and
never come near me again while you live."

The orator's wife happened to put her head out of the window at that instant, when, seeing a man who doubted
whether the Pope was Antichrist, she discharged upon his
head a chamber pot full of ——. Good heavens, to what excess does religious zeal transport the female kind!

A man who had never been christened, an honest Anabaptist ° named James, was witness to the cruel and igno-
minious treatment showed to one of his brethren, to a two-
footed featherless being, who had a soul. °° Moved with pity,
he carried him to his own house, cleaned him up, gave him
meat and drink, and made him a present of two florins, at the
same time proposing to instruct him in his own trade of weav-
ing Persian silks which are fabricated in Holland. Candide
threw himself at his feet, crying:

"Now I am convinced that Master Pangloss told me truth,
when he said that everything was for the best in this world,
for I am infinitely more affected by your extraordinary generosity than by the inhumanity of that gentleman in the black
cloak and his wife."

The next day, as Candide was walking out, he met a beg-

° Voltaire looked with favor on the sixteenth-century sect.
°° The Anabaptist adds the soul to the famous definition of man of a Greek
philosopher, to whom Antisthenes, the Cynic, thereupon presented a plucked
chicken.

gar all covered with scabs, his eyes were sunk in his head, the end of his nose was eaten off, his mouth drawn on one side, his teeth as black as coal, snuffling and coughing most violently, and every time he attempted to spit, out dropped a tooth.

CHAPTER IV

HOW CANDIDE FOUND HIS OLD MASTER IN PHILOSOPHY, DR. PANGLOSS, AGAIN AND WHAT HAPPENED TO THEM

CANDIDE, divided between compassion and horror, but giving way to the former, bestowed on this shocking figure the two florins which the honest Anabaptist James had just before given to him. The specter looked at him very earnestly, shed tears, and threw his arms about his neck. Candide started back aghast.

"Alas!" said the one wretch to the other, "don't you know your dear Pangloss?"

"What do I hear? Is it you, my dear master! You I behold in this piteous plight? What dreadful misfortune has befallen you? What has made you leave the most magnificent and delightful of all castles? What is become of Miss Cunegund, the mirror of young ladies and nature's masterpiece?"

"Oh, Lord!" cried Pangloss, "I am so weak I cannot stand."

Thereupon Candide instantly led him to the Anabaptist's stable, and procured him something to eat. As soon as Pangloss had a little refreshed himself, Candide began to repeat his inquiries concerning Miss Cunegund.

"She is dead," replied the other.

Candide immediately fainted away. His friend recovered him by the help of a little bad vinegar which he found by chance in the stable. Candide opened his eyes.

"Dead! Miss Cunegund dead!" he said. "Ah, where is the best of worlds now? But of what illness did she die? Was it for grief upon seeing her father kick me out of his magnificent castle?"

"No," replied Pangloss, "her belly was ripped open by the Bulgarian soldiers after they had ravished her as much as it was possible for damsel to be ravished. They knocked the Baron her father on the head for attempting to defend her; my lady her mother was cut in pieces; my poor pupil was served just in the same manner as his sister; and as for the castle, they have not left one stone upon another; they have destroyed all the ducks, and the sheep, the barns, and the trees. But we have had our revenge, for the Abares have done the very same thing in a neighboring barony, which belonged to a Bulgarian lord."

At hearing this, Candide fainted away a second time, but having come to himself again, he said all that it became him to say. He inquired into the cause and effect, as well as into the sufficient reason, that had reduced Pangloss to so miserable a condition.

"Alas!" replied the other. "It was love: love, the comfort of the human species; love, the preserver of the universe, the soul of all sensible beings. Love! Tender love!"

"Alas," replied Candide, "I have had some knowledge of love myself, this sovereign of hearts, this soul of souls. Yet it never cost me more than a kiss and twenty kicks on the backside. But how could this beautiful cause produce in you so hideous an effect?"

Pangloss made answer in these terms: "Oh, my dear Candide, you must remember Pacquette, that pretty wench, who waited on our noble Baroness. In her arms I tasted the pleasures of paradise, which produced these hell-torments with which you see me devoured. She was infected with the disease and perhaps is since dead of it. She received this present of a learned Franciscan monk, who derived it from the fountainhead; he was indebted for it to an old countess, who had it of a captain of horse, who had it of a marchioness, who had it of a page; the page had it of a Jesuit, who, during his novitiate, had it in a direct line from one of the fellow-adventurers of Christopher Columbus. For my part I shall give it to nobody, I am a dying man."

"Oh, Pangloss," cried Candide, "what a strange genealogy is this! Is not the devil the root of it?"

"Not at all," replied the great man. "It was a thing unavoidable, a necessary ingredient in the best of worlds,* for if Columbus had not, in an island of America, caught this disease, which contaminates the source of generation, and frequently impedes propagation itself, and is evidently opposite to the great end of nature, we should have had neither chocolate nor cochineal.** It is also to be observed that, even to the present time in this continent of ours, this malady, like our religious controversies, is peculiar to ourselves. The Turks, the Indians, the Persians, the Chinese, the Siamese, and the Japanese are entirely unacquainted with it; but there is a sufficient reason for them to know it in a few centuries. In the meantime, it is making prodigious progress among us, especially in those armies composed of well-disciplined hirelings, who determine the fate of nations; for we may safely affirm that, when an army of thirty thousand men fights another equal in number, there are about twenty thousand of them poxed on each side."

"Very surprising, indeed," said Candide. "But you must get cured."

"How can I?" said Pangloss. "My dear friend, I have not

---

* Voltaire mocks Pope's "all partial evil, universal good."
** A dye made from insects indigenous to Central America.

a penny in the world; and you know one cannot be bled or have a clyster without a fee."

This last speech had its effect on Candide. He flew to the charitable Anabaptist James, he flung himself at his feet, and gave him so touching a picture of the miserable situation of his friend that the good man, without any further hesitation, agreed to take Dr. Pangloss into his house and to pay for his cure. The cure was effected with only the loss of one eye and an ear. As he wrote a good hand and understood accounts tolerably well, the Anabaptist made him his bookkeeper. At the expiration of two months, being obliged to go to Lisbon about some mercantile affairs, he took the two philosophers with him in the same ship. Pangloss, during the voyage, explained to him how everything was so constituted that it could not be better. James did not quite agree with him on this point.

"Mankind," said he, "must, in some things, have deviated from their original innocence; for they were not born wolves, and yet they worry one another like those beasts of prey. God never gave them twenty-four pounders nor bayonets, and yet they have made cannon and bayonets to destroy one another. To this account I might add not only bankruptcies but the law, which seizes on the effects of bankrupts only to cheat the creditors."

"All this was indispensably necessary," replied the one-eyed doctor, "for private misfortunes are public benefits; so that the more private misfortunes there are, the greater is the general good."

While he was arguing in this manner, the sky was overcast, the winds blew from the four quarters of the compass, and the ship was assailed by a most terrible tempest, within sight of the port of Lisbon.

CHAPTER V

A TEMPEST, A SHIPWRECK, AN EARTHQUAKE;
AND WHAT ELSE BEFELL DR. PANGLOSS,
CANDIDE, AND JAMES THE ANABAPTIST

ONE half of the passengers, weakened and half dead with the inconceivable anguish which the rolling of a vessel at sea occasions to the nerves and all the humors of the body, tossed about in opposite directions, were lost to all sense of the danger that surrounded them. The other made loud outcries, or betook themselves to their prayers. The sails were blown into shivers, and the masts were brought by the board. The vessel leaked. Everyone was busily employed, but nobody could be either heard or obeyed. The Anabaptist, being upon deck, lent a helping hand as well as the rest, when a brutish sailor gave him a blow and laid him speechless. But, with the violence of the blow, the tar himself tumbled head-foremost overboard and fell upon a piece of the broken mast, which he immediately grasped. Honest James flew to his assistance and hauled him in again, but in the attempt was thrown overboard himself in sight of the sailor, who left him to perish without taking the least notice of him. Candide, who beheld all that passed and saw his benefactor one moment rising above water, and the next swallowed up by the merciless waves, was preparing to jump after him, but was prevented by the philosopher Pangloss, who demonstrated to him that the coast of Lisbon had been made on purpose for the Anabaptist to be drowned there. While he was proving his argument *a priori*, the ship foundered and the whole crew perished except Pangloss, Candide, and the brute of a sailor who had been the means of drowning the good Anabaptist. The villain swam ashore, but Pangloss and Candide got to land upon a plank.

As soon as they had recovered a little, they walked toward Lisbon. With what little money they had left they thought to save themselves from starving after having escaped drowning.

Scarce had they done lamenting the loss of their benefactor and set foot in the city, when they perceived the earth to tremble under their feet, and the sea, swelling and foaming in the harbor, dash in pieces the vessels that were riding at anchor.° Large sheets of flames and cinders covered the streets and public places. The houses tottered, and were tumbled topsy-turvy, even to their foundations, which were themselves destroyed, and thirty thousand inhabitants of both sexes, young and old, were buried beneath the ruins.

The sailor, whistling and swearing, cried, "Damn it, there's something to be got here."

"What can be the sufficient reason of this phenomenon?" said Pangloss.

"It is certainly the day of judgment," said Candide.

The sailor, defying death in the pursuit of plunder, rushed into the midst of the ruin, where he found some money with which he got drunk, and after he had slept himself sober, he purchased the favors of the first good-natured wench that came his way, amid the ruins of demolished houses, and the groans of half-buried and expiring persons. Pangloss pulled him by the sleeve.

"Friend," said he, "this is not right, you trespass against universal reason, and have chosen an improper time."

"Death and zounds!" answered the other, "I am a sailor, and born at Batavia, and have trampled four times upon the

---

° The great Lisbon earthquake occurred on November 1, 1755.

crucifix in as many voyages to Japan.* You have picked the right person with your universal reason."

Candide, who had been wounded by some pieces of stone that fell from the houses, lay stretched in the street almost covered with rubbish.

"For God's sake," said he to Pangloss, "get me a little wine and oil. I am dying."

"This concussion of the earth is no new thing," replied Pangloss. "The city of Lima in America experienced the same last year. The same cause, the same effects. There is certainly a train of sulphur all the way under ground from Lima to Lisbon."**

"Nothing more probable," said Candide, "but, for the love of God, a little oil and wine."

"Probable!" replied the philosopher. "I maintain that the thing is demonstrable."

Candide fainted away, and Pangloss fetched him some water from a neighboring spring.

The next day, in search among the ruins, they found some eatables with which they repaired their exhausted strength. After this, they assisted the inhabitants in relieving the distressed and wounded. Some, whom they had humanely assisted, gave them as good a dinner as could be expected under such terrible circumstances. The repast, indeed, was mournful, and the company moistened their bread with their tears, but Pangloss endeavored to comfort them under this affliction by affirming that things could not be otherwise than they were.

"For," said he, "all this is for the very best end. For if there is a volcano at Lisbon, it could be on no other spot. For

---

* An act required for admission to Japan, ever since the Portuguese had been implicated in a plot in 1637.

** Satire of current theory of earthquakes, propounded by Buffon and others.

it is impossible for things not to be as they are, for everything is for the best."

By his side sat a little man dressed in black, who was one of the familiars of the Inquisition. This person, taking him up with great politeness, said, "Possibly, my good sir, you do not believe in original sin. For if everything is best, there could have been no such thing as the fall or punishment of man."

"I humbly ask your Excellency's pardon," answered Pangloss, still more politely. "For the fall of man and the curse consequent thereupon necessarily entered into the system of the best of worlds."*

"That is as much as to say, sir," rejoined the familiar, "you do not believe in free will."

"Your Excellency will be so good as to excuse me," said Pangloss. "Free will is consistent with absolute necessity, for it was necessary we should be free, for in that the will—"

Pangloss was in the midst of his proposition, when the familiar made a sign to the armed attendant who was helping him to a glass of port wine.

---

* Voltaire mocks controversies that actually took place between Christian opponents of optimism and Leibniz's disciples.

CHAPTER VI

HOW THE PORTUGUESE MADE A SUPERB AUTO-DA-FÉ* TO PREVENT ANY FUTURE EARTHQUAKES, AND HOW CANDIDE UNDERWENT PUBLIC FLAGELLATION

AFTER the earthquake which had destroyed three-quarters of the city of Lisbon, the sages of that country could think of no means more effectual to preserve the kingdom from utter ruin, than to entertain the people with an *auto-da-fé*, it having been decided by the University of Coimbra that burning a few people alive by a slow fire and with great ceremony is an infallible secret to prevent earthquakes.

In consequence thereof they had seized on a Biscayan for marrying his godmother,** and on two Portuguese for taking out the bacon of a larded pullet they were eating.† After dinner, they came and secured Dr. Pangloss and his pupil Candide, the one for speaking his mind and the other for seeming to approve what he had said. They were conducted to separate apartments, extremely cool, where they were never incommoded with the sun. Eight days afterward they were each dressed in a *sanbenito*,†† and their heads were adorned with paper miters. The miter and *sanbenito* worn by

---

* A ceremonial public execution held by the Inquisition. The one referred to here took place on June 20, 1756.

** This was held to contravene the established spiritual relationship.

† This was considered by the Inquisition to be an infallible sign of belonging to the Jewish faith.

†† A black sackcloth garment, painted with figures of devils, etc., identifying the several crimes.

Candide were painted with flames reversed and with devils that had neither tails nor claws; but Dr. Pangloss' devils had both tails and claws, and his flames were upright. In these habits they marched in procession, and heard a very pathetic sermon, which was followed by a chant, beautifully intoned. Candide was flogged in regular cadence while the chant was being sung. The Biscayan and the two men who would not eat bacon were burned, and Pangloss was hanged, although this is not a common custom at these solemnities. The same day there was another earthquake, which made most dreadful havoc.*

Candide, amazed, terrified, confounded, astonished, and trembling from head to foot, said to himself, "If this is the best of all possible worlds, what are the others? If I had only been whipped, I could have put up with it, as I did among the Bulgarians. But, O my dear Pangloss! You greatest of philosophers! That ever I should live to see you hanged, without knowing for what! O my dear Anabaptist, you best of men, that it should be your fate to be drowned in the very harbor! O Miss Cunegund, you mirror of young ladies! That it should be your fate to have your belly ripped open."

He was making the best of his way from the place where he had been preached to, whipped, absolved, and received benediction, when he was accosted by an old woman, who said to him, "Take courage, my son, and follow me."

---

* A second tremor had actually occurred on December 21, 1755. Voltaire takes poetic license with the dates.

CHAPTER VII

HOW THE OLD WOMAN TOOK CARE OF CANDIDE, AND HOW HE FOUND THE OBJECT OF HIS LOVE

CANDIDE followed the old woman, though without taking courage, to a decayed house where she gave him a pot of ointment· to anoint his sores, showed him a very neat bed with a suit of clothes hanging up by it, and set victuals and drink before him.

"There," said she, "eat, drink, and sleep, and may our blessed Lady of Atocha and the great St. Anthony of Padua and the illustrious St. James of Compostella° take you under their protection. I shall be back tomorrow."

Candide, struck with amazement at what he had seen, at what he had suffered, and still more with the charity of the old woman, tried to show his acknowledgment by kissing her hand.

"It is not my hand you ought to kiss," said the old woman. "I shall be back tomorrow. Anoint your back, eat and take your rest."

Candide, notwithstanding so many disasters, ate and slept. The next morning, the old woman brought him his breakfast, examined his back and rubbed it herself with another ointment. She returned at the proper time and brought him his dinner, and at night she visited him again with his supper. The next day she observed the same ceremonies.

° Respectively, a shrine in Madrid, the patron saint of Portugal, and the patron saint of Spain.

"Who are you?" said Candide to her. "What god has inspired you with so much goodness? What return can I ever make you?"

The good old beldame kept a profound silence. In the evening she returned, but without his supper.

"Come along with me," said she, "but do not speak a word."

She took him by the arm and walked with him about a quarter of a mile into the country, till they came to a lonely house surrounded with moats and gardens. The old woman knocked at a little door, which was immediately opened, and she showed him up a pair of back stairs into a small but richly furnished apartment. There she made him sit down on a brocaded sofa, shut the door upon him and left him. Candide thought himself in a trance. He looked upon his whole life hitherto as a frightful dream and the present moment as a very agreeable one.

The old woman soon returned, supporting with great difficulty a young lady, who appeared scarce able to stand. She was of a majestic mien and stature. Her dress was rich and glittering with diamonds, and her face was covered with a veil.

"Take off that veil," said the old woman to Candide.

The young man approached, and, with a trembling hand, took off her veil. What a happy moment! What surprise! He thought he beheld Miss Cunegund. He did behold her, it was she herself. His strength failed him, he could not utter a word, he fell at her feet. Cunegund fainted upon the sofa. The old woman bedewed them with spirits, they recovered, they began to speak. At first they could express themselves only in broken accents. Their questions and answers were alternately interrupted with sighs, tears, and exclamations. The old woman urged them to make less noise and left them together.

"Good heavens!" cried Candide, "is it you? Is it Miss Cunegund I behold, and alive? Do I find you again in Portugal? Then you have not been ravished? They did not rip open your belly as the philosopher Pangloss informed me?"

"Indeed they did," replied Miss Cunegund, "but these two accidents do not always prove mortal."

"But were your father and mother killed?"

"Alas!" answered she. "It is but too true!" And she wept.

"And your brother?"

"And my brother also."

"And how did you come to Portugal? And how did you know of my being here? And by what strange adventure did you contrive to have me brought into this house?"

"I will tell you all," replied the lady, "but first you must acquaint me with all that has befallen you since the innocent kiss you gave me and the rude kicking you received."

Candide, with the greatest submission, obeyed her, and though he was still wrapped in amazement, though his voice was low and tremulous, though his back pained him, yet he gave her a most ingenuous account of everything that had befallen him since the moment of their separation. Cunegund, with her eyes uplifted to heaven, shed tears when he related the death of the good Anabaptist James and of Pangloss, after which, she thus related her adventures to Candide, who lost not one syllable she uttered and seemed to devour her with his eyes all the time she was speaking.

CHAPTER VIII

THE HISTORY OF CUNEGUND

"I was in bed and fast asleep, when it pleased heaven to send the Bulgarians to our delightful castle of Thunder-ten-tronckh, where they murdered my father and brother and cut my mother in pieces. A tall Bulgarian soldier, six feet high, perceiving that I had fainted away at this sight, started to ravish me. The operation brought me to my senses. I cried, I struggled, I bit, I scratched, I would have torn the tall Bulgarian's eyes out, not knowing that what had happened at my father's castle was a customary thing. The brutal soldier gave me a cut in the left groin with his knife, the mark of which I still carry."

"I hope I shall see it," said Candide, with all imaginable simplicity.

"You shall," said Cunegund. "But let me proceed."

"Pray do," replied Candide.

She continued. "A Bulgarian captain came in and saw me weltering in my blood, and the soldier still as busy as if no one had been present. The officer, enraged at the fellow's want of respect to him, killed him with one stroke of his saber as he lay upon me. This captain took care of me, had me cured and carried me prisoner of war to his quarters. I washed what little linen he was master of and dressed his victuals. He thought me very pretty it must be confessed. Neither can I deny that he was well made and had a white soft skin, but he was very stupid and knew nothing of philosophy. It might plainly be perceived that he had not been educated under Doctor Pangloss. In three months' time, having gamed away all his money and being grown tired of me, he sold me to a Jew named Don Issachar, who traded in Holland and Portugal and was passionately fond of women. This Jew showed me great kindness in hopes to gain my favors, but he never could prevail on me. A modest woman may be once ravished, but her virtue is greatly strengthened thereby. In order to make sure of me, he brought me to this country house you now see. I had hitherto believed that nothing could equal the beauty of the castle of Thunder-ten-tronckh, but I found I was mistaken.

"The Grand Inquisitor saw me one day at Mass, ogled me all the time of service and when it was over sent to let me know he wanted to speak with me about some private business. I was conducted to this palace, where I told him of my parentage. He represented to me how much it was beneath a person of my birth to belong to an Israelite. He caused a proposal to be made to Don Issachar that he should resign me to his lordship. Don Issachar, being the court banker and a man of credit, was not easily to be prevailed upon. His lordship threatened him with an *auto-da-fé*. In short, my Jew was frightened into a compromise, and it was agreed between them that the house and myself should belong to both in common; that the Jew should have Monday, Wednesday, and the Sabbath to himself; and the Inquisitor the other days of the week. This agreement has lasted almost six months, but not without several disputes whether the space from Saturday night to Sunday morning belonged to the old or the new law. For my part, I have hitherto withstood them both, and truly I believe this is the very reason why they both still love me.

"At length, to turn aside the scourge of earthquakes and to intimidate Don Issachar, my lord Inquisitor was pleased to celebrate an *auto-da-fé*. He did me the honor to invite me to the ceremony. I had a very good seat, and refreshments were offered the ladies between Mass and the execution. I was dreadfully shocked at the burning of the two Jews and of the honest Biscayan who married his godmother; but how great was my surprise, my consternation, and concern, when I beheld a figure so like Pangloss, dressed in a *sanbenito* and miter! I rubbed my eyes, I looked at him attentively. I saw him hanged, and I fainted away. Scarce had I recovered my senses, when I beheld you stark naked. This was the height of horror, grief, and despair. I must confess to you for a truth that your skin is far whiter and more blooming than that of the Bulgarian captain. This spectacle worked me up to a pitch of distraction. I screamed out and would have said, 'Hold, barbarians!' but my voice failed me, and indeed my cries would have been useless. After you had been severely whipped I said to myself, 'How is it possible that the lovely Candide and the sage Pangloss should be at Lisbon, the one to receive a hundred lashes and the other to be hanged by order of my lord Inquisitor, of whom I am so great a favorite? Pangloss deceived me most cruelly in saying that everything is fittest and best.'

"Thus agitated and perplexed, now distracted and lost, now half dead with grief, I revolved in my mind the murder of my father, mother, and brother; the insolence of the rascally Bulgarian soldier; the wound he gave me in the groin; my servitude; my being a cook wench to my Bulgarian captain; my subjection to the villainous Don Issachar, and my cruel Inquisitor; the hanging of Doctor Pangloss; the *Miserere* sung while you were whipped; and particularly the kiss I gave you behind the screen the last day I ever beheld you. I returned thanks to God for having brought you to the place where I was after so many trials. I charged the old woman who attends me to bring you hither as soon as possible. She has carried out my orders well, and I now enjoy the inexpressible satisfaction of seeing you, hearing you and speaking to you.

But you must certainly be half dead with hunger. I myself have got a good appetite, and so let us sit down to supper."

Upon this the two lovers immediately placed themselves at table, and, after having supped, they returned to seat themselves again on the magnificent sofa already mentioned. They were there when Signor Don Issachar, one of the masters of the house, entered unexpectedly. It was the Sabbath day, and he came to enjoy his privilege and sigh forth his tender passion.

CHAPTER IX

WHAT HAPPENED TO CUNEGUND, CANDIDE, THE GRAND INQUISITOR, AND THE JEW

THIS same Issachar was the most choleric little Hebrew that had ever been in Israel since the captivity in Babylon.

"What," said he, "you Galilean bitch, my lord Inquisitor was not enough for you, but this rascal must come in for a share with me?"

Uttering these words, he drew out a long poniard which he always carried about him, and never dreaming that his adversary had any arms, he attacked him most furiously. But our honest Westphalian had received a handsome sword from the old woman with the suit of clothes. Candide drew his rapier; and though he was the most gentle, sweet-tempered young man breathing, he whipped it into the Israelite and laid him sprawling on the floor at the fair Cunegund's feet.

"Holy Virgin!" cried she. "What will become of us? A

man killed in my apartment! If the peace officers come, we are undone."

"Had not Pangloss been hanged," replied Candide, "he would have given us most excellent advice in this emergency, for he was a profound philosopher. But since he is not here, let us consult the old woman."

She was very intelligent and was beginning to give her advice when another door opened suddenly. It was now one o'clock in the morning, and of course the beginning of Sunday, which, by agreement, fell to the lot of my lord Inquisitor. Entering, he discovered the flagellated Candide with his drawn sword in his hand, a dead body stretched on the floor, Cunegund frightened out of her wits and the old woman giving advice.

At that very moment a sudden thought came into Candide's head.

"If this holy man," thought he, "should call assistance, I shall most undoubtedly be consigned to the flames, and Miss Cunegund may perhaps meet with no better treatment. Besides, he was the cause of my being so cruelly whipped. He is my rival. And I have now begun to dip my hands in blood. There is no time to hesitate."

This whole train of reasoning was clear and instantaneous. So that without giving time to the Inquisitor to recover from his surprise, he ran him through the body and laid him by the side of the Jew.

"Good God!" cried Cunegund. "Here's another fine piece of work! Now there can be no mercy for us. We are excommunicated. Our last hour is come. But how in the name of wonder could you, who are of so mild a temper, dispatch a Jew and a prelate in two minutes' time?"

"Beautiful lady," answered Candide, "when a man is in love, is jealous and has been flogged by the Inquisition, he becomes lost to all reflection."

The old woman then put in her word.

"There are three Andalusian horses in the stable," said she, "with as many bridles and saddles. Let the brave Candide get them ready. Madam has moidores* and jewels. Let us mount immediately, though I have only one buttock to sit upon. Let us set out for Cadiz. It is the finest weather in the world, and there is great pleasure in traveling in the cool of the night."

Candide, without any further hesitation, saddled the three horses; and Miss Cunegund, the old woman, and he set out, and traveled thirty miles without once stopping. While they were making the best of their way, the Holy Brotherhood** entered the house. My Lord the Inquisitor was interred in a magnificent manner, and Issachar's body was thrown upon a dunghill.

Candide, Cunegund, and the old woman had, by this time, reached the little town of Aracena, in the midst of the mountains of Sierra Morena, and were engaged in the following conversation in an inn.

CHAPTER X

IN WHAT DISTRESS CANDIDE, CUNEGUND, AND THE OLD WOMAN ARRIVE AT CADIZ; AND OF THEIR EMBARKATION

"Who could it be who has robbed me of my moidores and jewels?" exclaimed Miss Cunegund, all bathed in tears. "How shall we live? What shall we do? Where shall I find Inquisitors and Jews who can give me more?"

---

* Gold Portuguese coin.
** The gendarmes.

"Alas!" said the old woman, "I have a shrewd suspicion of a reverend Franciscan, who lay last night in the same inn with us at Badajoz. God forbid I should condemn any one wrongfully, but he came into our room twice, and he set off in the morning long before us."

"Alas!" said Candide. "Pangloss has often demonstrated to me that the goods of this world are common to all men and that every one has an equal right to the enjoyment of them,* but according to these principles the friar ought to have left us enough to carry us to the end of our journey. Have you nothing at all left, my beautiful Cunegund?"

"Not a farthing," replied she.

"What is to be done then?" said Candide.

"Sell one of the horses," replied the old woman. "I will get behind my young lady though I have only one buttock to ride on, and we shall reach Cadiz, never fear."

In the same inn there was a Benedictine prior who bought the horse very cheap. Candide, Cunegund, and the old woman, after passing through Lucena, Chellas, and Lebrija, arrived at length at Cadiz. A fleet was then getting ready, and troops were assembling in order to reduce the reverend fathers, the Jesuits of Paraguay, who were accused of having excited one of the Indian tribes in the neighborhood of the town of the Holy Sacrament to revolt against the Kings of Spain and Portugal.** Candide, having been in the Bulgarian service, performed the military drill of that nation before the general of this little army with so intrepid an air, and with such agility and expedition that he gave him the command of a company of foot. Being now made a captain, he embarked with Miss Cunegund, the old woman, two valets, and the two Andalusian horses which had belonged to the Grand Inquisitor of Portugal.

---

* Satire of Hobbes's and Rousseau's theories of the state of nature.
** The Jesuit rebellion took place in 1757.

During their voyage they amused themselves with many profound reasonings on poor Pangloss's philosophy.

"We are now going into another world," said Candide, "and surely it must be there that everything is best. For I must confess that we have had some little reason to complain of what goes on in ours, both as to the physical and moral part."

"Though I have a sincere love for you," said Miss Cunegund, "yet I still shudder at the reflection of what I have seen and experienced."

"All will be well," replied Candide. "The sea of this new world is already better than our European seas. It is smoother, and the winds blow more regularly."

"God grant it," said Cunegund, "but I have met with such terrible treatment in this that I have almost lost all hopes of a better."

"What murmuring and complaining is here indeed!" cried the old woman. "If you had suffered half what I have done, there might be some reason for it."

Miss Cunegund could scarcely refrain from laughing at the good old woman and thought it droll enough to pretend to a greater share of misfortunes than herself.

"Alas, my good dame," said she, "unless you have been ravished by two Bulgarians, have received two deep wounds in your belly, have seen two of your own castles demolished, and beheld two fathers and two mothers barbarously murdered before your eyes, and, to sum up all, have had two lovers whipped at an *auto-da-fé,* I cannot see how you could be more unfortunate than I. Add to this, though born a baroness and bearing seventy-two quarterings, I have been reduced to a cook wench."

"Miss," replied the old woman, "you do not know my family as yet; but if I were to show you my backside, you would not talk in this manner, but suspend your judgment."

This speech raised a high curiosity in Candide and Cunegund; and the old woman continued as follows.

CHAPTER XI

THE HISTORY OF THE OLD WOMAN

"I HAVE not always been blear-eyed. My nose did not always touch my chin, nor was I always a servant. You must know that I am the daughter of Pope Urban X° and of the Princess of Palestrina. Up to the age of fourteen I was brought up in a castle, compared with which all the castles of the German barons would not have been fit for stabling, and one of my robes would have bought half the province of Westphalia. I grew in beauty, in wit, and in every graceful accomplishment, in the midst of pleasures, homage, and the highest expectations. I already began to inspire the men with love: my breasts began to take form; and such breasts! white, firm, and formed like those of Venus of Medici. My eyebrows were as black as jet; and as for my eyes, they darted flames and eclipsed the luster of the stars, as I was told by the poets of our part of the world. My maids, when they dressed and undressed me, used to fall into an ecstasy in viewing me before and behind, and all the men longed to be in their places.

"I was engaged to a sovereign prince of Massa-Carrara.°° Such a prince! As handsome as myself, sweet-tempered, charming, of brilliant wit, and in love with me over head and

---

° Voltaire commented: "Observe the extreme discretion of the author; up till now there hasn't been any Urban X; he is afraid to attribute a bastard to a known pope. What circumspection! What delicacy of conscience!"

°° A small duchy south of Tuscany.

ears. I loved him too, as our sex generally do for the first time, with transport and idolatry. The nuptials were prepared with surprising pomp and magnificence; the ceremony was attended with a succession of feasts, carousals, and burlesques. All Italy composed sonnets in my praise, though not one of them was tolerable. I was on the point of reaching the summit of bliss, when an old marchioness who had been mistress to the Prince my husband invited him to drink chocolate. In less than two hours after he returned from the visit he died of most terrible convulsions, but this is a mere trifle. My mother, in despair, and yet less afflicted than me, determined to absent herself for some time from so fatal a place. As she had a very fine estate in the neighborhood of Gaeta,* we embarked on board a galley which was gilded like the high altar of St. Peter's at Rome. Then a Sallee** corsair swooped down on us and boarded us. Our men defended themselves like true Pope's soldiers; they flung themselves upon their knees, laid down their arms and begged the corsair to give them absolution *in articulo mortis.*

"The Moors presently stripped us as bare as monkeys. My mother, my maids of honor, and myself were served all in the same manner. It is amazing how quick these gentry are at undressing people. But what surprised me most was that they thrust their fingers into that part of our bodies where we women seldom permit anything but enemas to enter. I thought it a very strange kind of ceremony, for thus we are generally apt to judge of things when we have not seen the world. I afterward learned that it was to discover if we had any diamonds concealed. This practice has been established since time immemorial among those civilized nations that scour the seas. I was informed that the religious Knights of Malta never fail to make this search whenever any Moors of

* A town near Naples.
** A town near Rabat, Morocco.

either sex fall into their hands. It is a part of the law of nations from which they never deviate.

"I need not tell you how great a hardship it was for a young princess and her mother to be made slaves and carried to Morocco. You may easily imagine what we must have suffered on board a corsair. My mother was still extremely handsome, our maids of honor, and even our common waiting-women had more charms than were to be found in all Africa. As to myself, I was enchanting; I was beauty itself, and then I had my virginity. But, alas! I did not retain it long; this precious flower, which was reserved for the lovely Prince of Massa-Carrara, was cropped by the captain of the Moorish vessel, who was a hideous Negro, and thought he did me infinite honor. Indeed, both the Princess of Palestrina and myself must have had very strong constitutions to undergo all we went through till our arrival at Morocco. But I will not detain you any longer with such common things; they are hardly worth mentioning.

"Upon our arrival at Morocco, we found that kingdom bathed in blood. Fifty sons of the Emperor Muley Ishmael* were each at the head of a party. This produced fifty civil wars of blacks against blacks, of blacks against tawnies, of tawnies against tawnies, and of mulattoes against mulattoes. In short, the whole empire was one continual scene of carnage.

"No sooner were we landed than a party of blacks, of a contrary faction to that of my captain, came to rob him of his booty. Next to the money and jewels, we were the most valuable things he had. I was witness on this occasion to such a battle as you never beheld in your cold European climates. The northern nations have not that fermentation in their blood, nor that raging lust for women that is so common in Africa. The natives of Europe seem to have their veins filled with milk only, but fire and vitriol circulate in

---

* The father of many children, he died in 1727.

those of the inhabitants of Mount Atlas and the neighboring provinces. They fought with the fury of the lions, tigers, and serpents óf their country to know who should have us. A Moor seized my mother by the right arm, while my captain's lieutenant held her by the left; another Moor laid hold of her by one leg, and one of our corsairs held her by the other. In this manner were almost every one of our women dragged between soldiers. My captain kept me concealed behind him, and with his drawn scimitar cut down everyone who opposed him. At length I saw all our Italian women and my mother mangled and torn in pieces by the monsters who contended for them. The captives, my companions, the Moors who had taken them, the soldiers, the sailors, the blacks, the tawnies, the whites, the mulattoes, and lastly my captain himself were all slain, and I remained alone expiring upon a heap of dead bodies. The like barbarous scenes were enacted every day over the whole country, which is an extent of three hundred leagues, and yet they never missed the five stated times of prayer enjoined by their prophet Mahomet.

"I disentangled myself with great difficulty from such a heap of slaughtered bodies and made shift to crawl to a large orange tree that stood on the bank of a neighboring rivulet, where I fell down exhausted with terror, and overwhelmed with horror, despair, and hunger. My senses being overpowered, I fell asleep, or rather seemed to be in a trance. Thus I lay in a state of weakness and insensibility between life and death, when I felt myself pressed by something that moved up and down upon my body. This brought me to myself; I opened my eyes, and saw a pretty fair-faced man, who sighed and muttered these words between his teeth, *'O che sciagura d'essere senza coglioni!'*"

CHAPTER XII

THE ADVENTURES OF THE OLD WOMAN
CONTINUED

"Astonished and delighted to hear my native language, and no less surprised at the young man's words, I told him that there were far greater misfortunes in the world than what he complained of. And to convince him of it, I gave him a short history of the horrible disasters that had befallen me, and again fell into a swoon. He carried me in his arms to a neighboring cottage, where he had me put to bed, procured me something to eat, waited on me, comforted me, caressed me, told me that he had never seen anything so perfectly beautiful as myself, and that he had never so much regretted the loss of what no one could restore to him.

" 'I was born at Naples,' said he, 'where they caponize two or three thousand children every year. Several die of the operation; some acquire voices far beyond the most tuneful of your ladies; and others are sent to govern states and empires.* I underwent this operation very happily, and was one of the singers in the Princess of Palestrina's chapel.'

" 'How,' cried I, 'in my mother's chapel!'

" 'The Princess of Palestrina, your mother!' cried he, bursting into a flood of tears. 'Can you be the beautiful young princess whom I had the care of bringing up till she was six years old, and who, at that tender age, promised to be as fair as I now behold you?'

---

* The allusion is to the notorius singer Farinelli, who was the power behind the throne in Spain from 1736 to 1761.

" 'I am the same,' I replied. 'My mother lies about a hundred yards from here, cut in pieces, and buried under a heap of dead bodies.'

"I then related to him all that had befallen me, and he in return acquainted me with all his adventures, and how he had been sent to the court of the King of Morocco by a Christian prince to conclude a treaty with that monarch; in consequence of which he was to be furnished with military stores and ships to enable him to destroy the commerce of other Christian governments.

" 'I have executed my commission,' said the eunuch. 'I am going to take shipping at Ceuta, and I'll take you along with me to Italy. *Ma che sciagura d'essere senza coglioni!'*

"I thanked him with tears of joy. But, instead of taking me with him into Italy, he carried me to Algiers and sold me to the dey of that province. I had not been long a slave when the plague, which had made the tour of Africa, Asia, and Europe, broke out at Algiers with redoubled fury. You have seen an earthquake, but tell me, miss, have you ever seen the plague?"

"Never," answered the young Baroness.

"If you ever had," continued the old woman, "you would own an earthquake was a trifle to it. It is very common in Africa, I was seized with it. Try to imagine what a situation for the daughter of a pope, only fifteen years old, and who in less than three months had felt the miseries of poverty and slavery, had been ravished almost every day, had beheld her mother cut into four quarters, had experienced the scourges of famine and war and was now dying of the plague at Algiers. I did not, however, die of it; but my eunuch, and the dey, and almost the whole seraglio of Algiers were swept off.

"As soon as the first fury of this dreadful pestilence was over, a sale was made of the dey's slaves. I was purchased by a merchant, who carried me to Tunis. This man sold me to another merchant, who sold me again to another at Tripoli.

From Tripoli I was sold to Alexandria, from Alexandria to Smyrna, and from Smyrna to Constantinople. After many changes, I at length became the property of an aga of the janissaries, who, soon after I came into his possession, was ordered away to the defense of Azov, then besieged by the Russians.*

"The aga being fond of women, took his whole seraglio with him, and lodged us in a small fort on Lake Maeotis, with two black eunuchs and twenty soldiers for our guard. Our army made a great slaughter among the Russians, but they soon returned us the compliment. Azov was taken by storm, and the enemy spared neither age nor sex, but put all to the sword and laid the city in ashes. Our little fort alone held out; they resolved to reduce us by famine. The twenty janissaries had bound themselves by an oath never to surrender the place. Being reduced to the extremity of famine, they found themselves obliged to eat two eunuchs rather than violate their oath. After a few days they determined to devour the women.

"We had a very pious and humane imam,** who made them a most excellent sermon on this occasion, exhorting them not to kill us all at once.

" 'Only cut off one of the buttocks of each of those ladies,' said he, 'and you will fare extremely well. If you are still under the necessity of having recourse to the same expedient again, you will find the like supply a few days hence. Heaven will approve of so charitable an action and work your deliverance.'

"By the force of this eloquence he easily persuaded them, and all underwent the operation. The imam applied the same balsam as they do to children after circumcision. We were all ready to give up the ghost.

---

* Azov was captured from the Turks by Peter the Great in 1696.
** A priest.

"The janissaries had scarcely time to finish the repast with which we had supplied them when the Russians attacked the place by means of flat-bottomed boats, and not a single janissary escaped. The Russians paid no regard to the condition we were in; but as there are French surgeons in all parts of the world, a skillful operator took us under his care and made a cure of us; and I shall never forget, while I live, that as soon as my wounds were perfectly healed, he made me certain proposals. Besides, he desired us all to have a good heart, assuring us that the like had happened in many sieges and that it was the law of war.

"As soon as my companions were in a condition to walk, they were sent to Moscow. As for me, I fell to the lot of a boyard,° who put me to work in his garden, and gave me twenty lashes a day. But this nobleman having, in about two years afterward, been broken alive upon the wheel with about thirty others for some court intrigues, I took advantage of the event and made my escape. I traveled over a great part of Russia. I was a long time an innkeeper's servant at Riga, then at Rostock, Wismar, Leipsic, Cassel, Utrecht, Leyden, The Hague, and Rotterdam. I have grown old in misery and disgrace, living with only one buttock, and in the perpetual remembrance that I was a pope's daughter. I have been a hundred times upon the point of killing myself, but still was fond of life. This ridiculous weakness is, perhaps, one of the dangerous principles implanted in our nature. For what can be more absurd than to persist in carrying a burden of which we wish to be eased?°° To detest, and yet to strive to preserve our existence? In a word, to caress the serpent that devours us, and hug him close to our bosoms till he has gnawed into our hearts?

° The boyards, or boyars, were a Russian aristocratic order that had been suppressed by Peter the Great, in 1698, after a rebellion.
°° A possible reference to Hamlet. Suicide was a much discussed subject at the time.

"In the different countries which it has been my fate to traverse and the many inns where I have been a servant, I have observed a prodigious number of people who held their existence in abhorrence, and yet I never knew more than twelve who voluntarily put an end to their misery; namely, three Negroes, four Englishmen, as many Genevans, and a German professor named Robeck.* My last place was with the Jew, Don Issachar, who placed me near your person, my fair lady. To your fortunes I have attached myself and have been more affected by your adventures than my own. I should never have even mentioned the latter to you, had you not a little piqued me, and if it were not customary to tell stories on board a ship in order to pass away the time. In short, my dear miss, I have a great deal of knowledge and experience of the world, therefore take my advice. Divert yourself and prevail upon each passenger to tell his story. And if there is one of them all that has not cursed his existence many times, and said to himself over and over again that he was the most wretched of mortals, I give you leave to throw me head-foremost into the sea."

* Robeck had drowned himself in 1735, shortly after writing a defense of suicide. The English were supposed to be inclined to suicide, due to a malady called "spleen," induced by the climate. "Genevans" was added later as a barb against Rousseau's *La Nouvelle Héloïse*, whose hero contemplates suicide.

CHAPTER XIII

HOW CANDIDE WAS OBLIGED TO LEAVE THE FAIR
CUNEGUND AND THE OLD WOMAN

THE fair Cunegund, being thus made acquainted with the history of the old woman's life and adventures, paid her all the respect and civility due to a person of her rank and merit. She accepted her proposal of engaging every one of the passengers to relate their adventures in turn, and was at length, as well as Candide, compelled to acknowledge that the old woman was in the right.

"It is a thousand pities," said Candide, "that the sage Pangloss should have been hanged contrary to the custom of an *auto-da-fé,* for he would have read us a most admirable lecture on the moral and physical evil which overspreads the earth and sea. And I think I should have courage enough to presume to offer (with all due respect) some few objections."

While everyone was reciting his adventures, the ship continued her way and at length arrived at Buenos Aires, where Cunegund, Captain Candide, and the old woman, landed and went to wait upon the Governor Don Fernando d'Ibaraa y Figueora y Mascarenas y Lampourdos y Souza. This nobleman carried himself with a haughtiness suitable to a person who bore so many names. He spoke with the most noble disdain to everyone, carried his nose so high, strained his voice to such a pitch, assumed so imperious an air, and stalked with so much loftiness and pride that everyone who had the honor of conversing with him was violently tempted to bastinade his Excellency. He was immoderately fond of women, and Cunegund appeared in his eyes a paragon of beauty. The first thing he did was to ask her if she was the captain's wife. The air with which he made this demand alarmed Candide. He did not dare to say he was married to her because, indeed, he was not. Neither dared he say she was his sister because she was not that either. And though this white lie had once been very fashionable among the ancients,* and might possibly be useful to some of the moderns, yet the purity of his heart would not permit him to violate the truth.

"Miss Cunegund," replied he, "is to do me the honor of marrying me, and we humbly beseech your Excellency to condescend to grace the ceremony with your presence."

Don Fernando d'Ibaraa y Figueora y Mascarenas y Lampourdos y Souza, twirling his mustachio and putting on a sarcastic smile, ordered Captain Candide to go and review his company. Candide obeyed, and the Governor was left with Miss Cunegund. He made her a strong declaration of love, protesting that he was ready on the morrow to give her his hand in the face of the Church, or otherwise, as should appear most agreeable to a young lady of her prodigious beauty. Cunegund desired leave to retire a quarter of an hour to consult the old woman and determine how she should proceed.

The old woman gave her the following counsel: "Miss, you have seventy-two quarterings in your arms, it is true, but you have not a penny to bless yourself with. It is your own fault if you are not wife to one of the greatest noblemen in South America, with an exceeding fine mustachio. What business have you to pride yourself upon an unshaken constancy? You have been ravished by a Bulgarian soldier; a Jew and an Inquisitor have both tasted of your favors.

---

* The allusion is to the story of Abraham and Sarah, which was involved in the contemporary polemics over truth and falsehood.

Misfortunes confer privileges. I must confess, were I in your place, I should, without the least scruple, give my hand to the Governor, and thereby make the fortune of the brave Captain Candide."

While the old woman was thus haranguing, with all the prudence that old age and experience furnish, a small bark entered the harbor, in which was a magistrate and his algua-zils.° Matters had fallen out as follows.

The old woman rightly guessed that the Franciscan with the long sleeves was the person who had taken Cunegund's money and jewels while they and Candide were at Badajoz, in their hasty flight from Lisbon. This same friar attempted to sell some of the diamonds to a jeweler, who at once knew them to have belonged to the Grand Inquisitor. The prior, be-fore he was hanged, confessed that he had stolen them and described the persons and the road they had taken. The flight of Cunegund and Candide was already the town talk. They sent in pursuit of them to Cadiz; and the vessel which had been sent, to make the greater dispatch, had now reached the port of Buenos Aires. A report was spread that a magis-trate was going to land, and that he was in pursuit of the murderers of my lord the Grand Inquisitor. The wise old woman immediately saw what was to be done.

"You cannot run away," said she to Cunegund, "but you have nothing to fear. It was not you who killed my lord Inquisitor. Besides, as the Governor is in love with you, he will not suffer you to be ill-treated, therefore stand your ground."

Then hurrying away to Candide, "Be gone," said she, "from hence this instant, or you will be burned alive."

Candide found there was no time to be lost. But how could he part from Cunegund and whither must he fly for shelter?

° Constables.

CHAPTER XIV

THE RECEPTION CANDIDE AND CACAMBO MET
WITH AMONG THE JESUITS IN PARAGUAY

CANDIDE had brought with him from Cadiz such a valet as one often meets with on the coasts of Spain and in the colonies. He was the fourth part of a Spaniard, of a mongrel breed, and born in Tucuman. He had successively gone through the profession of a choirboy, sexton, sailor, monk, pedlar, soldier, and lackey. His name was Cacambo. He had a great affection for his master because his master was a mighty good man. He immediately saddled the two Andalusian horses.

"Come, my good master," he said, "let us follow the old woman's advice, and make all the haste we can from this place without staying to look behind us."

Candide burst into a flood of tears.

"Oh, my dear Cunegund, must I then be compelled to quit you, just as the Governor was going to honor us with his presence at our wedding! Cunegund, so long lost, and found again, what will become of you?"

"Lord!" said Cacambo, "she must do as well as she can; women are never at a loss. God takes care of them, and so let us make the best of our way."

"But whither will you carry me? Where can we go? What can we do without Cunegund?" cried the disconsolate Candide.

"By St. James of Compostella," said Cacambo, "you were going to fight against the Jesuits of Paraguay. Now, let us go and fight for them. I know the road perfectly well; I'll conduct you to their kingdom.* They will be delighted with a captain that understands the Bulgarian drill; you will certainly make a prodigious fortune. If we cannot find our account in one world, we'll find it in another. It is a great pleasure to see new objects, and perform new exploits."

"Then you have been in Paraguay?" said Candide.

"Aye, marry, have I," replied Cacambo. "I was a drill master in the College of the Assumption, and I am as well acquainted with the new government of Los Padres as I am with the streets of Cadiz. Oh, it is an admirable government, that is most certain! The kingdom is at present upward of three hundred leagues in diameter and divided into thirty provinces. The fathers there have everything, and the people nothing; this is the masterpiece of justice and reason. For my part, I see nothing so divine as the good fathers, who wage war in this part of the world against the King of Spain and the King of Portugal, at the same time that they hear the confessions of those very princes in Europe; who kill Spaniards in America, and send them to Heaven in Madrid. This pleases me exceedingly, but let us push forward. You are going to be most fortunate of all mortals. How charmed will those fathers be to hear that a captain who understands the Bulgarian drill is coming among them!"

As soon as they reached the first barrier, Cacambo called to the advance guard and told them that a captain wanted to speak to my Lord the General. Notice was given to the main guard, and immediately a Paraguayan officer ran to throw himself at the feet of the Commandant to impart this news to him. Candide and Cacambo were immediately disarmed, and their two Andalusian horses were seized. The two strangers were now conducted between two files of musketeers; the Commandant was at the farther end with a

---

* The Jesuits had established a kind of totalitarian, communistic State of which Voltaire disapproved.

three-cornered cap on his head, his gown tucked up, a sword by his side, and a half-pike in his hand. He made a sign, and instantly four-and-twenty soldiers drew up round the newcomers. A sergeant told them that they must wait, the Commandant could not speak to them, and that the Reverend Father Provincial did not suffer any Spaniard to open his mouth but in his presence, or to stay above three hours° in the province.

"And where is the Reverend Father Provincial?" said Cacambo.

"He is just come from Mass and is at the parade," replied the sergeant, "and in about three hours' time, you may possibly have the honor to kiss his spurs."

"But," said Cacambo, "the captain, who, as well as myself, is perishing with hunger, is no Spaniard, but a German; therefore, pray, might we not be permitted to break our fast till we can be introduced to his Reverence?"

The sergeant immediately went and acquainted the Commandant with what he heard.

"God be praised," said the Reverend Commandant, "since he is a German, I will hear what he has to say. Let him be brought to my arbor."

Immediately they conducted Candide to a beautiful pavilion, adorned with a colonnade of green and gold marble, and with trellises of vines, which served as a kind of cage for parrots, hummingbirds, fly-birds, guinea hens, and all other curious kinds of birds. An excellent breakfast was provided in vessels of gold. And while the Paraguayans ate corn out of wooden dishes in the open air, and exposed to the burning heat of the sun, the Reverend Father Commandant retired to his cool arbor.

He was a very handsome young man, round-faced, fair, and fresh-colored, his eyebrows were finely arched, he had

---

° Voltaire exaggerates; three days were allowed.

a piercing eye, the tips of his ears were red, his lips vermilion, and he had a bold and commanding air; but such a boldness as neither resembled that of a Spaniard nor of a Jesuit. He ordered Candide and Cacambo to have their arms restored to them together with their two Andalusian horses. Cacambo gave the poor beasts some oats to eat close by the arbor, keeping a strict eye upon them all the while for fear of surprise.

Candide having kissed the hem of the Commandant's robe, they sat down to table.

"It seems you are a German?" said the Jesuit to him in that language.

"Yes, Reverend Father," answered Candide.

As they pronounced these words, they looked at each other with great amazement, and with an emotion that neither could conceal.

"From what part of Germany do you come?" said the Jesuit.

"From the dirty province of Westphalia," answered Candide. "I was born in the castle of Thunder-ten-tronckh."

"Oh heavens! Is it possible?" said the Commandant.

"What a miracle!" cried Candide.

"Can it be you?" said the Commandant.

On this they both retired a few steps backward, then embraced and let fall a shower of tears.

"Is it you then, Reverend Father? You are the brother of the fair Cunegund? You who were slain by the Bulgarians! You the Baron's son! You a Jesuit in Paraguay! I must confess this is a strange world we live in. Oh, Pangloss! Pangloss! What joy would this have given you, if you had not been hanged."

The Commandant dismissed the Negro slaves and the Paraguayans who were presenting them with liquor in crystal goblets. He returned thanks to God and St. Ignatius a thousand times. He clasped Candide in his arms, and both their faces were bathed in tears.

"You will be more surprised, more affected, more transported," said Candide, "when I tell you that Miss Cunegund, your sister, whose belly was supposed to have been ripped open, is in perfect health."

"Where?"

"In your neighborhood, with the Governor of Buenos Aires; and I myself was going to fight against you."

Every word they uttered during this long conversation was productive of some new matter of astonishment. Their souls fluttered on their tongues, listened in their ears and sparkled in their eyes. Like true Germans, they continued a long time at table, waiting for the Reverend Father Provincial; and the Commandant spoke to his dear Candide as follows:

CHAPTER XV

HOW CANDIDE KILLED THE BROTHER OF
HIS DEAR CUNEGUND

"NEVER while I live shall I lose the remembrance of that horrible day on which I saw my father and mother barbarously butchered before my eyes and my sister ravished. When the Bulgarians retired, we found no sign of my dear sister; but the bodies of my father, mother, and myself, with two servant maids, and three little boys with their throats cut were thrown into a cart to be buried in a chapel belonging to the Jesuits, within two leagues of our family seat. A Jesuit sprinkled us with some holy water, which was confoundedly salt, and a few drops of it went into my eyes. The father perceived that my eyelids stirred a little; he put his hand on my breast and felt my heart beat; upon which he gave me proper assistance, and at the end of three weeks I was perfectly recovered. You know, my dear Candide, I was very handsome; I became still more so, and the Reverend Father Kroust, Superior of the House, took a great fancy to me. He gave me a novice's habit, and some years afterward I was sent to Rome. Our general stood in need of new levies of young German Jesuits. The sovereigns of Paraguay admit as few Spanish Jesuits as possible; they prefer those of other nations, as being more obedient to command. The Reverend Father General looked upon me as a proper person to work in that vineyard. I set out in company with a Pole and a Tyrolese. Upon my arrival, I was honored with a subdeaconship and a lieutenancy. Now I am colonel and priest. We shall give a warm reception to the King of Spain's troops; I can assure you, they will be well excommunicated and beaten. Providence has sent you here to assist us. But is it true that my dear sister Cunegund is in the neighborhood with the Governor of Buenos Aires?"

Candide swore that nothing could be more true, and the tears began again to trickle down their cheeks.

The Baron knew no end of embracing Candide. He called him his brother, his deliverer.

"Perhaps," said he, "my dear Candide, we shall be fortunate enough to enter the town sword in hand and rescue my sister Cunegund."

"Ah! That would crown my wishes," replied Candide, "for I intended to marry her, and I hope I shall still be able to do so."

"Insolent fellow!" replied the Baron. "You! You have the impudence to marry my sister, who bears seventy-two quarterings! I think you are quite insolent to dare so much as mention such an audacious design to me."

Candide, thunderstruck by this speech, answered, "Reverend Father, all the quarterings in the world are of no significance. I have delivered your sister from a Jew and an Inquisitor. She is under many obligations to me, and she is resolved to give me her hand. Master Pangloss always told me that mankind are by nature equal. Therefore, you may depend upon it that I will marry your sister."

"We shall see about that, villain!" said the Jesuit Baron of Thunder-ten-tronckh and struck him across the face with the flat side of his sword.

Candide, in an instant, drew his rapier and plunged it up to the hilt in the Jesuit's body; but, in pulling it out reeking hot, he burst into tears.

"Good God!" cried he, "I have killed my old master, my friend, my brother-in-law. I am the mildest man in the world, and yet I have already killed three men, and of these three two were priests."

Cacambo, standing sentry near the door of the arbor, instantly ran up.

"Nothing remains," said his master, "but to sell our lives as dearly as possible. They will undoubtedly look into the arbor. We must die sword in hand."

Cacambo, who had been through far worse, did not lose his head. He stripped the Baron of his Jesuit's habit and put it upon Candide, then gave him the dead man's three-cornered cap and made him mount on horseback. All this was done as quick as thought.

"Gallop, master," cried Cacambo. "Everybody will take you for a Jesuit going to give orders, and we shall have passed the frontiers before they are able to overtake us."

He flew as he spoke these words, crying out aloud in Spanish, "Make way, make way for the Reverend Father Colonel."

CHAPTER XVI

WHAT HAPPENED TO OUR TWO TRAVELERS WITH
TWO GIRLS, TWO MONKEYS, AND
THE SAVAGES CALLED OREILLONS

CANDIDE and his servant had already passed the frontiers
before it was known that the German Jesuit was dead. The
wary Cacambo had taken care to fill his wallet with bread,
chocolate, ham, fruit, and a few bottles of wine. They penetrated with their Andalusian horses into a strange country
where they could discover no beaten path. At length, a beautiful meadow, intersected with streams, opened to their view.
Our two travelers allowed their steeds to graze. Cacambo
urged his master to take some food, and he set him an
example.

"How can you desire me to eat ham, when I have killed the
son of my Lord the Baron and am doomed never more to see
the beautiful Cunegund? What will it avail me to prolong a
wretched life that might be spent far from her in remorse and
despair. And then, what will the *Journal de Trévoux* say?"[*]

While he was making these reflections, he still continued
eating. The sun was now on the point of setting, when the
ears of our two wanderers were assailed with cries which
seemed to be uttered by a female voice. They could not
tell whether these were cries of grief or joy. However, they
instantly started up, full of that uneasiness and apprehension

---

[*] The Jesuit periodical, with which Voltaire was to have increasingly bad
relations.

which a strange place inspires. The cries proceeded from two young women who were tripping stark naked on the edge of the prairie, while two monkeys followed close at their heels biting their buttocks. Candide was touched with compassion. He had learned to shoot while he was among the Bulgarians, and he could hit a filbert in a hedge without touching a leaf. Accordingly, he took up his double-barreled Spanish musket, pulled the trigger and laid the two monkeys lifeless on the ground.

"God be praised, my dear Cacambo, I have rescued two poor girls from a most perilous situation. If I have committed a sin in killing an Inquisitor and a Jesuit, I made ample amends by saving the lives of these two girls. Who knows but they may be young ladies of a good family and that this assistance I have been so happy to give them may procure us great advantage in this country."

He was about to continue, when he felt himself struck speechless at seeing the two girls embracing the dead bodies of the monkeys in the tenderest manner, bathing their wounds with their tears and rending the air with the most doleful lamentations.

"Really," said he to Cacambo, "I should not have expected to see such a prodigious share of good nature."

"Master," replied Cacambo, "you have made a precious piece of work of it. Do you know that you have killed the lovers of these two ladies?"

"Their lovers! Cacambo, you are jesting! It cannot be! I can never believe it."

"Dear sir," replied Cacambo, "you are surprised at everything. Why should you think it so strange that there should be a country where monkeys insinuate themselves into the good graces of the ladies? They are the fourth part of a man as I am the fourth part of a Spaniard."

"Alas!" replied Candide, "I remember to have heard Master Pangloss say that such accidents as these frequently came to pass in former times and that these commixtures are productive of centaurs, fauns, and satyrs and that many of the ancients had seen such monsters, but I looked upon the whole as fabulous."

"Now you are convinced," said Cacambo, "that it is very true, and you see what use is made of those creatures by persons who have not had a proper upbringing. All I am afraid of is that these same ladies will play us some ugly trick."

These judicious reflections operated so far on Candide as to make him quit the meadow and strike into a thicket. There he and Cacambo supped, and after heartily cursing the Grand Inquisitor, the Governor of Buenos Aires, and the Baron, they fell asleep on the ground. When they awoke, they were surprised to find that they could not move. The reason was that the Oreillons who inhabit that country, and to whom the two girls had denounced them, had bound them with cords made of the bark of trees. They were surrounded by fifty naked Oreillons armed with bows and arrows, clubs, and hatchets of flint. Some were making a fire under a large cauldron, and others were preparing spits, crying out one and all, "A Jesuit! A Jesuit! We shall be revenged; we shall have excellent fare; let us eat Jesuit! Let us eat Jesuit!"

"I told you, master," cried Cacambo mournfully, "that those two wenches would play us some scurvy trick."

Candide, seeing the cauldron and the spits, cried out, "I suppose they are going either to boil or roast us. Ah! What would Master Pangloss say if he were to see what pure nature is like! Everything is right. It may be so, but I must confess it is something hard to be bereft of Miss Cunegund and to be spitted by these Oreillons."

Cacambo, who never lost his presence of mind in distress, said to the disconsolate Candide, "Do not despair. I understand a little of the jargon of these people. I will speak to them."

"Ay, pray do," said Candide, "and be sure you make them sensible of the horrid barbarity of boiling and roasting human creatures and how little of Christianity there is in such practices."

"Gentlemen," said Cacambo, "you think perhaps you are going to feast upon a Jesuit. If so, it is mighty well, nothing can be more agreeable to justice than thus to treat your enemies. Indeed, the law of nature teaches us to kill our neighbor, and accordingly we find this practiced all over the world. And if we do not indulge ourselves in eating human flesh, it is because we have much better fare. But you have not such resources as we have; it is certainly much better judged to feast upon your enemies than to abandon to ravens and crows the fruits of your victory. But surely, gentlemen, you would not choose to eat your friends. You imagine you are going to roast a Jesuit, whereas my master is your friend, your defender, and you are going to spit the very man who has been destroying your enemies. As to myself, I am your countryman. This gentleman is my master, and so far from being a Jesuit, he has very lately killed one of that order, whose spoils he now wears and which have probably occasioned your mistake. To convince you of the truth of what I say, take the habit he now has on, and carry it to the first barrier of the Jesuits' kingdom and inquire whether my master did not kill one of their officers. There will be little or no time lost by this, and you may still reserve our bodies in your power to feast on, if you should find what we have told you to be false. But, on the contrary, if you find it to be true, I am persuaded you are too well acquainted with the principles of the laws of society, humanity, and justice, not to use us courteously."*

---

* The contrast between the pleas of Candide and Cacambo plays up the eighteenth century belief that men are not motivated by abstract ideas, but by passion and self-interest.

This speech appeared very reasonable to the Oreillons. They deputed two of their people with all expedition to inquire into the truth of this affair. The two delegates acquitted themselves of their commission like men of sense and soon returned with good tidings. Upon this the Oreillons released their two prisoners, showed them all sorts of civilities, offered them girls, gave them refreshments and reconducted them to the confines of their country, crying before them all the way, in token of joy, "He is no Jesuit, he is no Jesuit."

Candide could not help admiring the cause of his deliverance.

"What men! What manners!" cried he. "If I had not fortunately run my sword up to the hilt in the body of Miss Cunegund's brother, I should have infallibly been eaten alive. But, after all, pure nature is an excellent thing, since these people, instead of eating me, showed me a thousand civilities as soon as they knew I was not a Jesuit."

CHAPTER XVII

CANDIDE AND HIS SERVANT ARRIVE IN
THE COUNTRY OF EL DORADO.
WHAT THEY SAW THERE

boring life

WHEN they got to the frontiers of the Oreillons, Cacambo said to Candide, "You see, this hemisphere is no better than the other. Take my advice, and let us return to Europe by the shortest way possible."

"But how can we get back?" said Candide, "and whither shall we go? To my own country? The Bulgarians and the Abares are laying that waste with fire and sword. Or shall we go to Portugal? There I shall be burned. And if we abide here, we are every moment in danger of being spitted. But how can I bring myself to quit that part of the world where Miss Cunegund has her residence?"

"Let us turn toward Cayenne," said Cacambo. "There we shall meet with some Frenchmen, for they ramble all over the world. Perhaps they will assist us, and God will look with pity on our distress."

It was not so easy to get to Cayenne. They knew pretty nearly whereabouts it lay; but the mountains, rivers, precipices, robbers, savages, were dreadful obstacles in the way. Their horses died with fatigue, and their provisions were at an end. They subsisted a whole month upon wild fruit, till at length they came to a little river bordered with coconut palms, the sight of which at once sustained life and hope.

Cacambo, who was always giving as good advice as the old woman herself, said to Candide, "We are utterly exhaust-

57

ed; we have traveled enough on foot. I see an empty canoe near the riverside; let us fill it with coconuts, get into it and go down with the stream; a river always leads to some inhabited place. If we do not meet with agreeable things, we shall at least meet with something new."

"Agreed," replied Candide. "Let us recommend ourselves to Providence."

They drifted a few leagues down the river, the banks of which were in some places covered with flowers; in others barren; in some parts smooth and level, and in others steep and rugged. The stream widened as they went further on, till at length it passed under a vault of frightful rocks whose summits seemed to reach the clouds. Here our two travelers had the courage to commit themselves to the stream beneath this vault, which, contracting in this part, hurried them along with a dreadful noise and rapidity. At the end of twenty-four hours, they saw daylight again, but their canoe was dashed to pieces against the rocks. They were obliged to creep along from rock to rock for the space of a league, till at last a spacious plain presented itself to their sight, bound by inaccessible mountains. The country appeared cultivated equally for pleasure and to produce the necessaries of life. The useful and agreeable° were here equally blended. The roads were covered, or rather adorned, with carriages formed of glittering materials, in which were men and women of a surprising beauty, drawn with great rapidity by red sheep°° of a very large size, which far surpassed in speed the finest coursers of Andalusia, Tetuàn, or Mequinez.

"Here is a country," said Candide, "which seems preferable to Westphalia."

He and Cacambo landed near the first village they saw, at the entrance of which they perceived some children cov-

---

° These two adjectives summarize the ideal of value of Voltaire and most of the eighteenth century.

°° Llamas.

ered with tattered garments of the richest gold brocade, playing at quoits. Our two inhabitants of the other hemisphere amused themselves greatly with what they saw. The quoits were large round pieces, yellow, red, and green, which cast a most glorious luster. Our travelers picked some of them up, and they proved to be gold, emeralds, rubies, and diamonds, the least of which would have been the greatest ornament to the superb throne of the great Mogul.

"Without doubt," said Cacambo, "these children must be the King's sons, that are playing at quoits."

As he was uttering those words, the schoolmaster of the village appeared, who came to call them to school.

"There," said Candide, "is the preceptor of the royal family."

The little ragamuffins immediately quitted their game, leaving the quoits on the ground with all their other playthings. Candide gathered them up, ran to the schoolmaster, and, with a most respectful bow, presented them to him, giving him to understand by signs that their Royal Highnesses had forgotten their gold and precious stones. The schoolmaster, with a smile, flung them upon the ground, then, having examined Candide from head to foot with an air of great surprise, went on his way.

Our travelers took care, however, to gather up the gold, the rubies, and the emeralds.

"Where are we?" cried Candide. "The King's children in this country must have an excellent upbringing, since they are taught to show such a contempt for gold and precious stones."

Cacambo was as much surprised as his master.

They at length drew near the first house in the village, which was built after the manner of a European palace. There was a crowd of people round the door and a still greater number in the house. The sound of the most delightful musical instrument was heard, and the most agreeable smell came from the kitchen. Cacambo went up to the door and heard those within talking in the Peruvian language, which was his mother tongue; for everyone knows that Cacambo was born in a village of Tucuman where no other language is spoken.

"I will be your interpreter here," said he to Candide. "Let us go in; this is an eating-house."

Immediately two waiters and two servant-girls, dressed in cloth of gold, and their hair braided with ribbons of tissue, accosted the strangers and invited them to sit down to the ordinary. Their dinner consisted of four dishes of different soups, each garnished with two young paroquets, a boiled condor that weighed two hundredweight, two roasted monkeys of a delicious flavor, three hundred hummingbirds in one dish, and six hundred hummingbirds in another; some excellent stews, delicate tarts, and the whole served up in dishes of rock-crystal. Several sorts of liquors, extracted from the sugar cane, were handed about by the servants who attended.

Most of the company were merchants and wagoners, all extremely polite. They asked Cacambo a few questions, with the utmost discretion and circumspection, and replied to his in a most obliging and satisfactory manner.

As soon as dinner was over, both Candide and Cacambo thought they would pay very handsomely for their entertainment by laying down two of those large gold pieces which they had picked off the ground; but the landlord and landlady burst into a fit of laughing and held their sides for some time before they were able to speak.*

"Gentlemen," said the landlord, "I plainly perceive you are strangers, and such we are not accustomed to see. Pardon

---

* Voltaire uses the then common technique of considering conventional values and beliefs from the "naive" viewpoint of an uncivilized person.

us, therefore, for laughing when you offered us the common pebbles of our highways for payment of your reckoning. To be sure, you have none of the coin of this kingdom; but there is no necessity to have any money at all to dine in this house. All the inns, which are established for the convenience of those who carry on the trade of this nation, are maintained by the government. You have found but very indifferent entertainment here, because this is only a poor village; but in almost every other of these public houses you will meet with a reception worthy of persons of your merit."

Cacambo explained the whole of this speech of the land-lord to Candide, who listened to it with the same astonishment with which his friend communicated it.

"What sort of a country is this," said the one to the other, "that is unknown to all the world, and in which Nature has everywhere so different an appearance from what she has in ours? Possibly this is that part of the globe where every-thing is right, for there must certainly be some such place; and, for all that Master Pangloss could say, I often perceived that things went very ill in Westphalia."

CHAPTER XVIII

WHAT THEY SAW IN THE COUNTRY OF
EL DORADO

CACAMBO vented all his curiosity upon the landlord by a thousand different questions.

The honest man answered him thus: "I am very ignorant, sir, but I am contented with my ignorance. However, we have in this neighborhood an old man* retired from court, who is the most learned and communicative person in the whole kingdom."

He then directed Cacambo to the old man. Candide acted now only a second character and attended his servant. They entered a quite plain house, for the door was nothing but silver, and the ceiling was only of beaten gold, but wrought in so elegant a taste as to vie with the richest. The ante-chamber, indeed, was only incrusted with rubies and emer-alds, but the order in which everything was disposed made amends for this great simplicity.

The old man received the strangers on a sofa, which was stuffed with hummingbirds' feathers, and ordered his servants to present them with liquors in golden goblets, after which he satisfied their curiosity in the following terms:

"I am now one hundred and seventy-two years old; and I learned from my late father who was equerry to the king of the amazing revolutions of Peru, to which he had been an eye-witness. This kingdom is the ancient patrimony of the Incas, who very imprudently quitted it to conquer another part of the world, and were at length conquered and destroyed them-selves by the Spaniards.

"Those princes of their family who remained in their native country acted more wisely. They ordained, with the consent of their whole nation, that none of the inhabitants of our little kingdom should ever quit it; and to this wise ordinance we owe the preservation of our innocence and happiness. The Spaniards had some confused notion of this country, to which they gave the name of El Dorado, and Sir Walter Raleigh, an Englishman, actually came very near it, about a hundred years ago. But the inaccessible rocks and precipices with which our country is surrounded on all sides

---

* A stock character in Utopian literature. Voltaire's Utopia is not a primi-tivist one. It has every luxury, including servants.

have hitherto secured us from the rapacious fury of the people of Europe, who have an unaccountable fondness for the pebbles and dirt of our land, for the sake of which they would murder us all to the very last man."*

The conversation lasted some time and turned chiefly on the form of government, the customs, the women, the public diversions, and the arts. At length, Candide, who had always had a taste for metaphysics, asked whether the people of that country had any religion.

The old man reddened a little at this question.

"Can you doubt it?" said he. "Do you take us for wretches lost to all sense of gratitude?"

Cacambo asked in a respectful manner what was the established religion of El Dorado. The old man blushed again.

"Can there be two religions then?" he said. "Ours, I apprehend, is the religion of the whole world. We worship God from morning till night."

"Do you worship but one God?" said Cacambo, who still acted as the interpreter of Candide's doubts.

"Certainly," said the old man. "There are not two, nor three, nor four Gods. I must confess the people of your world ask very extraordinary questions."

However, Candide could not refrain from making many more inquiries of the old man; he wanted to know in what manner they prayed to God in El Dorado.

"We do not pray to him at all," said the reverend sage. "We have nothing to ask of him, he has given us all we want, and we give him thanks incessantly."

Candide had a curiosity to see some of their priests, and desired Cacambo to ask the old man where they were.

At this he, smiling, said, "My friends, we are all of us priests. The King and all the heads of families sing solemn

---

* The humanitarian *philosophes* were deeply perturbed by the cruelty of the Spanish conquerors.

hymns of thanksgiving every morning, accompanied by five or six thousand musicians."

"What!" said Cacambo. "Have you no monks among you, to dispute, to govern, to intrigue and to burn people who are not of the same opinion with themselves?"

"Do you take us for fools?" said the old man. "Here we are all of one opinion and know not what you mean by your monks."

During the whole of this discourse Candide was in raptures, and he said to himself:

"What a prodigious difference is there between this place and Westphalia, and this house and the Baron's castle! If our friend Pangloss had seen El Dorado, he would no longer have said that the castle of Thunder-ten-tronckh was the finest of all possible edifices: there is nothing like seeing the world, that's certain."

This long conversation being ended, the old man ordered six sheep to be harnessed and put to the coach and sent twelve of his servants to escort the travelers to Court.

"Excuse me," said he, "for not waiting on you in person; my age deprives me of that honor. The King will receive you in such a manner that you will have no reason to complain; and doubtless you will make a proper allowance for the customs of the country, if they should not happen altogether to please you."

Candide and Cacambo got into the coach, the six sheep flew and in less than a quarter of an hour they arrived at the King's palace, which was situated at the further end of the capital. At the entrance was a portal two hundred and twenty feet high, and one hundred wide; but it is impossible for words to express the materials of which it was built. The reader, however, will readily conceive they must have a prodigious superiority over the pebbles and sand which we call gold and precious stones.

Twenty beautiful young virgins-in-waiting received Candide and Cacambo at their alighting from the coach, conducted them to the bath, and clad them in robes woven of the down of hummingbirds. After this they were introduced by the great officers of the crown of both sexes to the King's apartment, between two files of musicians, each file consisting of a thousand, according to the custom of the country. When they drew near to the presence chamber, Cacambo asked one of the officers in what manner they were to pay their obeisance to his Majesty: whether it was the custom to fall upon their knees, or to prostrate themselves upon the ground? whether they were to put their hands upon their heads, or behind their backs? whether they were to lick the dust off the floor? In short, what was the ceremony usual on such occasions?

"The custom," said the great officer, "is to embrace the King, and kiss him on each cheek."

Candide and Cacambo accordingly threw their arms round his Majesty's neck. And he received them in the most gracious manner imaginable and very politely asked them to sup with him.

While supper was preparing, orders were given to show them the city, where they saw public structures that reared their lofty heads to the clouds; the market places decorated with a thousand columns; fountains of spring water, besides others of rose water, and of liquors drawn from the sugar cane, incessantly flowing in the great squares. These were paved with a kind of precious stone that emitted an odor like that of cloves and cinnamon. Candide asked to see the high court of justice, the parlement; but was answered that they have none in that country, being utter strangers to lawsuits. He then inquired if they had any prisons. They replied, "None." But what gave him at once the greatest surprise and pleasure was the Palace of Sciences, where he saw a gallery two thousand feet long, filled with the various apparatus of mathematics and natural philosophy.

After having spent the whole afternoon in seeing only about the thousandth part of the city, they were brought back to the King's palace. Candide sat down at the table with his Majesty, his servant Cacambo, and several ladies of the Court. Never was entertainment more elegant, nor could anyone possibly show more wit than his Majesty displayed while they were at supper. Cacambo explained all the King's *bons mots* to Candide, and although they were translated they still appeared to be *bons mots*. Of all the things that surprised Candide, this was not the least. They spent a whole month in this hospitable place, during which time Candide was continually saying to Cacambo:

"I own, my friend, once more, that the castle where I was born is a mere nothing in comparison with the place where we now are; but still Miss Cunegund is not here, and you yourself have doubtless some mistress in Europe. If we remain here, we shall only be as others are. Whereas, if we return to our own world with only a dozen of El Dorado sheep, loaded with the pebbles of this country, we shall be richer than all the kings in Europe. We shall no longer need to stand in awe of the Inquisitors, and we may easily recover Miss Cunegund."

This speech pleased Cacambo. We have such a fondness for roving, for making a figure in our own country and for boasting of what we have seen in our travels, that the two happy wanderers resolved to be happy no longer, and demanded permission of his Majesty to quit the country.

"You are about to do a rash and silly action," said the King. "I am sensible my kingdom is an inconsiderable spot; but when people are tolerably at their ease in any place, I should think it would be their interest to remain there. Most assuredly, I have no right to detain you or any strangers against your wills; this is an act of tyranny to which our manners and our laws are equally repugnant. All men are free; you have an undoubted liberty to depart whenever you please, but you will have many difficulties in passing the frontiers. It is impossible to ascend that rapid river which runs under high and vaulted rocks and by which you were conveyed hither by a miracle. The mountains by which my kingdom is hemmed in on all sides are ten thousand feet high and perfectly perpendicular. They are above ten leagues over each, and the descent from them is one continued precipice. However, since you are determined to leave us, I will immediately give orders to the superintendent of machines to cause one to be made that will convey you safely. When they have conducted you to the back of the mountains, nobody can attend you further; for my subjects have made a vow never to quit the kingdom, and they are too prudent to break it. Ask me whatever else you please."

"All we shall ask of your Majesty," said Cacambo, "is a few sheep laden with provisions, pebbles, and the clay of your country."

The King smiled at the request, and said, "I cannot imagine what pleasure you Europeans find in our yellow clay; but take away as much of it as you will, and much good may it do you."

He immediately gave orders to his engineers to make a machine to hoist these two extraordinary men out of the kingdom. Three thousand good mathematicians went to work and finished it in about fifteen days, and it did not cost more than twenty millions sterling of that country's money. Candide and Cacambo were placed on this machine, and they took with them two large red sheep, bridled and saddled, to ride upon when they got on the other side of the mountains; twenty others to serve as pack-horses for carrying provisions; thirty laden with presents of whatever was most curious in the country; and fifty with gold, diamonds, and other precious stones. The King embraced the two wanderers with the greatest cordiality.

It was a curious sight to behold the manner of their setting off and the ingenious method by which they and their sheep were hoisted to the top of the mountains. The mathematicians and engineers took leave of them as soon as they had conveyed them to a place of safety, and Candide was wholly occupied with the thoughts of presenting his sheep to Miss Cuneg..nd.

"Now," said he, "thanks to heaven, we have more than sufficient to pay the Governor of Buenos Aires for Miss Cunegund, if she is redeemable. Let us make the best of our way to Cayenne, where we will take ship, and then we may at leisure think of what kingdom we shall purchase."

CHAPTER XIX

WHAT HAPPENED TO THEM AT SURINAM, AND HOW CANDIDE BECAME ACQUAINTED WITH MARTIN

OUR travelers' first day's journey was very pleasant; they were elated with the prospect of possessing more riches than were to be found in Europe, Asia, and Africa together. Candide, in amorous transports, cut the name of Miss Cunegund on the trees. The second day, two of their sheep sank into a morass, and were swallowed up with their loads; two more died of fatigue some few days afterward; seven or eight perished with hunger in a desert, and others, at different times, tumbled down precipices; so that, after traveling about a hundred days, they had only two sheep left.

Said Candide to Cacambo, "You see, my dear friend, how perishable the riches of this world are; there is nothing solid but virtue and the joy of seeing Miss Cunegund again."

"Very true," said Cacambo, "but we have still two sheep remaining, with more treasure than ever the King of Spain will be possessed of; and I espy a town at a distance, which I take to be Surinam, a town belonging to the Dutch. We are now at the end of our troubles and at the beginning of happiness."

As they drew near the town, they saw a Negro stretched on the ground with only one-half of his habit, which was a pair of blue cotton drawers, for the poor man had lost his left leg and his right hand.

"Good God," said Candide in Dutch, "what are you doing here, friend, in this deplorable condition?"

"I am waiting for my master, Mynheer Vanderdendur, the famous trader,"* answered the Negro.

"Was it Mynheer Vanderdendur that used you in this cruel manner?"

"Yes, sir," said the Negro. "It is the custom here. They give a pair of cotton drawers twice a year, and that is all our covering. When we labor in the sugar-works, and the mill happens to snatch hold of a finger, they instantly chop off our hand. And when we attempt to run away, they cut off a leg. Both these cases have happened to me, and it is at this expense that you eat sugar in Europe. And yet when my mother sold me for ten pattacoons on the coast of Guinea, she said to me, 'My dear child, bless our fetishes; adore them forever; they will make you live happy; you have the honor to be a slave to our lords the whites, by which you will make the fortune of us your parents.' Alas! I know not whether I have made their fortunes, but they have not made mine. Dogs, monkeys, and parrots are a thousand times less wretched than me. The Dutch fetishes who converted me tell me every Sunday that, blacks and whites, we are all children of Adam. As for me, I do not understand anything of genealo-

---

* Voltaire is jibing at a Dutch publisher, Van Düren, who had kept increasing the amount stipulated for printing a book.

gies; but if what these preachers say is true, we are all second cousins; and you must allow, that it is impossible to be worse treated by our relations than we are."

"Oh, Pangloss!" cried out Candide, "such horrid doings never entered your imagination. Here is an end of the matter; I find myself, after all, obliged to renounce your Optimism."

"Optimism!" said Cacambo. "What is that?"

"Alas!" replied Candide. "It is the obstinacy of maintaining that everything is best when it is worst." And so saying, he turned his eyes toward the poor Negro and shed a flood of tears, and in this weeping mood he entered the town of Surinam.

Immediately upon their arrival, our travelers inquired if there was any vessel in the harbor which they might send to Buenos Aires. The person they addressed themselves to happened to be the master of a Spanish bark, who offered to agree with them on moderate terms and appointed them a meeting at a publichouse. There Candide and his faithful Cacambo went to wait for him, taking with them their two sheep.

Candide, who was all frankness and sincerity, made an ingenuous recital of his adventures to the Spaniard, declaring to him at the same time his resolution of carrying off Miss Cunegund.

"In that case," said the shipmaster, "I'll take good care not to take you to Buenos Aires. It would prove a hanging matter to us all. The fair Cunegund is the Governor's favorite mistress."

These words were like a clap of thunder to Candide. He wept bitterly for a long time, and, taking Cacambo aside, he said to him:

"I'll tell you, my dear friend, what you must do. We have each of us in our pockets to the value of five or six millions in diamonds. You are cleverer at these matters than I; you

must go to Buenos Aires and bring off Miss Cunegund. If the
Governor makes any difficulty, give him a million. If he holds
out, give him two. As you have not killed an Inquisitor, they
will have no suspicion of you. I'll fit out another ship and go
to Venice, where I will wait for you. Venice is a free country,* where we shall have nothing to fear from Bulgarians,
Abares, Jews, or Inquisitors."

Cacambo greatly applauded this wise resolution. He was
inconsolable at the thought of parting with so good a master,
who treated him more like an intimate friend than a servant;
but the pleasure of being able to do him a service soon got
the better of his sorrow. They embraced each other with a
flood of tears. Candide charged him not to forget the old
woman. Cacambo set out the same day. This Cacambo was a
very honest fellow.

Candide continued some days longer at Surinam, waiting
for any captain to carry him and his two remaining sheep to
Italy. He hired domestics and purchased many things necessary for a long voyage. At length, Mynheer Vanderdendur,
skipper of a large Dutch vessel, came and offered his service.

"What will you take," said Candide, "to carry me, my
servants, my baggage, and these two sheep you see here
direct to Venice?"

The skipper asked ten thousand piastres, and Candide
agreed to his demand without hesitation.

"Oh, ho!" said the cunning Vanderdendur to himself, "this
stranger must be very rich. He agrees to give me ten thousand
piastres without hesitation."

Returning a little while after, he told Candide that upon
second consideration he could not undertake the voyage for
less than twenty thousand.

"Very well, you shall have them," said Candide.

---

* The Venetian republic remained independent until conquered by Napo-
leon in 1797.

"Zounds!" said the skipper to himself, "this man agrees to pay twenty thousand piastres with as much ease as ten."

Accordingly he went back again, and told him roundly that he would not carry him to Venice for less than thirty thousand piastres.

"Then you shall have thirty thousand," said Candide.

"Odso!" said the Dutchman once more to himself. "Thirty thousand piastres seem a trifle to this man. Those sheep must certainly be laden with an immense treasure. I'll stop here and ask no more, but make him pay down the thirty thousand piastres, and then we shall see."

Candide sold two small diamonds, the least of which was worth more than all the skipper asked. He paid him beforehand, and the two sheep were put on board, and Candide followed in a small boat to join the vessel in the road. The skipper took his opportunity, hoisted his sails and put out to sea with a favorable wind. Candide, confounded and amazed, soon lost sight of the ship.

"Alas!" said he, "this is a trick like those in our old world!"

He returned back to the shore overwhelmed with grief. And indeed, he had lost what would have been the fortune of twenty monarchs.

Immediately upon his landing, he applied to the Dutch magistrate. Being transported with passion, he thundered at the door, which being opened, he went in, told his case, and talked a little louder than was necessary. The magistrate began with fining him ten thousand piastres for his petulance and then listened very patiently to what he had to say, promised to examine into the affair at the skipper's return and ordered him to pay ten thousand piastres more for the fees of the court.

This treatment put Candide out of all patience. It is true he had suffered misfortunes a thousand times more grievous, but the cool insolence of the judge and of the skipper who robbed him raised his choler and threw him into a deep melancholy. The villainy of mankind presented itself to his mind in all its deformity, and his soul was a prey to the most gloomy ideas. After some time, hearing that the captain of a French ship was ready to set sail for Bordeaux, as he had no more sheep loaded with diamonds to put on board, he hired the cabin at the usual price and made it known in the town that he would pay the passage and board of any honest man who would give him his company during the voyage, besides making him a present of ten thousand piastres, on condition that such person was the most dissatisfied with his condition and the most unfortunate in the whole province.

Upon this there appeared such a crowd of candidates that a large fleet could not have contained them. Candide, willing to choose from among those who appeared most likely to answer his intention, selected twenty, who seemed to him the most sociable, and who all pretended to merit the preference. He invited them to his inn and promised to treat them with a supper, on condition that every man should bind himself by an oath to relate his own history. He declared at the same time that he would make choice of that person who should appear to him the most deserving of compassion and the most justly dissatisfied with his condition of life, and that he would make a present to the rest.

This extraordinary assembly continued sitting till four in the morning. Candide, while he was listening to their adventures, called to mind what the old woman had said to him on their voyage to Buenos Aires and the wager she had laid that there was not a person on board the ship but had met with very great unhappiness. Every story he heard put him in mind of Pangloss.

"My old master," said he, "would be confoundedly put to it to demonstrate his favorite system. Would he were here! Certainly if everything is for the best, it is in El Dorado, and not in the other parts of the world."

At length he determined in favor of a poor scholar who

had labored ten years for the booksellers at Amsterdam, being of opinion that no employment could be more detestable.°

This scholar, who was in fact a very honest man, had been robbed by his wife, beaten by his son and forsaken by his daughter, who had run away with a Portuguese. He had been likewise deprived of a small employment on which he subsisted, and he was persecuted by the clergy of Surinam, who took him for a Socinian.°° It must be acknowledged that the other competitors were, at least, as wretched as he, but Candide was in hopes that the company of a man of letters would relieve the tediousness of the voyage. All the other candidates complained that Candide had done them great injustice, but he stopped their mouths by a present of a hundred piastres to each.

CHAPTER XX

WHAT BEFELL CANDIDE AND MARTIN
ON THEIR VOYAGE

THE old scholar, whose name was Martin, embarked with Candide for Bordeaux. They both had seen and suffered a great deal; and if the ship had been destined to sail from Surinam to Japan round the Cape of Good Hope, they could have found sufficient entertainment for each other during the whole voyage in discoursing upon moral and natural evil.

° A subject of frequent complaints and harsh words in Voltaire's correspondence. Copyright and royalties had not yet been introduced; a writer was often at the publisher's mercy and was often cheated.

°° The Socinian heresy denies Original Sin and the need for Grace, as well as the Trinity.

Candide, however, had one advantage over Martin. He lived in the pleasing hopes of seeing Miss Cunegund once more, whereas the poor philosopher had nothing to hope for. Besides, Candide had money and jewels, and, notwithstanding he had lost a hundred red sheep, laden with the greatest treasure on the earth, and though he still smarted from the reflection of the Dutch skipper's knavery, yet when he considered what he had still left and repeated the name of Cunegund, especially after meal-times, he inclined to Pangloss's doctrine.

"And pray," said he to Martin, "what is your opinion of the whole of this system? What notion have you of moral and natural evil?"

"Sir," replied Martin, "our priests accused me of being a Socinian, but the real truth is I am a Manichæan."*

"Nay, now you are jesting," said Candide; "there are no Manichæans existing at present in the world."

"And yet I am one," said Martin, "but I cannot help it. I cannot for the soul of me think otherwise."

"Surely the devil must be in you," said Candide.

"He concerns himself so much," replied Martin, "in the affairs of this world that it is very probable he may be in me as well as everywhere else; but I must confess, when I cast my eye on this globe, or rather globule, I cannot help thinking that God has abandoned it to some malignant being. I always except El Dorado. I scarce ever knew a city that did not wish the destruction of its neighboring city, nor a family that did not desire to exterminate some other family. The poor, in all parts of the world, bear an inveterate hatred to the rich, even while they creep and cringe to them; and the rich treat the poor like sheep, whose wool and flesh they barter for money. A million of regimented assassins traverse

* A third century heresy which maintained co-equal principles of good and evil in the universe.

Europe from one end to the other to get their bread by regular depredation and murder, because it is the most gentlemanlike profession. Even in those cities which seem to enjoy the blessings of peace and where the arts flourish, the inhabitants are devoured with envy, care, and anxiety, which are greater plagues than any experienced in a town besieged. Private chagrins are still more dreadful than public calamities. In a word, I have seen and suffered so much, that I am a Manichæan."

"And yet there is some good in the world," replied Candide.

"Maybe," said Martin, "but it has escaped my knowledge."

While they were deeply engaged in this dispute they heard the report of cannon, which redoubled every moment. Each took out his glass, and they spied two ships warmly engaged at the distance of about three miles. The wind brought them both so near the French ship that those on board her had the pleasure of seeing the fight with great ease. At last one of the two vessels gave the other a shot between wind and water, which sank her outright. Then could Candide and Martin plainly perceive a hundred men on the deck of the vessel which was sinking, who, with hands uplifted to heaven, sent forth piercing cries and were in a moment swallowed up by the waves.

"Well," said Martin, "you now see in what manner mankind treat each other."

"It is certain," said Candide, "that there is something diabolical in this affair."

As he was speaking thus, he saw something of a shining red hue, which swam close to the vessel. The boat was hoisted out to see what it might be, when it proved to be one of his sheep. Candide felt more joy at the recovery of this one animal than he did grief when he lost the other hundred, though laden with the large diamonds of El Dorado.

The French captain quickly perceived that the victorious ship belonged to the crown of Spain, that the other which sank was a Dutch pirate and the very same captain who had robbed Candide. The immense riches which this villain had amassed were buried with him in the deep, and only this one sheep saved out of the whole.

"You see," said Candide to Martin, "that vice is sometimes punished. This villain, the Dutch skipper, has met with the fate he deserved."

"Very truly," said Martin, "but why should the passengers be doomed also to destruction? God has punished the knave, and the devil has drowned the rest."

The French and Spanish ships continued their cruise, and Candide and Martin their conversation. They disputed fourteen days successively, at the end of which they were just as far advanced as the first moment they began. However, they had the satisfaction of disputing, of communicating their ideas and of mutually comforting each other. Candide embraced his sheep.

"Since I have found thee again," said he, "I may possibly find my Cunegund once more."

CHAPTER XXI

CANDIDE AND MARTIN, WHILE THUS REASONING WITH EACH OTHER, DRAW NEAR TO THE COAST OF FRANCE

At length they sighted the coast of France.

"Pray, Mr. Martin," said Candide, "have you ever been in France?"

"Yes, sir," said Martin, "I have been in several provinces

of that kingdom. In some, one-half of the people are mad-men; and in some, they are too artful; in others, again, they are in general either very good-natured or very brutal; while in others, they affect to be witty, and in all, their ruling pas-sion is love, the next is slander and the last is to talk non-sense."

"But pray, Mr. Martin, were you ever in Paris?"

"Yes, sir, I have been in that city, and it is a place that contains the several species just described. It is a chaos, a confused multitude, where everyone seeks for pleasure with-out being able to find it, at least, as far as I have observed during my short stay in that city. At my arrival, I was robbed of all I had in the world by pickpockets and sharpers at the fair of St. Germain. I was taken up myself for a robber and confined in prison a whole week. After that I hired myself as proofreader to a press in order to get a little money toward defraying my expenses back to Holland on foot. I knew the whole tribe of scribblers, intriguers, and religious convul-sionaries.* It is said the people of that city are very polite; I believe they may be so."

"For my part, I have no curiosity to see France," said Candide. "You may easily conceive, my friend, that, after spending a month at El Dorado, I can desire to behold noth-ing upon earth but Miss Cunegund. I am going to wait for her at Venice. I intend to pass through France on my way to Italy; will you not bear me company?"

"With all my heart," said Martin. "They say Venice is agreeable to none but noble Venetians, but that, neverthe-less, strangers are well received there when they have plenty of money. Now I have none, but you have, therefore I will attend you wherever you please."

"Now we are upon this subject," said Candide, "do you

---

* Refers to the "miracles" on the grave of the Jansenist deacon Pâris (1725), which induced hypnotic convulsions in the throngs.

think that the earth was originally sea, as we read in that great book which belongs to the captain of the ship?"

"I believe nothing of it," replied Martin, "any more than I do of the many other chimeras which have been related to us for some time past."

"But then, to what end," said Candide, "was the world formed?"

"To make us mad," said Martin.

"Are you not surprised," continued Candide, "at the love which the two girls in the country of the Oreillons had for those two monkeys?—You know, I have told you the story."

"Surprised!" replied Martin. "Not in the least. I see nothing strange in this passion. I have seen so many extraordinary things, that there is nothing extraordinary to me now."

"Do you think," said Candide, "that mankind always massacred each other as they do now? Were they always guilty of lies, fraud, treachery, ingratitude, inconstancy, envy, ambition, and cruelty? Were they always thieves, fools, cowards, gluttons, drunkards, misers, calumniators, debauchees, fanatics, and hypocrites?"

"Do you believe," said Martin, "that hawks have always been accustomed to eat pigeons when they found them?"

"Yes, of course," said Candide.

"Well then," replied Martin, "if hawks have always had the same nature, why should you pretend that mankind change theirs?"

"Oh!" said Candide. "There is a great deal of difference, for free will . . ."

Reasoning thus, they arrived at Bordeaux.

CHAPTER XXII

WHAT HAPPENED TO CANDIDE AND MARTIN
IN FRANCE

CANDIDE stayed no longer at Bordeaux than was necessary to dispose of a few of the pebbles he had brought from El Dorado and to provide himself with a post-chaise for two persons, for he could no longer stir a step without his philosopher Martin. The only thing that gave him concern was the being obliged to leave his sheep behind him, which he entrusted to the care of the Academy of Sciences at Bordeaux. The academicians proposed, as a prize subject for the year, to prove why the wool of this sheep was red. And the prize was adjudged to a northern sage, who demonstrated by A plus B, minus C, divided by Z, that the sheep must necessarily be red and die of the rot.

In the meantime, all the travelers whom Candide met with in the inns, or on the road, told him to a man that they were going to Paris. This general eagerness gave him likewise a great desire to see this capital, and it was not much out of his way to Venice.

He entered the city by the suburbs of St. Marceau, and thought himself in one of the vilest hamlets in all Westphalia.

Candide had not been long at his inn before he was seized with a slight disorder owing to the fatigue he had undergone. As he wore a diamond of an enormous size on his finger, and had, among the rest of his equipage, a strong box that seemed very weighty, he soon found himself between two physicians whom he had not sent for, a number of intimate friends whom he had never seen, and who would not quit his bedside, and two female devotees who warmed his soup for him.

"I remember," said Martin to him, "that the first time I came to Paris I was likewise taken ill. I was very poor, and, accordingly, I had neither friends, nurses, nor physicians, and yet I did very well."

However, by dint of purging and bleeding Candide's disorder became very serious. The priest of the parish came with all imaginable politeness to desire a note of him, payable to the bearer in the other world.* Candide refused to comply with his request, but the two devotees assured him that it was a new fashion. Candide replied that he was not one that followed the fashion. Martin was for throwing the priest out of the window. The cleric swore Candide should not have Christian burial. Martin swore in his turn that he would bury the cleric alive if he continued to plague them any longer. The dispute grew warm. Martin took him by the shoulders and turned him out of the room, which gave great scandal, and occasioned a lawsuit.

Candide recovered; and, till he was in a condition to go abroad, had a great deal of very good company to pass the evenings with him in his chamber. They played for high stakes. Candide was surprised to find he never got the aces, and Martin was not at all surprised at the matter.

Among those who did him the honors of the place was a little spruce Abbé from Périgord, one of those insinuating, busy, fawning, impudent, accommodating fellows, who lie in wait for strangers at their arrival, tell them all the scandal of the town and offer to minister to their pleasures at various prices. This man conducted Candide and Martin to the play-

* Priests sometimes refused absolution to the dying unless they signed a "confessional note" acknowledging adherence to the Bull (*Unigenitus*) condemning the Jansenists.

house. They were acting a new tragedy. Candide found himself placed near a cluster of wits. This, however, did not prevent him from shedding tears at some scenes which were perfectly acted. One of these talkers said to him between the acts:

"You are greatly to blame in shedding tears. That actress plays horribly, and the man who plays with her still worse, and the piece itself is still more execrable than the performance. The author* does not understand a word of Arabic, and yet he has laid his scene in Arabia. And what is more, he is a fellow who does not believe in innate ideas. Tomorrow I will bring you a score of pamphlets that have been written against him."

"Pray, sir," said Candide to the Abbé, "how many theatrical pieces have you in France?"

"Five or six thousand," replied the other.

"Indeed! That is a great number," said Candide, "but how many good ones may there be?"

"About fifteen or sixteen."

"Oh! That is a great number," said Martin.

Candide was greatly taken with an actress who performed the part of Queen Elizabeth in a dull kind of tragedy that is played sometimes.

"That actress," said he to Martin, "pleases me greatly. She has a slight resemblance to Miss Cunegund. I should be very glad to pay my respects to her."

The Abbé of Périgord offered his services to introduce him to her at her own house. Candide, who was brought up in Germany, desired to know what might be the ceremonial used on those occasions and how a Queen of England was treated in France.

"There is a necessary distinction to be observed in these matters," said the Abbé. "In a country town we take them to

---

* Voltaire is referring to himself and to his tragedy, *Mahomet*.

a tavern; here in Paris, they are treated with great respect during their lifetime, provided they are handsome, and when they die, we throw their bodies upon a dunghill."

"How," said Candide, "throw a queen's body upon a dunghill!"

"The gentleman is quite right," said Martin. "He tells you nothing but the truth. I happened to be in Paris when Mlle. Monime* made her exit, as one may say, out of this world into another. She was refused what they call here the rights of sepulture; that is to say, she was denied the privilege of rotting in a churchyard by the side of all the beggars in the parish. She was buried alone by her troupe at the corner of Burgundy Street, which must certainly have shocked her extremely, as she had very exalted notions of things."

"This is acting very impolitely," said Candide.

"Lord!" said Martin. "What can be said to it? It is the way of these people. Imagine all the contradictions, all the inconsistencies possible, and you may meet with them in the government, the courts of justice, the churches, and the public spectacles of this odd nation."

"Is it true," said Candide, "that the people of Paris are always laughing?"

"Yes," replied the Abbé, "but it is with anger in their hearts. They express all their complaints by loud bursts of laughter and commit the most detestable crimes with a smile on their faces."

"Who was that fat swine," said Candide, "who spoke so ill to me of the piece with which I was so much affected, and of the players who gave me so much pleasure?"

"A good-for-nothing sort of a man," answered the Abbé, "one who gets his livelihood by abusing every new book and play. He abominates to see anyone meet with success, like

---

* The famous actress, Adrienne Lecouvreur, was refused sacred burial in 1730, to Voltaire's great indignation. There was considerable polemic over the excommunication of actors.

eunuchs who detest everyone that possesses those powers they are deprived of. He is one of those vipers in literature who nourish themselves with their own venom, a pamphlet-monger."

"A pamphlet-monger!" said Candide. "What is that?"

"Why, a pamphlet-monger," replied the Abbé, "is a writer of pamphlets, a Fréron."*

Candide, Martin, and the Abbé of Périgord argued thus on the staircase, while they stood to see people go out of the playhouse.

"Though I am very eager to see Miss Cunegund again," said Candide, "yet I have a great inclination to sup with Mlle. Clairon,** for I am really much taken with her."

The Abbé was not a person to show his face at this lady's house, which was frequented by none but the best company.

"She is engaged this evening," said he, "but I will do myself the honor of introducing you to a lady of quality of my acquaintance, at whose house you will see as much of the manners of Paris as if you had lived here for four years."

Candide, who was naturally curious, suffered himself to be conducted to this lady's house, which was in the suburb of St. Honoré. The company were engaged at faro; twelve melancholy punters!† each held in his hand a small pack of cards, the corners of which doubled down†† were so many registers of their ill fortune. A profound silence reigned throughout the assembly; a pallid dread was in the countenances of the punters and restless anxiety in the face of him who kept the

---

* Voltaire and the journalist-critic Elie Fréron, were bitter enemies. Voltaire was extremely sensitive to criticism.

** Renowned actress to whom Voltaire was grateful for her moving performance in his tragedy *Tancrède*. Much of this chapter is a later interpolation.

† Those who play against the banker, or dealer.

†† Bending the corner of the card indicated a multiplication of the bet by seven ("sept-et-le-va"). A "parole" *(paroli)* was a dishonest trick, made after the first bet had been won. The contrived name, "Parolignac," is comically built on the word *paroli.*

bank. And the lady of the house, who was seated next to him, observed pitilessly with lynx's eyes every parole, and sept-et-le-va as they were going, as likewise those who tallied, and made them undouble their cards with a severe exactness, though mixed with a politeness which she thought necessary not to frighten away her customers. This lady assumed the title of Marchioness of Parolignac. Her daughter, a girl of about fifteen years of age, was one of the punters and took care to give her mamma a wink, when any one of them attempted to repair the rigor of their ill fortune by a little innocent deception. The company were thus occupied, when Candide, Martin, and the Abbé made their entrance. Not a creature rose to salute them, or indeed took the least notice of them, being wholly intent upon the business in hand.

"Ah!" said Candide, "my lady Baroness of Thunder-ten-tronckh would have behaved more civilly."

However, the Abbé whispered in the ear of the Marchioness, who half rose and honored Candide with a gracious smile and Martin with a dignified inclination of her head. She then ordered a seat for Candide and a hand of cards. He lost fifty thousand francs in two rounds. After that, they supped very elegantly, and everyone was astounded that Candide was not disturbed at his loss. The servants said to each other in their servants' language:

"This must be some English lord!"

Supper was like most others of this kind in Paris. At first there was silence, then there was an indistinguishable babel of words, then jokes, most of them insipid, false reports, bad reasonings, a little political talk, and much scandal. They spoke also of new books.

"Have you seen," said the Abbé of Périgord, "the romance written by Monsieur Gauchat, the doctor of theology?"

"Yes," replied one of the guests, "but I had not the patience to go through it. We have a throng of impertinent writers, but all of them together do not approach Gauchat, the doctor of theology, in impertinence. I am so sated with reading these piles of vile stuff that flood upon us that I even resolved to come here and make a party at faro."

"But what say you to Archdeacon Trublet's miscellanies?" said the Abbé.

"Oh," cried the Marchioness of Parolignac, "tedious creature. What pains he is at to tell one things that all the world knows. How he labors an argument that is hardly worth the slightest consideration! How absurdly he makes use of other people's wit! How he mangles what he pilfers from them! How he disgusts me! But he will disgust me no more. It is enough to have read a few pages of the Archdeacon."

There was at the table a person of learning and taste, who supported what the Marchioness had advanced. They next began to talk of tragedies. The lady desired to know how it came about that there were several tragedies which still continued to be played, but which were unreadable. The man of taste explained very clearly how a piece may be in some manner interesting, without having a grain of merit. He showed, in a few words, that it is not sufficient to throw together a few incidents that are to be met with in every romance and that dazzle the spectator. The thoughts should be new without being far-fetched; frequently sublime, but always natural; the author should have a thorough knowledge of the human heart and make it speak properly. He should be a great poet, without showing an affectation of it in any of the characters of his piece; he should be a perfect master of his language, speak it with all its purity and with the utmost harmony, and yet not so as to make the sense a slave to the rhyme.

"Whoever," added he, "neglects any of these rules, though he may write two or three tragedies with tolerable success, will never be reckoned in the number of good authors. There are a few good tragedies, some are idylls, in well-written and harmonious dialogue, and others a chain of political reasonings that send one to sleep, or else pompous and high-flown amplifications that disgust rather than please. Others again are the ravings of an enthusiast, in an uncouth style, with unmeaning flights, or long apostrophes to the deities, for want of knowing how to address mankind; in a word, a collection of false maxims and turgid commonplaces."

Candide listened to this discourse with great attention, and conceived a high opinion for the person who delivered it. And as the Marchioness had taken care to place him at her side, he took the liberty to whisper softly in her ear and ask who this person was who spoke so well.

"He is a man of letters," replied her ladyship, "who never plays and whom the Abbé brings with him to my house sometimes to spend an evening. He is a great judge of writing, especially in tragedy; he has composed one himself which was a flop, and has written a book which was never seen out of his bookseller's shop, excepting only one copy, which he sent me with a dedication."

"What a great man," cried Candide. "He is a second Pangloss."

Then, turning toward him, "Sir," said he, "you are doubtless of opinion that everything is for the best in the physical and moral world and that nothing could be otherwise than it is?"

"I, sir," replied the man of letters, "I think no such thing, I assure you. I find that all in this world is topsy-turvy. No one knows what is his rank, his office, nor what he does, nor what he should do; and that except for our evenings which we generally pass tolerably merrily, the rest of our time is spent in idle disputes and quarrels, Jansenists against Molinists,* the Parlement against the Church, men of letters against men of letters, countries against countries, financiers against the people, wives against husbands, relations against relations. In short, there is eternal warfare."

---

* Molinism was a branch of Jesuitism, which explained grace and free will by God's foreknowledge.

"Yes," said Candide, "and I have seen worse than all that. And yet a learned man, who had the misfortune to be hanged, taught me that everything was marvelously well and that these evils you are speaking of were only so many shadows in a beautiful picture."*

"Your hempen sage," said Martin, "laughed at you. These shadows as you call them are most horrible blemishes."

"It is men who make these blemishes," rejoined Candide, "and they cannot do otherwise."

"Then it is not their fault," added Martin.

The greater part of the gamesters, who did not understand a syllable of this discourse, continued to drink, while Martin reasoned with the learned gentleman, and Candide recounted some of his adventures to the lady of the house.

After supper, the Marchioness conducted Candide into her dressing-room, and made him sit down on a sofa.

"Well," said she, "are you still so violently fond of Miss Cunegund of Thunder-ten-tronckh?"

"Yes, madam," replied Candide.

The Marchioness said to him with a tender smile, "You answer like a young man from Westphalia. A Frenchman would have said, 'It is true, madam, I have a great passion for Miss Cunegund, but since I have seen you, I fear I can no longer love her as I did.'"

"Alas, madam," replied Candide, "I'll make you what answer you please."

"You fell in love with her, I find, in picking up her handkerchief. You shall pick up my garter."

"With all my heart," said Candide.

"But you must tie it on," said the lady, and Candide tied it on.

"Look you," said the lady, "you are a stranger. I make some of my lovers here in Paris languish for me a fortnight,

---

* A reference to Leibnitz's *Theodicy.*

but I surrender to you the first night, because I am willing to do the honors of my country to a young Westphalian."

The fair one having cast her eye on two large diamonds on the young stranger's finger, praised them in so earnest a manner that they passed from Candide's fingers to those of the Marchioness.

As Candide was going home with the Abbé, he felt some qualms of conscience for having been guilty of infidelity to Miss Cunegund. The Abbé shared with him in his uneasiness. He had but an inconsiderable share in the fifty thousand francs that Candide had lost at play and in the value of the two jewels, half given, half extorted from him. His plan was to profit as much as he could from the advantages which his acquaintance with Candide could procure for him. He spoke to him much of Miss Cunegund, and Candide assured him that he would heartily ask pardon of that fair one for his infidelity to her when he saw her at Venice.

The Abbé redoubled his civilities and seemed to interest himself warmly in everything that Candide said, did or seemed inclined to do.

"And so, sir, you have a rendezvous at Venice?"

"Yes, Monsieur l'Abbé," answered Candide. "I must indeed go and find Miss Cunegund."

Then the pleasure he took in talking about the object he loved led him insensibly to relate, according to custom, part of his adventures with the illustrious Westphalian beauty.

"I fancy," said the Abbé, "Miss Cunegund has a great deal of wit and that her letters must be very entertaining."

"I never received any from her," said Candide, "for you are to consider that being kicked out of the castle on her account, I could not write to her; especially as, soon after my departure, I heard she was dead; that though I found her again, I lost her, and that I have sent a messenger to her two thousand five hundred leagues from here, and I wait here for his return with an answer from her."

The Abbé listened attentively—and seemed a little thought-ful. He soon took leave of the two strangers, after having embraced them tenderly. The next day, immediately on wak-ing, Candide received a letter couched in these terms:

"My dearest lover, I have been ill in this city these eight days. I have heard of your arrival and should fly to your arms, were I able to move a limb of me. I was informed of your procedure at Bordeaux. I left there the faithful Cacambo and the old woman who will soon follow me. The Governor of Buenos Aires has taken everything from me, but I still have your heart. Come. Your presence will restore me to life or will make me die with pleasure."

At the receipt of this charming, this unexpected, letter, Candide felt the utmost joy, though the malady of his beloved Cunegund overwhelmed him with grief. Distracted between these two passions, he took his gold and his diamonds and procured a person to direct him with Martin to the house where Miss Cunegund lodged. He entered, trembling with emotion, his heart fluttered, his tongue faltered. He attempted to draw the curtain apart, and called for a light to the bed-side.

"Take care," said the servant. "The light is unbearable to her," and immediately she closed the curtains again.

"My beloved," said Candide, weeping, "how are you? If you cannot see me, at least speak to me."

"She cannot speak," said the servant. The lady then put from the bed a plump hand which Candide bathed with his tears, then filled with diamonds, leaving a purse full of gold on the armchair.

In the midst of his transports there arrived a police officer, followed by the Abbé of Périgord and a file of musketeers.

"There," said he, "are the two suspected foreigners."

He had them seized forthwith and bade the soldiers carry them off to prison.

"Travelers are not treated in this manner in El Dorado," said Candide.

"I am more of a Manichæan now than ever," said Martin.

"But pray, good sir, where are you taking us?" asked Candide.

"To a dungeon," said the officer.

Martin having recovered his calm judged that the lady who pretended to be Cunegund was a cheat, that the Abbé of Périgord was a sharper, who had imposed upon Candide's simplicity as quickly as he could, and the officer another knave whom they might easily get rid of.

Candide, following the advice of his friend Martin, and burning with impatience to see the real Cunegund, rather than be obliged to appear at a court of justice, proposed to the officer to make him a present of three small diamonds, each of them worth three thousand pistoles.

"Ah, sir," said this understrapper of justice, "had you committed ever so much villainy, this would render you the honestest man living in my eyes. Three diamonds, worth three thousand pistoles. Why, my dear sir, so far from leading you to jail, I would lose my life to serve you. There are orders to arrest all strangers, but leave it to me. I have a brother at Dieppe in Normandy. I myself will conduct you there, and if you have a diamond left to give him, he will take as much care of you as I myself should."

"But why," said Candide, "do they arrest all strangers?"

The Abbé of Périgord answered that it was because a poor devil of the province of Atrébatie* heard somebody tell foolish stories and this induced him to commit a parricide; not such a one as that in the month of May, 1610, but such as that in the month of December in the year 1594, and such

---

* The province of Artois, home of Damiens, who in 1757 attempted to assassinate Louis XV. In 1610, Ravaillac had assassinated Henri IV, after a previous attempt in 1594 by Jean Chastel.

as many that have been perpetrated in other months and years by other poor devils who had heard foolish stories.

The officer then explained to them what the Abbé meant.

"Monsters," exclaimed Candide. "Is it possible that such horrors should pass among a people who are continually singing and dancing? Is there no immediate means of flying this abominable country, where monkeys provoke tigers?* I have seen bears in my country, but men I have beheld nowhere but in El Dorado. In the name of God, sir," said he to the officer, "do me the kindness to conduct me to Venice, where I am to wait upon Miss Cunegund."

"I cannot conduct you further than Lower Normandy," said the officer.

So saying, he ordered Candide's irons to be struck off, said he had made an error, and sent his followers about their business, after which he conducted Candide and Martin to Dieppe and left them to the care of his brother. There happened just then to be a small Dutch ship in the roads. The Norman, whom the other three diamonds had converted into the most obliging, serviceable being that ever breathed, took care to see Candide and his attendants safe on board the vessel that was just ready to sail for Portsmouth in England. This was not the nearest way to Venice indeed, but Candide thought himself escaped out of hell and did not in the least doubt but he should quickly find an opportunity of resuming his voyage to Venice.

---

* Monkeys, i.e., priests; tigers, i.e., assassins.

CHAPTER XXIII

CANDIDE AND MARTIN TOUCH UPON THE
ENGLISH COAST. WHAT THEY SAW THERE

"Ah, Pangloss! Pangloss! Ah, Martin! Martin! Ah, my dear Miss Cunegund! What is this world of ours?" Thus exclaimed Candide as soon as he had got on board the Dutch ship.

"Why, something very insane, and very abominable," said Martin.

"You are acquainted with England," said Candide. "Are they as great fools in that country as in France?"

"Yes, but in a different manner," answered Martin. "You know that these two nations are at war about a few acres of snow in the neighborhood of Canada and that they have expended much greater sums in the contest than all Canada is worth. To say exactly whether there are a greater number fit to be inhabitants of a madhouse in the one country than the other exceeds the limits of my imperfect capacity. I know, in general, that the people we are going to visit are of a very dark and gloomy disposition."

As they were chatting thus together, they arrived at Portsmouth. The shore, on each side of the harbor, was lined with a multitude of people, whose eyes were steadfastly fixed on a rather large man, who was kneeling down on the deck of one of the men-of-war, with his eyes bound.° Opposite to this personage stood four soldiers, each of whom shot three

---

° Admiral John Byng was executed on March 14, 1757, for the loss of Minorca. Voltaire, who had met Byng during his stay in England, was greatly aroused by this injustice.

bullets into his skull, with all the composure imaginable. And when it was done, the whole company went away perfectly well satisfied.

"What the devil is all this for?" said Candide. "And what demon lords it thus over all the world?"

He then asked who was that stout man who had been sent out of the world with so much ceremony, and he received for answer that it was an admiral.

"And pray," he said, "why do you put your admiral to death?"

"Because he did not put a sufficient number of his fellow creatures to death. You must know, he had an engagement with a French admiral, and it has been proved against him that he was not near enough to his antagonist."

"But," replied Candide, "the French admiral must have been as far from him."

"There is no doubt of that. But in this country it is found requisite, now and then, to put one admiral to death in order to spirit up the others."

Candide was so shocked at what he saw and heard that he would not set foot on shore, but made a bargain with the Dutch skipper (were he even to rob him like the captain of Surinam) to carry him directly to Venice.

The skipper was ready in two days. They sailed along the coast of France and passed within sight of Lisbon, at which Candide trembled. From there they proceeded to the straits, entered the Mediterranean and at length arrived at Venice.

"God be praised," said Candide, embracing Martin. "This is the place where I am to behold my beloved Cunegund once again. I can rely on Cacambo, like another self. All is well, all very well, all as well as possible."

CHAPTER XXIV

OF PACQUETTE AND FRIAR GIROFLÉE

UPON their arrival at Venice, he went in search of Cacambo at every inn and coffeehouse and among all the ladies of pleasure, but could hear nothing of him. He sent every day to inquire of every ship and every vessel that came in. Still no news of Cacambo.

"It is strange!" said he to Martin. "Very strange! That I should have had time to sail from Surinam to Bordeaux; to travel from there to Paris, to Dieppe, to Portsmouth; to sail along the coast of Portugal and Spain, and up the Mediterranean, to spend some months in Venice; and that my lovely Cunegund should not have arrived! Instead of her, I only met with a Parisian impostor, and a rascally Abbé of Périgord. Cunegund is probably dead, and I have nothing to do but to follow her. Alas! How much better would it have been for me to have remained in the paradise of El Dorado than to have returned to this cursed Europe! You are in the right, my dear Martin; you are certainly in the right; all is misery and deceit."

He fell into a deep melancholy and neither went to the opera in vogue, nor partook of any of the diversions of the Carnival. Not a woman caused him even a moment's temptation.

Martin said to him, "Upon my word, I think you are very simple to imagine that a rascally valet, with five or six millions in his pocket, would go in search of your mistress to the further end of the world and bring her to Venice to meet you. If he finds her, he will take her for himself; if he does not, he will take another. Let me advise you to forget your valet Cacambo and your mistress Cunegund."

Martin's speech was not consoling. Candide's melancholy increased, and Martin never left proving to him that there is very little virtue or happiness in this world, except perhaps in El Dorado where hardly anybody can gain admittance.

While they were disputing on this important subject, and still expecting Miss Cunegund, Candide perceived a young Theatine friar in St. Mark's Place, with a girl under his arm. The Theatine looked fresh-colored, plump, and vigorous; his eyes sparkled; his air and gait were bold and lofty. The girl was very pretty and was singing a song; and every now and then gave her Theatine an amorous ogle and wantonly pinched his ruddy cheeks.

"You will at least allow," said Candide to Martin, "that these two are happy. Hitherto I have met with none but unfortunate people in the whole habitable globe, except in El Dorado; but, as to this couple, I would venture to lay a wager they are happy."

"Done," said Martin. "I wager they are not."

"Well, we have only to ask them to dine with us," said Candide, "and you will see whether I am mistaken."

Thereupon he accosted them and with great politeness invited them to his inn to eat some macaroni, with Lombard partridges and caviar, and to drink a bottle of Montepulciano, Lacrima Christi, Cyprus and Samos wine. The girl blushed; the Theatine accepted the invitation, and she followed him, eyeing Candide every now and then with a mixture of surprise and confusion, while the tears stole down her cheeks. No sooner did she enter his apartment than she cried out:

"How, Mr. Candide, have you quite forgotten poor Pacquette? Do you not know her again?"

Candide, who had not regarded her with any degree of attention before, being wholly occupied with the thoughts of his dear Cunegund, exclaimed:

"Ah! Is it you, child? Was it you that reduced Dr. Pangloss to that fine condition I saw him in?"

"Alas, sir," answered Pacquette, "it was I, indeed. I find you are acquainted with everything, and I have been informed of all the misfortunes that happened to the whole family of my lady Baroness and the fair Cunegund. But I can safely swear to you that my lot was no less deplorable. I was innocence itself when you saw me last. A Franciscan, who was my confessor, easily seduced me. The consequences proved terrible. I was obliged to leave the castle some time after the Baron kicked you out by the backside from there, and if a famous surgeon had not taken compassion on me, I had been a dead woman. Gratitude obliged me to live with him some time as a mistress. His wife, who was a very devil for jealousy, beat me unmercifully every day. Oh! she was a perfect fury. The doctor himself was the most ugly of all mortals, and I the most wretched creature existing, to be continually beaten for a man whom I did not love. You are sensible, sir, how dangerous it was for an ill-natured woman to be married to a physician. Incensed at the behavior of his wife, he one day gave her so affectionate a remedy for a slight cold she had caught that she died in less than two hours in most dreadful convulsions. Her relations prosecuted the husband, who was obliged to fly, and I was sent to prison. My innocence would not have saved me, if I had not been tolerably handsome. The judge gave me my liberty on condition he should succeed the doctor. However, I was soon supplanted by a rival, turned off without a farthing and obliged to continue the abominable trade which you men think so pleasing, but which to us unhappy creatures is the most dreadful of all sufferings. At length I came to follow the business at Venice. Ah, sir, did you but know what it is to be obliged to lie indifferently with old tradesmen, with counselors, with monks, gondoliers, and abbés; to be exposed to all their insolence and abuse; to find it often necessary to borrow a skirt, only that it may be lifted by some disgusting wretch; to be robbed by one gallant of what we get from another; to be subject to the extortions of civil magistrates; and to have forever before one's eyes the prospect of old age, a poorhouse, or a dunghill, you would conclude that I am one of the most unhappy wretches breathing."

Thus did Pacquette unbosom herself to honest Candide in his closet, in the presence of Martin, who took occasion to say to him:

"You see I have half won the wager already."

Friar Giroflée was all this time in the parlor refreshing himself with a glass or two of wine till dinner was ready.

"But," said Candide to Pacquette, "you looked so gay and content when I met you. You were singing and caressing the Theatine with so much fondness that I absolutely thought you as happy as you say you are now miserable."

"Ah, dear sir," said Pacquette, "this is one of the miseries of the trade. Yesterday I was robbed and beaten by an officer, yet today I must appear good-humored and gay to please a friar."

Candide was convinced and acknowledged that Martin was in the right. They sat down to table with Pacquette and the Theatine. The meal was very pleasant, and toward the end they began to converse together with some freedom.

"Father," said Candide, to the friar, "you seem to me to enjoy a state of happiness that even kings might envy, joy and health are painted in your countenance. You have a pretty wench for your pleasure, and you seem to be perfectly well contented with your condition as a Theatine."

"Faith, sir," said Friar Giroflée, "I wish with all my soul the Theatines were every one of them at the bottom of the sea. I have been tempted a thousand times to set fire to the convent and go and turn Turk. My parents obliged me, at the age of fifteen, to put on this detestable habit only to increase the fortune of an elder brother of mine, whom God confound! Jealousy, discord, and fury reside in our convent. It is true, I have preached some paltry sermons, by which I have got a little money, half of which the prior robs me of, and the remainder helps to pay my girls. But, at night, when I go to my convent, I am ready to dash my brains against the walls of the dormitory, and this is the case with all the rest of our fraternity."

Martin, turning toward Candide, with his usual indifference, said, "Well, what think you now? Have I won the wager entirely?"

Candide gave two thousand piastres to Pacquette and a thousand to Friar Giroflée, saying, "I will answer that this will make them happy."

"I am not of your opinion," said Martin. "Perhaps this money will only make them much more wretched."

"Be that as it may," said Candide, "one thing comforts me. I see that one often meets with those whom we expected never to see again, so that, perhaps, as I have found my red sheep and Pacquette, I may be lucky enough to find Miss Cunegund also."

"I wish," said Martin, "she one day may make you happy, but I doubt it much."

"You are very hard," said Candide.

"It is because," said Martin, "I have seen the world."

"Observe those gondoliers," said Candide. "Are they not perpetually singing?"

"You do not see them," answered Martin, "at home with their wives and brats. The doge has his chagrin, gondoliers theirs. Nevertheless, in the main, I look upon the gondolier's life as preferable to that of the doge; but the difference is so trifling that it is not worth the trouble of examining into."

"I have heard great talk," said Candide, "of the senator

Pococurante,* who lives in that fine house at the Brenta, where, they say, he entertains foreigners in the most polite manner. They claim that this man is a perfect stranger to trouble."

"I should be glad to see so extraordinary a being," said Martin.

Candide thereupon sent a messenger to Signor Pococurante, desiring permission to wait on him the next day.

CHAPTER XXV

CANDIDE AND MARTIN PAY A VISIT TO SIGNOR POCOCURANTE, A NOBLE VENETIAN

CANDIDE and his friend Martin went in a gondola on the Brenta, and arrived at the palace of the noble Pococurante. The gardens were laid out in an elegant taste and adorned with beautiful marble statues. His palace was architecturally magnificent. The master of the house, who was a man of sixty and very rich, received our two travelers with great politeness, but without much ceremony, which somewhat disconcerted Candide, but was not at all displeasing to Martin.

First, two very pretty girls, neatly dressed, brought in chocolate, which was extremely well frothed. Candide could not help praising their beauty and graceful carriage.

"The creatures are well enough," said the senator. "I make them go to bed with me sometimes, for I am heartily tired of the women of the town, their coquetry, their jealousy, their quarrels, their humors, their meannesses, their pride, and their

---

* The name involves a double play on words: "caring little, indifferent," and "cuckold."

folly. I am weary of making sonnets, or of paying for sonnets to be made on them, but after all, these two girls begin to bore me."

After having refreshed himself, Candide walked into a large gallery, where he was struck with the sight of a fine collection of paintings. He asked what master had painted the two first.

"They are Raphael's," answered the senator. "I gave a great deal of money for them some years ago, purely out of conceit, as they were said to be the finest pieces in Italy, but I cannot say they please me. The coloring is dark and heavy; the faces are not rounded and do not stand out enough, and the drapery has no resemblance to the actual material. In short, notwithstanding the encomiums lavished upon them, they are not, in my opinion, a true representation of nature. I approve of no paintings but where I think I behold nature herself, and there are none of that kind to be met with. I have what is called a fine collection, but I take no manner of delight in them."

While dinner was getting ready, Pococurante ordered a concert. Candide praised the music to the skies.

"This noise," said the noble Venetian, "may amuse one for a little time, but if it was to last above half an hour, it would grow tiresome to everybody, though perhaps no one would care to own it. Music is become the art of executing what is difficult; now, whatever is difficult cannot be long pleasing. I believe I might take more pleasure in an opera, if they had not made such a monster of it as perfectly shocks me. And I am amazed how people can bear to see wretched tragedies set to music, where the scenes are contrived for no other purpose than to lug in, as it were by the ears, three or four ridiculous songs, to give a favorite actress an opportunity of exhibiting her pipe. Let who will, or can, die away in raptures at the trills of an eunuch quavering the majestic part of Cæsar or Cato, and strutting in a foolish manner upon the stage; for my part, I have long ago renounced these paltry entertainments which constitute the glory of modern Italy, and are so dearly purchased by crowned heads."

Candide opposed these sentiments, but he did it in a discreet manner. As for Martin, he was entirely of the old senator's opinion.

Dinner being served they sat down to table, and after a very hearty repast returned to the library. Candide, observing Homer richly bound, commended the noble Venetian's taste.

"This," said he, "is a book that was once the delight of the great Pangloss, the best philosopher in Germany."

"Homer is no favorite of mine,*" answered Pococurante, very coolly. "I was made to believe once that I took a pleasure in reading him; but his continual repetitions of battles have all such a resemblance with each other; his gods that are forever in a hurry and bustle, without ever doing anything; his Helen, that is the cause of the war, and yet hardly acts in the whole performance; his Troy, that holds out so long, without being taken. In short, all these things together make the poem very insipid to me. I have asked some learned men, whether they are not in reality as much bored as myself with reading this poet. Those who were sincere assured me that he had made them fall asleep; and yet, that they could not well avoid giving him a place in their libraries as a monument of antiquity or like those rusty medals which are of no use in commerce."

"But your Excellency does not surely form the same opinion of Virgil?" said Candide.

"Why, I grant," replied Pococurante, "that the second, third, fourth, and sixth book of his *Æneid* are excellent; but as for his pious Æneas, his strong Cloanthus, his friendly Achates, his boy Ascanius, his silly king Latinus, his ill-bred

---

* An echo of the Quarrel of the Ancients and the Moderns, which had put Homer out of fashion.

Amata, his insipid Lavinia, I think there cannot in nature be anything more flat and disagreeable. I must confess, I prefer Tasso and Ariosto's cock-and-bull stories."

"May I take the liberty to ask if you do not receive great pleasure from reading Horace?" said Candide.

"There are maxims in this writer," replied Pococurante, "from which a man of the world may reap some benefit; and the short and forceful measure of the verse makes them more easily to be retained in the memory. But I see nothing extraordinary in his journey to Brundisium, and his account of his bad dinner; nor in his dirty low quarrel between one Pupilus, whose words, as he expresses it, were full of pus, and another, whose language was dipped in vinegar.* His indelicate verses against old women and witches have frequently given me great offense; nor can I discover the great merit of his telling his friend Mæcenas that if he will but rank him in the class of lyric poets, his lofty head shall touch the stars. Ignorant readers are apt to praise everything by the lump in a writer of reputation. For my part, I read only to please myself. I like nothing but what makes for my purpose."

Candide, who had been brought up with a notion of never making use of his own judgment, was astonished at what he had heard, but Martin found there was a good deal of reason in the senator's remarks.

"Oh! Here is a Cicero," said Candide. "This great man, I fancy, you are never tired of reading?"

"Indeed, I never read him at all," replied Pococurante. "What the deuce is it to me whether he pleads for Rabirius or Cluentius? I try causes enough myself. I had once some liking for his philosophical works, but when I found he doubted of everything, I thought I knew as much as he and had no need of a guide to learn ignorance."

"Ha!" cried Martin, "here are fourscore volumes of the

---

* Rupilius, in Horace's seventh satire.

memoirs of the Academy of Science. Perhaps there may be something valuable in them."

"Yes," answered Pococurante, "so there might if any one of the compilers of this rubbish had only invented the art of pin-making. But all these volumes are filled with mere chimerical systems without one single article conducive to real utility."

"I see a prodigious number of plays," said Candide, "in Italian, Spanish, and French."

"Yes," replied the Venetian, "there are I think three thousand, and not three dozen of them good for anything. As to these huge volumes of divinity and those enormous collections of sermons, they are altogether not worth one single page in Seneca; and I fancy you will readily believe that neither myself, nor anyone else, ever looks into them."

Martin noticed some shelves filled with English books.

"I fancy," he said, "that a republican must be highly delighted with those books, which are most of them written with a noble spirit of freedom."

"It is noble to write as we think," said Pococurante. "It is the privilege of humanity. Throughout Italy we write only what we do not think, and the present inhabitants of the country of the Cæsars and Antoninuses dare not acquire a single idea without the permission of a Dominican friar. I should be enamored of the spirit of the English nation did it not utterly frustrate the good effects it would produce, by passion and the spirit of party."

Candide, seeing a Milton, asked the senator if he did not think that author a great man.

"Who?" said Pococurante sharply. "That barbarian who writes a tedious commentary in ten books of harsh verse on the first chapter of Genesis? That slovenly imitator of the Greeks, who disfigures the creation, by making the Messiah take a pair of compasses from a cupboard in heaven to plan the world; whereas Moses represented the Deity as producing the whole universe by his fiat? Can I, think you, have any esteem for a writer who has spoiled Tasso's hell and the devil? who transforms Lucifer sometimes into a toad, and, at others, into a pigmy? who makes him rehash the same thing over again a hundred times? who makes him argue over theology? and who, by an absurdly serious imitation of Ariosto's comic invention of firearms, represents the devils and angels cannonading each other in heaven? Neither I nor any other Italian can possibly take pleasure in such melancholy reveries; but the marriage of Sin and Death, and snakes issuing from the womb of the former, are enough to make any person sick that is not lost to all sense of delicacy, while his long description of a public hospital is fit only for a gravedigger. This obscene, whimsical and disagreeable poem met with neglect at its first publication, and I only treat the author now as he was treated in his own country by his contemporaries."

Candide was sensibly grieved at this speech as he had a great respect for Homer and was very fond of Milton.

"Alas!" said he softly to Martin. "I am afraid this man holds our German poets in great contempt."

"There would be no such great harm in that," said Martin.

"O what a remarkable man!" said Candide, still to himself. "What a prodigious genius is this Pococurante! Nothing can please him."

After finishing their survey of the library, they went down into the garden, when Candide commended all its beauties.

"I know nothing upon earth laid out in such bad taste," said Pococurante; "everything about it is childish and trifling, but I shall have another laid out tomorrow upon a nobler plan."

As soon as our two travelers had taken leave of his Excellency, Candide said to Martin:

"Surely now, you will own that this man is the happiest of all mortals, for he is above everything he possesses."

"But do not you see," answered Martin, "that he likewise

dislikes everything he possesses? It was an observation of Plato, long since, that those are not the best stomachs that reject, without distinction, all sorts of aliments."

"True," said Candide, "but still there must certainly be a pleasure in criticizing everything, and in perceiving faults where others think they see beauties."

"That is," replied Martin, "there is a pleasure in having no pleasure."

"Well, well," said Candide, "I find that I shall be the only happy man at last, when I am blessed with the sight of my dear Cunegund."

"It is good to hope," said Martin.

In the meanwhile, days and weeks slipped away, and no news of Cacambo. Candide was so overwhelmed with grief that he did not reflect on the behavior of Pacquette and Friar Giroflée, who never returned to thank him for the presents he had so generously made them.

CHAPTER XXVI

CANDIDE AND MARTIN SUP WITH SIX STRANGERS, AND WHO THEY WERE

ONE evening when Candide, with his attendant Martin, was going to sit down to supper with some foreigners who lodged in the same inn, a man, with a face the color of soot, came behind him, and taking him by the arm, said:

"Hold yourself in readiness to go along with us, be sure you do not fail."

He turned and beheld Cacambo. Nothing but the sight of

Cunegund could have given greater joy and surprise. He was almost beside himself with joy. After embracing this dear friend, he said:

"Cunegund must be here. Where, where is she? Carry me to her this instant, that I may die with joy in her presence."

"Cunegund is not here," answered Cacambo. "She is at Constantinople."

"Good heavens, at Constantinople! But no matter if she was in China, I would fly there. Let us be gone."

"We depart after supper," said Cacambo. "I cannot at present stay to say anything more to you. I am a slave, and my master waits for me. I must go and attend him at table. But say not a word, only get your supper, and hold yourself in readiness."

Candide, divided between joy and grief, charmed to have thus met with his faithful agent again and surprised to hear he was a slave, his heart palpitating, his senses confused, but full of the hopes of recovering his mistress, sat down to table with Martin, who beheld all these scenes with great unconcern, and with six strangers who had come to spend the carnival at Venice.

Cacambo waited at table upon one of these strangers. When supper was nearly over, he drew near to his master, and whispered to him in the ear:

"Sire, your Majesty may go when you please, the ship is ready."

Having said these words, he left the room. The guests, surprised at what they had heard, looked at each other without speaking a word; then another servant drawing near to his master, in like manner said:

"Sire, your Majesty's post-chaise is at Padua, and the bark is ready."

His master made him a sign, and he instantly withdrew. The company all stared at each other again, and the general astonishment was increased. A third servant then approached another of the strangers, and said:

"Sire, if your Majesty will be advised by me, you will not stay any longer in this place. I will go and get everything ready"—and he instantly disappeared.

Candide and Martin then took it for granted that this was some of the diversions of the carnival, and that these were characters in masquerade. Then a fourth domestic said to the fourth stranger:

"Your Majesty may set out when you please." Saying this, he went away like the rest.

A fifth valet said the same to a fifth master. But the sixth domestic spoke in a different style to the person on whom he waited, and who sat next to Candide.

"Troth, sir," said he, "they will trust your Majesty no longer, nor myself neither; and we may both of us chance to be pinched this very night; and therefore I shall take care of myself, and so adieu."

The servants being all gone, the six strangers, with Candide and Martin, remained in a profound silence. At length Candide broke it by saying:

"Gentlemen, this is a very singular joke. Why, how came you all to be kings? For my part, I own frankly, that neither my friend Martin here nor myself have any claim to royalty."

Cacambo's master then began, with great gravity, to deliver himself thus in Italian:

"I am not joking in the least, my name is Achmet III. I was Grand Sultan for many years.* I dethroned my brother, my nephew dethroned me, my viziers lost their heads, and I am condemned to end my days in the old seraglio. My nephew, the Grand Sultan Mahmud, gives me permission to travel sometimes for my health, and I am come to spend the carnival at Venice."

---

* From 1703 to 1730.

A young man who sat by Achmet spoke next, and said:

"My name is Ivan.* I was once Emperor of all the Russias, but was dethroned in my cradle. My parents were confined, and I was brought up in a prison. Yet I am sometimes allowed to travel, though always with persons to keep a guard over me, and I am come to spend the carnival at Venice."

The third said:

"I am Charles Edward, King of England.** My father has renounced his right to the throne in my favor. I have fought in defense of my rights, and eight hundred of my followers have had their hearts taken out of their bodies alive and thrown in their faces. I have myself been confined in a prison. I am going to Rome to visit the King my father, who was dethroned as well as myself and my grandfather, and I am come to spend the carnival at Venice."

The fourth spoke thus:

"I am the King of Poland. The fortune of war has stripped me of my hereditary dominions. My father experienced the same vicissitudes of fate. I resign myself to the will of Providence, in the same manner as Sultan Achmet, the Emperor Ivan, and King Charles Edward, whom God long preserve, and I am come to spend the carnival at Venice."

The fifth said:

"I am King of Poland also.† I have twice lost my kingdom, but Providence has given me other dominions, where I have done more good than all the Sarmatian kings put together were ever able to do on the banks of the Vistula. I resign myself likewise to Providence, and am come to spend the carnival at Venice."

It now came the sixth monarch's turn to speak.

---

* Ivan VI (1740–1764), dethroned in 1741.

** The Pretender, grandson of James II, who was defeated by the Duke of Cumberland at Culloden (1746).

† Stanislas Leczinsky (1677–1766) having twice lost Poland, was made Duke of Lorraine. He was an enlightened ruler and popular among the *philosophes*.

"Gentlemen," said he, "I am not so great a prince as the rest of you, it is true; but I am, however, a crowned head. I am Theodore, elected King of Corsica. I have had the title of Majesty, and am now hardly treated with common civility. I have coined money, and am not now worth a single ducat. I have had two secretaries of state, and am now without a valet. I was once seatèd on a throne, and since that have lain upon a truss of straw in a common jail in London, and I very much fear I shall meet with the same fate here in Venice, where I come, like your Majesties, to divert myself at the carnival."

The other five kings listened to this speech with great attention. It excited their compassion. Each of them made the unhappy Theodore a present of twenty sequins to get clothes and shirts, and Candide gave him a diamond worth just a hundred times that sum.

"Who can this private person be," said the five kings, "who is able to give, and has actually given, a hundred times as much as any of us? Are you, sir, also a king?"

"No, gentlemen, and I have no wish to be one."

Just as they rose from table, in came four Serene Highnesses who had also been stripped of their territories by the fortune of war, and were come to spend the remainder of the carnival at Venice. Candide took no manner of notice of them, for his thoughts were wholly employed on his voyage to Constantinople, whither he intended to go in search of his beloved Cunegund.

CHAPTER XXVII

CANDIDE'S VOYAGE TO CONSTANTINOPLE

THE trusty Cacambo had already engaged the captain of the Turkish ship that was to carry Sultan Achmet back to Constantinople to take Candide and Martin on board. Accordingly, they both embarked, after paying their obeisance to his miserable Highness. As they were going on board, Candide said to Martin:

"You see we supped in company with six dethroned kings, and to one of them I gave charity. Perhaps there may be a great many other princes still more unfortunate. For my part, I have lost only a hundred sheep, and am now going to fly to the arms of Cunegund. My dear Martin, I must insist on it, that Pangloss was in the right. All is for the best."

"I wish it may be," said Martin.

"But this was an odd adventure we met with at Venice. I do not think there ever was an instance before of six dethroned monarchs supping together at a public inn."

"This is no more extraordinary," said Martin, "than most of what has happened to us. It is a very common thing for kings to be dethroned. And as for our having the honor to sup with six of them, it is a mere accident not deserving our attention. What does it matter with whom one sups, provided one has good fare?"

As soon as Candide set his foot on board the vessel, he flew to his old friend and servant Cacambo; and throwing his arms about his neck, embraced him with transports of joy.

111

"Well," said he, "what news of Cunegund? Does she still continue the paragon of beauty? Does she love me still? How is she? You have, doubtless, purchased a palace for her at Constantinople?"

"My dear master," replied Cacambo, "Cunegund washes dishes on the banks of the Sea of Marmora, in the house of a prince who has very few to wash. She is at present a slave in the family of an ancient sovereign, named Ragotsky,* whom the Grand Turk allows three crowns a day to maintain him in his exile. But the most melancholy circumstance of all is, that she has lost her beauty and turned horribly ugly."

"Ugly or handsome," said Candide, "I am a man of honor, and, as such, am obliged to love her still. But how could she possibly have been reduced to so abject a condition, when I sent five or six millions to her by you?"

"Lord bless me," said Cacambo, "was not I obliged to give two millions to Señor Don Fernando d'Ibaraa y Figueora y Mascarenas y Lampourdos y Souza, Governor of Buenos Aires, for liberty to take Miss Cunegund away with me? And then did not a brave fellow of a pirate very gallantly strip us of all the rest? And then did not this same pirate carry us with him to Cape Matapan, to Milo, to Nicaria, to Samos, to Petra, to the Dardanelles, to Marmora, to Scutari? Cunegund and the old woman are now servants to the prince I have told you of, and I myself am slave to the dethroned Sultan."

"What a chain of terrible calamities!" exclaimed Candide. "But, after all, I have still some diamonds left, with which I can easily procure Cunegund's liberty. It is a pity she is grown ugly."

Then turning to Martin, "What think you, friend," said he, "whose condition is most to be pitied, the Emperor Achmet's, the Emperor Ivan's, King Charles Edward's, or mine?"

---

* Rákóczy (1676–1735), prince of Transylvania, defeated by Joseph II of Austria, against whom the French had sent him.

"Faith, I cannot resolve your question," said Martin, "unless I had been in the breasts of you all."

"Ah!" cried Candide. "Was Pangloss here now, he would have known and satisfied me at once."

"I know not," said Martin, "in what balance your Pangloss could have weighed the misfortunes of mankind, and have set a just estimation on their sufferings. All that I pretend to know of the matter is that there are millions of men on the earth whose conditions are a hundred times more pitiable than those of King Charles Edward, the Emperor Ivan, or Sultan Achmet."

"Why, that may be," answered Candide.

In a few days they reached the Bosporus, and the first thing Candide did was to pay a high ransom for Cacambo. Then, without losing time, he and his companions went on board a galley in order to search for his Cunegund, on the banks of the Sea of Marmora, notwithstanding she was grown so ugly.

There were two slaves among the crew of the galley, who rowed very ill, and to whose bare backs the master of the vessel frequently applied a lash of oxhide. Candide, from natural sympathy, looked at these two slaves more attentively than at any of the rest, and drew near them with a look of pity. Their features, though greatly disfigured, appeared to him to bear a strong resemblance with those of Pangloss and the unhappy Baron Jesuit, Miss Cunegund's brother. This idea affected him with grief and compassion: he examined them more attentively than before.

"In troth," said he, turning to Martin, "if I had not seen my master Pangloss fairly hanged, and had not myself been unlucky enough to run the Baron through the body, I could believe these are they rowing in the galley."

No sooner had Candide uttered the names of the Baron and Pangloss than the two slaves gave a great cry, ceased rowing and let fall their oars out of their hands. The master of the vessel, seeing this, ran up to them and redoubled the discipline of the lash.

"Hold, hold," cried Candide. "I will give you what money you ask for these two persons."

"Good heavens! It is Candide," said one of the men.

"Candide!" cried the other.

"Do I dream," said Candide, "or am I awake? Am I actually on board this galley? Is this my lord Baron, whom I killed? And that my master Pangloss, whom I saw hanged?"

"It is I! It is I!" cried they both together.

"What? Is this your great philosopher?" said Martin.

"My dear sir," said Candide to the master of the galley, "how much do you ask for the ransom of the Baron of Thunder-ten-tronckh, who is one of the first barons of the empire, and of Mr. Pangloss, the most profound metaphysician in Germany?"

"Why then, Christian cur," replied the Turkish captain, "since these two dogs of Christian slaves are barons and metaphysicians, who no doubt are of high rank in their own country, you will give me fifty thousand sequins."

"You shall have them, sir. Carry me back as quick as thought to Constantinople, and you shall receive the money immediately. No! Carry me first to Miss Cunegund."

The captain, upon Candide's first proposal, had already tacked about, and he made the crew apply their oars so effectively that the vessel flew through the water quicker than a bird cleaves the air.

Candide bestowed a thousand embraces on the Baron and Pangloss.

"And so then, my dear Baron, I did not kill you? And you, my dear Pangloss, are come to life again after your hanging? But how came you slaves on board a Turkish galley?"

"And is it true that my dear sister is in this country?" said the Baron.

"Yes," said Cacambo.

"And do I once again behold my dear Candide?" said
Pangloss.

Candide presented Martin and Cacambo to them. They
embraced each other, and all spoke together. The galley flew
like lightning, and now they were got back to the port. Candide instantly sent for a Jew, to whom he sold for fifty
thousand sequins a diamond richly worth one hundred thousand, though the fellow swore to him all the time, by Abraham, that he gave him the most he could possibly afford. He
no sooner got the money into his hands than he paid it down
for the ransom of the Baron and Pangloss. The latter flung
himself at the feet of his deliverer and bathed him with his
tears. The former thanked him with a gracious nod and
promised to return him the money at the first opportunity.

"But is it possible," said he, "that my sister should be in
Turkey?"

"Nothing is more possible," answered Cacambo, "for she
scours the dishes in the house of a Transylvanian prince."

Candide sent directly for two Jews and sold more diamonds to them. And then he set out with his companions in
another galley, to deliver Cunegund from slavery.

CHAPTER XXVIII

WHAT BEFELL CANDIDE, CUNEGUND, PANGLOSS, MARTIN, &C.

"Pardon," said Candide to the Baron. "Once more let me entreat your pardon, Reverend Father, for running you through
the body."

"Say no more about it," replied the Baron. "I was a little

too hasty I must own. But as you seem to be anxious to know by what accident I came to be a slave on board the galley where you saw me, I will inform you. After I had been cured of the wound you gave me, by the apothecary of the college, I was attacked and carried off by a party of Spanish troops, who clapped me up in prison in Buenos Aires, at the very time my sister was setting out from there. I asked leave to return to Rome, to the general of my order, who appointed me chaplain to the French ambassador at Constantinople. I had not been a week in my new office, when I happened to meet one evening with a young Icoglan,* extremely handsome and well-made. The weather was very hot, the young man had an inclination to bathe. I took the opportunity to bathe likewise. I did not know it was a crime for a Christian to be found naked in company with a young Turk. A cadi** ordered me to receive a hundred blows on the soles of my feet and sent me to the galleys. I do not believe that there was ever an act of more flagrant injustice. But I would fain know how my sister came to be a scullion to a Transylvanian prince who has taken refuge among the Turks."

"But how happens it that I behold you again, my dear Pangloss?" said Candide.

"It is true," answered Pangloss, "you saw me hanged, though I ought properly to have been burned. But you may remember that it rained extremely hard when they were going to roast me. The storm was so violent that they found it impossible to light the fire, so they hanged me because they could do no better. A surgeon purchased my body, carried it home, and prepared to dissect me. He began by making a cruciform incision from my navel to the clavicle. It is impossible for anyone to have been more poorly hanged than I had been. The executioner of the Holy Inquisition was a subdeacon and knew how to burn people very well, but as for

* An officer of the sultan's palace.
** Magistrate.

hanging, he was a novice at it, being quite out of the way of his practice. The cord being wet, and not slipping properly, the noose did not join. In short, I still continued to breathe. The cruciform incision made me scream to such a degree that my surgeon fell flat upon his back and, imagining it was the devil he was dissecting, ran away and in his fright tumbled downstairs. His wife hearing the noise flew from the next room and, seeing me stretched upon the table with my cruciform incision, was still more terrified than her husband. She took to her heels and fell over him. When they had a little recovered themselves, I heard her say to her husband, 'My dear, how could you think of dissecting an heretic? Don't you know that the devil is always in them? I'll run directly to a priest to come and drive the evil spirit out.' I trembled from head to foot at hearing her talk in this manner, and exerted what little strength I had left to cry out, 'Have mercy on me!' At length the Portuguese barber took courage, sewed up my wound, and his wife nursed me; and I was upon my legs in a fortnight's time. The barber got me a place as lackey to a Knight of Malta who was going to Venice; but finding my master had no money to pay me my wages, I entered into the service of a Venetian merchant, and went with him to Constantinople.

"One day I happened to enter a mosque, where I saw no one but an old imam and a very pretty young female devotee, who was saying her prayers. Her bosom was rather exposed, and between her breasts she had a beautiful nosegay of tulips, roses, anemones, ranunculuses, hyacinths, and auriculas. She let fall her nosegay. I ran immediately to take it up, and presented it to her with a most respectful bow. I was so long in putting it back, that the imam began to be angry, and, perceiving I was a Christian, he cried out for help. They carried me before the cadi, who ordered me to receive one hundred bastinadoes and sent me to the galleys. I was chained in the very galley and to the very same bench with my lord the

Baron. On board this galley there were four young men from Marseilles, five Neapolitan priests, and two monks of Corfu, who told us that the like adventures happened every day. The Baron pretended that he had been worse used than myself, and I insisted that there was far less harm in taking up a nosegay and putting it into a woman's bosom than to be found stark naked with a young Icoglan. We were continually in dispute and received twenty lashes a day with a thong, when the universal concatenation of events brought you on board our galley to ransom us from slavery."

"Well, my dear Pangloss," said Candide to him, "when you were hanged, dissected, whipped and tugging at the oar, did you continue to think that everything in this world happens for the best?"

"I have always abided by my first opinion," answered Pangloss, "for, after all, I am a philosopher, and it would not become me to retract my sentiments. Especially, as Leibnitz could not be in the wrong, and that pre-established harmony is the finest thing in the world, as well as the *plenum* and the *materia subtilis*."*

CHAPTER XXIX

IN WHAT MANNER CANDIDE FOUND CUNEGUND AND THE OLD WOMAN AGAIN

WHILE Candide, the Baron, Pangloss, Martin, and Cacambo were relating their several adventures, and reasoning on the contingent or noncontingent events of this world; while they

---

* "Pre-established harmony" is Leibnitz's doctrine of mind-body synchronization. The "plenum" and "subtle matter" belong to Cartesian physics, mocked by Newtonians like Voltaire.

were disputing on causes and effects, on moral and physical evil, on free will and necessity, and on the consolation that may be felt by a person when a slave and chained to an oar in a Turkish galley, they arrived at the house of the Transylvanian prince on the coasts of the Propontis. The first objects they beheld there were Miss Cunegund and the old woman, who were hanging some tablecloths on a line to dry.

The Baron turned pale at the sight. Even the tender Candide, that affectionate lover, upon seeing his fair Cunegund sunburned, bleary-eyed, flat-breasted, her face wrinkled and her arms all covered with a red scurf, started back with horror. But, recovering himself, he advanced toward her out of good manners. She embraced Candide and her brother; they embraced the old woman, and Candide ransomed them both.

There was a small farm in the neighborhood, which the old woman proposed to Candide to make a shift with till the company should meet with a more favorable destiny. Cunegund, not knowing that she was grown ugly, as no one had informed her of it, reminded Candide of his promise in so peremptory a manner that the simple lad did not dare to refuse her. He then acquainted the Baron that he was going to marry his sister.

"I will never suffer," said the Baron, "my sister to be guilty of an action so derogatory to her birth and family, nor will I bear this insolence on your part. No, I never will be reproached that my nephews are not qualified for the first ecclesiastical dignities in Germany, nor shall a sister of mine ever be the wife of any person below the rank of a baron of the Empire."

Cunegund flung herself at her brother's feet and bedewed them with her tears, but he still continued inflexible.

"You crazy fool," said Candide, "have I not delivered you from the galleys, paid your ransom, and your sister's too who was a scullion and is very ugly, and yet I condescend to marry her? And will you make claim to oppose the match? If I were to listen only to the dictates of my anger, I should kill you again."

"You may kill me again," said the Baron, "but you shall not marry my sister while I am living."

CHAPTER XXX

CONCLUSION

CANDIDE had, in truth, no great inclination to marry Cunegund; but the extreme impertinence of the Baron determined him to conclude the match, and Cunegund pressed him so warmly that he could not recant. He consulted Pangloss, Martin, and the faithful Cacambo. Pangloss composed a fine memorial, by which he proved that the Baron had no right over his sister; and that she might, according to all the laws of the Empire, marry Candide without benefit of clergy. Martin concluded that they should throw the Baron into the sea. Cacambo decided that he must be delivered to the Turkish captain and sent to the galleys, after which he should be conveyed by the first ship to the Father General at Rome. This advice was found to be very good. The old woman approved of it, and not a syllable was said to his sister. The business was executed for a little money, and they had the pleasure of tricking a Jesuit and punishing the pride of a German baron.

It was altogether natural to imagine that after undergoing so many disasters, Candide, married to his mistress, and living with the philosopher Pangloss, the philosopher Martin, the prudent Cacambo, and the old woman, having besides brought home so many diamonds from the country of the ancient Incas, would lead the most agreeable life in the world. But he had been so much cheated by the Jews that he had nothing else left but his little farm. His wife, every day growing more and more ugly, became ill-natured and insupportable. The old woman was infirm, and more bad-tempered yet than Cunegund. Cacambo, who worked in the garden, and carried the produce of it to sell at Constantinople, was overworked and cursed his fate. Pangloss despaired of making a figure in any of the German universities. And as to Martin, he was firmly persuaded that a person is equally ill-situated everywhere. He took things with patience. Candide, Martin, and Pangloss disputed sometimes about metaphysics and morality. Boats were often seen passing under the windows of the farm fraught with effendis, pashas, and cadis, that were going into banishment to Lemnos, Mytilene, and Erzeroum. And other cadis, pashas, and effendis were seen coming back to succeed the place of the exiles, and were driven out in their turns. They saw several heads very curiously stuffed with straw, being carried as presents to the Sublime Porte. Such sights gave occasion to frequent dissertations; and when no disputes were carried on, the irksomeness was so excessive that the old woman ventured one day to say to them:

"I would be glad to know which is worse, to be ravished a hundred times by Negro pirates, to have one buttock cut off, to run the gauntlet among the Bulgarians, to be whipped and hanged at an *auto-da-fé*, to be dissected, to be chained to an oar in a galley, and in short to experience all the miseries through which every one of us passed—or to remain here doing nothing?"

"This," said Candide, "is a big question."

This discourse gave birth to new reflections, and Martin especially concluded that man was born to live in the con-

vulsions of disquiet, or in the lethargy of boredom. Though
Candide did not absolutely agree to this, yet he was sure of
nothing. Pangloss avowed that he had undergone dreadful
sufferings; but having once maintained that everything went
on as well as possible, he still maintained it, and at the same
time believed nothing of it.

There was one thing which, more than ever, confirmed
Martin in his detestable principles, made Candide hesitate and
embarrassed Pangloss. This was the arrival of Pacquette and
Friar Giroflée one day at their farm. This couple had been
in the utmost distress. They had very speedily made away
with their three thousand piastres; they had parted, been
reconciled; quarreled again, been thrown into prison; had
made their escape, and at last Brother Giroflée turned Turk.
Pacquette still continued to follow her trade wherever she
came; but she got little or nothing by it.

"I foresaw very well," said Martin to Candide, "that your
presents would soon be squandered and only make them
more miserable. You and Cacambo were stuffed with millions
of piastres, and yet you are not more happy than Brother
Giroflée and Pacquette."

"Ah!" said Pangloss to Pacquette. "It is Heaven who has
brought you here among us, my poor child! Do you know
that you have cost me the tip of my nose, one eye, and one
ear? What a sight you are! And what is this world!"

This new adventure engaged them more deeply than ever
in philosophical disputations.

In the neighborhood lived a very famous dervish, who
passed for the best philosopher in Turkey; him they went to
consult: Pangloss, who was their spokesman, addressed him
thus:

"Master, we come to intreat you to tell us why so strange
an animal as man has been formed?"

"Why do you trouble your head about it?" said the dervish.
"Is it any business of yours?"

"But, my Reverend Father," said Candide, "there is a horrible deal of evil on the earth."

"What signifies it," said the dervish, "whether there is evil or good? When his Highness sends a ship to Egypt, does he trouble his head whether the rats in the vessel are at their ease or not?"

"What must then be done?" said Pangloss.

"Be silent," answered the dervish.

"I flattered myself," replied Pangloss, "that we should have the pleasure of arguing with you on causes and effects, on the best of possible worlds, the origin of evil, the nature of the soul, and the pre-established harmony."

At these words the dervish shut the door in their faces.

During this conversation, news was spread abroad that two viziers of the bench and the mufti had just been strangled at Constantinople, and several of their friends impaled. This catastrophe made a great noise for some hours. Pangloss, Candide, and Martin, as they were returning to the little farm, met with a good-looking old man, who was taking the air at his door, under an alcove formed of orange-trees. Pangloss, who was as inquisitive as he was argumentative, asked him what was the name of the mufti who was lately strangled.

"I cannot tell," answered the good old man. "I never knew the name of any mufti or vizier breathing. I am entirely ignorant of the event you speak of. I presume that, in general, such as are concerned in public affairs sometimes come to a miserable end, and that they deserve it; but I never inquire what is happening at Constantinople. I am content with sending thither the produce of the garden which I cultivate."

After saying these words, he invited the strangers to come into his house. His two daughters and two sons presented them with diverse sorts of iced sherbet of their own making; besides *caymac*, heightened with the peel of candied citrons, oranges, lemons, pineapples, pistachio nuts, and Mocha coffee unadulterated with the bad coffee of Batavia or the West Indies. After which the two daughters of this good mussulman perfumed the beards of Candide, Pangloss, and Martin.

"You must certainly have a vast estate," said Candide to the Turk.

"I have no more than twenty acres of ground," he replied, "the whole of which I cultivate myself with the help of my children; and our labor keeps off from us three great evils, boredom, vice, and want."

Candide, as he was returning home, made profound reflections on the Turk's discourse.

"This good old man," he said to Pangloss and Martin, "appears to me to have chosen for himself a lot much preferable to that of the six kings with whom we had the honor to sup."

"Human grandeur," said Pangloss, "is very dangerous, if we believe the testimonies of almost all philosophers; for we find Eglon, King of the Moabites, was assassinated by Ehud; Absalom was hanged by the hair of his head, and run through with three darts; King Nadab, son of Jeroboam, was slain by Baasha; King Elah by Zimri; Ahaziah by Jehu; Athaliah by Jehoiada; the Kings Jehoiakim, Jechoniah, and Zedekiah were led into captivity. I need not tell you what was the fate of Croesus, Astyages, Darius, Dionysius of Syracuse, Pyrrhus, Perseus, Hannibal, Jugurtha, Ariovistus, Caesar, Pompey, Nero, Otho, Vitellius, Domitian, Richard II of England, Edward II, Henry VI, Richard III, Mary Stuart, Charles I, the three Henrys of France, and the Emperor Henry IV."

"I know too," said Candide, "that we must cultivate our garden."

"You are in the right," said Pangloss, "for when man was put into the Garden of Eden, it was so that he should work in it; and this proves that man was not born to be idle."

"Let us work then without disputing," said Martin. "It is the only way to render life supportable."

The little society, one and all, entered into this laudable design and set themselves to exert their different talents. The little piece of ground yielded them a plentiful crop. Cunegund indeed was very ugly, but she became an excellent hand at pastrywork; Pacquette embroidered; the old woman had the care of the linen. There was none, down to Brother Giroflée, but did some service; he was a very good carpenter and became an honest man. Pangloss used now and then to say to Candide:

"There is a concatenation of all events in the best of possible worlds; for, in short, had you not been kicked out of a fine castle by the backside for the love of Miss Cunegund, had you not been put into the Inquisition, had you not traveled over America on foot, had you not run the Baron through the body, and had you not lost all your sheep which you brought from the good country of El Dorado, you would not have been here to eat preserved citrons and pistachio nuts."

"Excellently observed," answered Candide, "but let us cultivate our garden."

God MaDE UNIVErSE, then
sat bAck and watcheD

let break away from Pangloss
dogma

biblical
cultivate mind - reason - through EXPERIENCE
don't leave your life to FatE - man is responsible
for his own actions
be prepared to work
much like Descartes

Candide - always talking

ZADIG*

OR

FATE

AN

ORIENTAL HISTORY

APPROBATION

[I, the underwritten, who have obtained the character of a learned and even of an ingenious man, have read this manuscript, which, in spite of myself, I have found to be curious, entertaining, moral, philosophical, and capable of affording pleasure even to those who hate romances. I have therefore decried it and have assured the Cadi-lesquier** that it is an abominable performance.]

---

* The name "Zadig" is probably related to the Hebrew word "Zadok," meaning "just."
** Turkish dignitary in charge of religion and laws.

EPISTLE DEDICATORY OF ZADIG TO THE
SULTANA SHERAH

By SADI[*]

The 18th of the Month SCHEWAL, *in the 837th Year of the* HEGIRA

DELIGHT of the eyes, torment of the heart, and light of the mind, I kiss not the dust of your feet, because you never walk, or walk only on the carpets of Iran, or in paths strewn with roses. I offer you the translation of a book, written by an ancient sage, who, having the happiness to have nothing to do, amused himself in composing the history of Zadig, a work which performs more than it promises. I beseech you to read and examine it; for, though you are in the spring of life, and every pleasure courts you to its embrace; though you are beautiful, and your beauty be embellished by your admirable talents; though you are praised from evening to morning, and, on all these accounts, have a right to be devoid of common sense; yet you have a sound judgment, and a fine taste; and I have heard you reason with more accuracy than the old dervishes, with their long beards and pointed bonnets. You are discreet without being distrustful; gentle without weakness; and beneficent with discernment. You love your friends, and make yourself no enemies. Your wit never borrows its charms from the shafts of detraction; you neither say nor do any ill, notwithstanding that both are so much in your power. In a

[*] Noted Persian poet.

129

word, your soul has always appeared to me to be as pure and unsullied as your beauty. Besides, you have some little knowledge in philosophy, which makes me believe that you will take more pleasure than others of your sex in perusing the work of this venerable sage.

It was originally written in the ancient Chaldee, a language which neither you nor I understand. It was afterward translated into the Arabic, to amuse the famous Sultan Ouloug-beg,* much about the time that the Arabians and the Persians began to write the *Thousand and One Nights*, the *Thousand and One Days*, &c. Ouloug was fond of reading about Zadig, but the sultanas were fonder of the *Thousand and One*.

"How can you prefer (would the wise Ouloug say to them) those stories which have neither sense nor meaning?"

"It is for that very reason (replied the sultanas) that we like them."

I flatter myself that you will not resemble these your predecessors; but that you will be a true Ouloug. I even hope that when you are tired with those general conversations, which differ from the *Thousand and One* in nothing but in being less agreeable, I shall have the honor to entertain you for a moment with a rational discourse. Had you been Thalestris** in the time of Alexander the son of Philip, had you been the Queen of Sheba in the time of Solomon, these are the very kings that would have paid you a visit.

I pray the heavenly powers that your pleasures may be unmixed, your beauty never fading and your happiness without end.

—SADI

---

* Reigned from 1416 to 1449.
** Queen of the Amazons who visited Alexander in order to have a child by him.

CHAPTER I

THE BLIND OF ONE EYE

THERE lived at Babylon, in the reign of King Moabdar, a young man, named Zadig, of a good natural disposition, strengthened and improved by education. Though rich and young, he had learned to moderate his passions: he had nothing affected in his behavior; he did not pretend to examine every action by the strict rules of reason, but was always ready to make proper allowances for the weakness of mankind. It was a matter of surprise that, notwithstanding his wit, he never exposed by his raillery those vague, incoherent, and noisy discourses, those rash censures, ignorant decisions, coarse jests, and all that empty jingle of words which at Babylon went by the name of conversation. He had learned, in the first book of Zoroaster, that self-love is a football swelled with wind, from which, when pierced, tempests issue forth. Above all, Zadig never boasted of his conquests among the women, nor affected to entertain a contemptible opinion of the fair sex. He was generous, and was never afraid of obliging the ungrateful, remembering the grand precept of Zoroaster: "When you eat, give to the dogs, should they even bite you." He was as wise as it is possible for a man to be, for he sought to live with the wise. Instructed in the sciences of the ancient Chaldeans, he understood the principles of natural philosophy, such as they were then supposed to be, and knew as much of metaphysics as has ever been known in any age, that is, little or nothing at all. He was firmly persuaded, notwithstanding the new philosophy of the times, that the year consisted of three hundred and sixty-five days and six hours and that the sun was in the center of the universe. But when the principal magi told him, with a haughty and contemptuous air, that his sentiments were of a dangerous tendency, and that it was to be an enemy of the state to believe that the sun revolved round its own axis, and that the year had twelve months, he held his tongue with great modesty and meekness.

Possessed as he was of great riches, and consequently of many friends, blessed with a good constitution, a handsome face, a mind just and moderate, and a heart noble and sincere, Zadig imagined that he might easily be happy. He was going to be married to Semira, who, in point of beauty, birth, and fortune, was the first match in Babylon. He had a real and virtuous affection for this lady, and she loved him with the most passionate fondness. The happy moment that was to unite them had almost arrived, when happening to take a walk together toward one of the gates of Babylon, under the palm trees that adorn the banks of the Euphrates, they saw some men approaching, armed with sabers and arrows. These were the attendants of young Orcan, the minister's nephew, whom his uncle's creatures had flattered into an opinion that he might do everything with impunity. He had none of the graces nor virtues of Zadig; but thinking himself a much more accomplished man, he was enraged to find that the other was preferred before him. This jealousy, which was merely the effect of his vanity, made him imagine that he was desperately in love with Semira. The ravishers seized her. In the violence of the outrage they wounded her, and made the blood flow from one, the sight of whom would have softened the tigers of Mount Imaus. She pierced the heavens with her complaints. She cried out:

"My dear husband! They tear me from the man I adore."

Regardless of her own danger, she was only concerned for the fate of her dear Zadig, who, in the meantime, defended himself with all the strength that courage and love could inspire. Assisted only by two slaves, he put the ravishers to flight and carried home Semira, insensible and covered with blood. On opening her eyes, she beheld her deliverer.

"O Zadig," said she, "I loved you formerly as my intended husband; I now love you as the preserver of my honor and my life."

Never was heart more deeply moved than that of Semira. Never did a mouth more charming express more moving sentiments, in these glowing words inspired by a sense of the greatest of all favors, and by the most tender transports of a lawful passion. Her wound was slight and was soon cured. Zadig was more dangerously wounded; an arrow had pierced him near his eye, and penetrated to a considerable depth. Semira wearied Heaven with her prayers for the recovery of her lover. Her eyes were constantly bathed in tears. She anxiously waited the happy moment when those of Zadig should be able to meet hers; but an abscess growing on the wounded eye, gave every cause for fear. A messenger was immediately dispatched to Memphis for the great physician Hermes, who came with a numerous retinue. He visited the patient and declared that he would lose his eye. He even foretold the day and hour when this fatal event would happen.

"Had it been the right eye," said he, "I could easily have cured it, but the wounds of the left eye are incurable."

All Babylon lamented the fate of Zadig and admired the profound knowledge of Hermes. In two days the abscess broke of its own accord, and Zadig was perfectly cured. Hermes wrote a book, to prove that it ought not to have been cured. Zadig did not read it; but, as soon as he was able to go abroad, he went to pay a visit to her in whom all his hopes of happiness were centered, and for whose sake alone he wished to have eyes. Semira had been in the country for three days past. He learned on the road that that fine lady, having openly declared that she had an unconquerable aversion to one-eyed men, had the night before given her hand to Orcan. At this news he fell speechless to the ground. His sorrows brought him almost to the brink of the grave. He was ill for a long time; but reason at last got the better of his affliction, and the severity of his fate served even to console him.

"Since," said he, "I have suffered so much from the cruel caprice of a woman educated at court, I must now think of marrying the daughter of a citizen."

He pitched upon Azora, a lady of the greatest prudence, and of the best family in town. He married her and lived with her for a month in all the delights of the most tender union. He only observed that she had a little levity, and that she was too apt to find that those young men who had the most handsome persons were likewise possessed of most wit and virtue.

CHAPTER II

THE NOSE

One morning Azora returned from a walk in a terrible passion and uttered the most violent exclamations.

"What ails you, my dear wife?" said he. "What is it that can thus have put you out of temper?"

"Alas," said she, "you would be as much enraged as I am, had you seen what I have just beheld. I have been to comfort the young widow Cosrou, who, within these two days, has raised a tomb to her young husband, near the rivulet that washes the skirts of this meadow. She vowed to Heaven, in the bitterness of her grief, to remain at this tomb, while the water of the rivulet should continue to run near it."

"Well," said Zadig, "she is an excellent woman and loved her husband with the most sincere affection."

"Ah," replied Azora, "did you but know in what she was employed when I went to wait upon her!"

"In what, pray, beautiful Azora?"

"She was turning the course of the rivulet."

Azora broke out into such long invectives and loaded the young widow with such bitter reproaches that Zadig was far from being pleased with this ostentation of virtue.

Zadig had a friend, named Cador, one of those young men in whom his wife discovered more probity and merit than in others. He made him his confidant and secured his fidelity, as much as possible, by a considerable present. Azora, having passed two days with a friend in the country, returned home on the third. The servants told her, with tears in their eyes, that her husband had died suddenly the night before, that they were afraid to send her an account of this mournful event, and that they had just been depositing his corpse in the tomb of his ancestors, at the end of the garden. She wept, she tore her hair, and swore she would follow him to the grave. In the evening, Cador begged leave to wait upon her and joined his tears with hers. Next day they wept less and dined together. Cador told her that his friend had left him the greater part of his estate, and that he would think himself extremely happy in sharing his fortune with her. The lady wept, fell into a passion and at last became more mild and gentle. They sat longer at supper than at dinner. They now talked with greater confidence. Azora praised the deceased, but owned that he had many failings from which Cador was free.

During supper, Cador complained of a violent pain in his side. The lady, greatly concerned and eager to serve him, caused all kinds of essences to be brought, with which she anointed him, to try if some of them might not possibly ease him of his pain. She lamented that the great Hermes was not still in Babylon. She even condescended to touch the side in which Cador felt such exquisite pain.

"Are you subject to this cruel disorder?" said she to him with a compassionate air.

"It sometimes brings me," replied Cador, "to the brink of the grave, and there is but one remedy that can give me relief, and that is to apply to my side the nose of a man who is lately dead."

"A strange remedy, indeed!" said Azora.

"Not more strange," replied he, "than the sachets of Arnoult against the apoplexy." *

This reason, added to the great merit of the young man, at last determined the lady.

"After all," says she, "when my husband shall cross the bridge Tchinavar,** in his journey from the world of yesterday to the world of tomorrow, the angel Asrael will not refuse him a passage because his nose is a little shorter in the second life than it was in the first."

She then took a razor, went to her husband's tomb, bedewed it with her tears and drew near to cut off the nose of Zadig, whom she found extended at full length in the tomb. Zadig arose, holding his nose with one hand and checking the razor with the other.

"Madam," said he, "don't exclaim so violently against young Cosrou: the project of cutting off my nose is equal to that of turning the course of a rivulet."

---

* There was at that time a Babylonian named Arnoult, who, according to his advertisements in the Gazettes, cured and prevented all kinds of apoplexies, by a little bag hung about the neck. [Voltaire's note. Arnoult was really a French charlatan.]

** Bridge leading to paradise.

CHAPTER III

THE DOG AND THE HORSE

ZADIG found by experience that the first month of marriage, as it is written in the book of Zend,* is the moon of honey, and that the second is the moon of wormwood. He was some time after obliged to repudiate Azora, who became too difficult to live with, and he then sought for happiness in the study of nature.

"No man," said he, "can be happier than a philosopher, who reads in this great book which God has placed before our eyes. The truths he discovers are his own, he nourishes and exalts his soul; he lives in peace; he fears nothing from men; and his tender spouse will not come to cut off his nose."

Possessed of these ideas, he retired to a country house on the banks of the Euphrates. There he did not employ himself in calculating how many inches of water flow in a second of time under the arches of a bridge, or whether there fell a cubic line of rain in the month of the mouse more than in the month of the sheep. He never dreamed of making silk of cobwebs, or porcelain of broken bottles; but he chiefly studied the properties of plants and animals, and soon acquired a sagacity that made him discover a thousand differences where other men see nothing but uniformity.

One day, as he was walking near a little wood, he saw one of the Queen's eunuchs running toward him, followed by several officers, who appeared to be in great perplexity, and

---

* The Zend Avesta, or Avesta, the Zoroastrian Scriptures.

who ran to and fro like men distracted, eagerly searching for something they had lost of great value.

"Young man," said the first eunuch, "have you seen the Queen's dog?"

"It is a bitch," replied Zadig with great modesty, "and not a dog."

"You are in the right," returned the first eunuch.

"It is a very small she-spaniel," added Zadig. "She has lately whelped; she limps on the left forefoot and has very long ears."

"You have seen her," said the first eunuch, quite out of breath.

"No," replied Zadig, "I have not seen her, nor did I so much as know that the Queen had a bitch."

Exactly at the same time, by one of the common freaks of fortune, the finest horse in the King's stable had escaped from the groom in the plains of Babylon. The chief huntsman, and all the other officers, ran after him with as much eagerness and anxiety as the first eunuch had done after the bitch. The chief huntsman addressed Zadig and asked him if he had not seen the King's horse passing by.

"He is the fleetest horse in the King's stable," replied Zadig. "He is five feet high, with very small hoofs, and a tail three feet and a half in length. The studs on his bit are gold of twenty-three carats, and his shoes are silver of eleven penny-weights."

"What way did he take? Where is he?" demanded the chief huntsman.

"I have not seen him," replied Zadig, "and never heard of him before."

The chief huntsman and the first eunuch never doubted that Zadig had stolen the King's horse and the Queen's bitch. They therefore had him conducted before the Assembly of the

Grand Desterham,* who condemned him to the knout and to spend the rest of his days in Siberia. Hardly was the sentence passed when the horse and the bitch were both found. The judges were reduced to the disagreeable necessity of reversing their sentence; but they condemned Zadig to pay four hundred ounces of gold for having said that he had not seen what he had seen. This fine he was obliged to pay. After this he was permitted to plead his cause before the Council of the Grand Desterham, when he spoke to the following effect:

"You stars of justice, mines of knowledge, mirrors of truth, who have the weight of lead, the hardness of iron, the splendor of the diamond, and many of the properties of gold. Since I am permitted to speak before this august assembly, I swear to you by Ormuzd** that I have never seen the Queen's respectable bitch, nor the sacred horse of the King of kings. The truth of the matter was as follows: I was walking toward the little wood, where I afterward met the venerable eunuch, and the most illustrious chief huntsman. I observed on the sand the traces of an animal and could easily perceive them to be those of a little dog. The light and long furrows impressed on little eminences of sand between the marks of the paws, plainly discovered that it was a bitch, whose dugs were hanging down, and that therefore she must have whelped a few days before. Other traces of a different kind that always appeared to have gently brushed the surface of the land near the marks of the forefeet showed me that she had very long ears; and as I remarked that there was always a slighter impression made on the sand by one foot than by the other three, I found that the bitch of our august Queen was a little lame, if I may be allowed the expression.

"With regard to the horse of the King of kings, you will be pleased to know that walking in the lanes of this wood, I

---

* For Defterdar, head of finances.
** The principle of Good.

observed the marks of a horse's shoes, all at equal distances. This must be a horse, said I to myself, that gallops excellently. The dust on the trees in a narrow road that was but seven feet wide was a little brushed off, at the distance of three feet and a half from the middle of the road. This horse, said I, has a tail three feet and a half long, which being whisked to the right and left has swept away the dust. I observed, under the trees that formed an arbor five feet in height, that the leaves of the branches were newly fallen; from whence I inferred that the horse had touched them, and that he must therefore be five feet high. As to his bit, it must be gold of twenty-three carats, for he had rubbed its bosses against a stone which I knew to be a touchstone, and which I had tested. In a word, from the marks made by his shoes on flints of another kind, I concluded that he was shod with silver eleven deniers fine."

All the judges admired Zadig for his acute and profound discernment. The news of this speech was carried even to the King and Queen. Nothing was talked of but Zadig in the ante-chambers, the chambers, and the cabinet; and though many of the magi were of opinion that he ought to be burned as a sorcerer, the King ordered his officers to restore him the four hundred ounces of gold which he had been obliged to pay. The registrar, the attorneys, and bailiffs went to his house, with great formality, to carry him back his four hundred ounces. They only retained three hundred and ninety-eight of them to defray the expenses of justice, and their servants demanded their fees.

Zadig saw how extremely dangerous it sometimes is to appear too knowing, and he therefore resolved that on the next occasion of the like nature he would not tell what he had seen.

Such an opportunity soon offered. A prisoner of state made his escape and passed under the windows of Zadig's house. Zadig was examined and made no answer. But it was proved that he had looked at the prisoner from this window. For this crime he was condemned to pay five hundred ounces of gold; and, according to the custom of Babylon, he thanked his judges for their indulgence.

"Great God!" said he to himself, "what a misfortune it is to walk in a wood through which the Queen's bitch or the King's horse has passed! How dangerous to look out of a window! And how difficult to be happy in this life!"

CHAPTER IV

THE ENVIOUS MAN

ZADIG resolved to comfort himself by philosophy and friendship for the evils he had suffered from fortune. He had in the suburbs of Babylon a house elegantly furnished, in which he assembled all the arts and all the pleasures worthy of the pursuit of a gentleman. In the morning, his library was open to the learned. In the evening, his table was surrounded by good company. But he soon found what very dangerous guests these men of letters are. A warm dispute arose on one of Zoroaster's laws, which forbids the eating of a griffin.

"Why," said some of them, "prohibit the eating of a griffin, if no such animal exists?"

"There must necessarily be such an animal," said the others, "since Zoroaster forbids us to eat it."

Zadig would fain have reconciled them by saying:

"If there are griffins, let us not eat them, and if there are no griffins, we cannot possibly eat them: and thus either way we shall obey Zoroaster."

A learned man, who had composed thirteen volumes on the

properties of the griffin, and was besides the chief theurgist,[*] hastened away to accuse Zadig before one of the principal magi, named Yebor,[**] the greatest blockhead and therefore the greatest fanatic among the Chaldeans. This man would have impaled Zadig to do honor to the sun, and would then have recited the breviary of Zoroaster with greater satisfaction. The friend Cador (a friend is better than a hundred priests) went to Yebor, and said to him:

"Long live the sun and the griffins; beware of punishing Zadig; he is a saint; he has griffins in his inner court and does not eat them; and his accuser is an heretic, who dares to maintain that rabbits have cloven feet and are not unclean."

"Well," said Yebor, shaking his bald pate, "we must impale Zadig for having thought contemptuously of griffins, and the other for having spoke disrespectfully of rabbits."

Cador hushed up the affair by means of a maid of honor who had borne him a child, and who had great influence in the college of the magi. Nobody was impaled. This lenience occasioned a great murmuring among some of the doctors, who from this predicted the fall of Babylon.

"Upon what does happiness depend?" said Zadig. "I am persecuted by everything in the world, even by beings that have no existence."

He cursed those men of learning and resolved for the future to live with none but good company.

He assembled at his house the most worthy men and the most beautiful ladies of Babylon. He gave them delicious suppers, often preceded by concerts of music, and always animated by polite conversation, from which he knew how to banish that affectation of wit, which is the surest method of not having any, thus spoiling the pleasure of the most agreeable society. Neither the choice of his friends nor that of the

---

[*] Magician, i.e., theologian.

[**] Anagram of Boyer, a monk who was powerful at the Court and who frequently made trouble for Voltaire.

dishes was made by vanity; for in everything he preferred substance to appearance; and by these means he procured that real respect to which he did not aspire.

Opposite to his house lived one Arimazes,* a man whose deformed countenance was but a faint picture of his still more deformed mind. He was tormented with malice and inflated with pride, and to crown all, he was of most tedious would-be wit. Having never been able to succeed in the world, he revenged himself by cursing it. Rich as he was, he found it difficult to procure a set of flatterers. The rattling of the chariots that entered Zadig's court in the evening filled him with uneasiness; the sound of his praises enraged him still more. He sometimes went to Zadig's house and sat down at table without being desired, where he spoiled all the pleasure of the company, as the harpies are said to infect the viands they touch. It happened one day he took it into his head to give an entertainment to a lady, who, instead of accepting it, went to sup with Zadig. At another time, as he was talking with Zadig at Court, a Minister of State came up to them and invited Zadig to supper, without inviting Arimazes. The most implacable hatred has seldom a more solid foundation. This man, who in Babylon was called the "Envious," resolved to ruin Zadig, because he was called the "Happy."

"The opportunity of doing mischief occurs a hundred times a day and that of doing good but once a year," says the wise Zoroaster.

The envious man went to see Zadig, who was walking in his garden with two friends and a lady, to whom he said many gallant things, without any other intention than that of saying them. The conversation turned upon a war which the King had just brought to a happy conclusion against the Prince of Hyrcania, his vassal. Zadig, who had signalized his courage in this short war, bestowed great praises on the King, but greater still on the lady. He took out his notebook, and wrote

---

* A name suggested by Ahriman, principle of Evil.

four lines extempore, which he gave to this beautiful person to read. His friends begged they might see them; but modesty, or rather a well-regulated self-love, would not allow him to grant their request. He knew that extemporary verses are never approved by any but the person in whose honor they are written. He therefore tore in two the leaf on which he had written them, and threw both the pieces into a thicket of rose bushes where the rest of the company sought for them in vain. A slight shower falling soon after obliged them to return to the house. The envious man, who stayed in the garden, continued to search, till at last he found a piece of the leaf. It had been torn in such a manner that each half of a line made sense, and even a verse of a shorter measure; but what was still more surprising, these short verses were found to contain the most injurious reflections on the King; they ran thus:

> to flagrant Crimes;
> his Crown he owes;
> to peaceful Times,
> the worst of Foes.

The envious man was now happy for the first time in his life. He had it in his power to ruin a person of virtue and merit. Filled with this fiendlike joy, he found means to convey to the King the satire written by the hand of Zadig, who, together with the lady and his two friends, was thrown into prison.

His trial was soon finished, without his being permitted to speak for himself. As he was going to receive his sentence, the envious man threw himself in his way and told him with a loud voice that his verses were good for nothing. Zadig did not value himself on being a good poet; but it filled him with inexpressible concern to find that he was condemned for high treason and that the fair lady and his two friends were confined in prison for a crime of which they were not guilty. He was not allowed to speak because his writing spoke for him. Such was the law of Babylon. Accordingly he was conducted to the place of execution, through an immense crowd of spectators, who dared not venture to express their pity for him, but who carefully examined his countenance to see if he died with a good grace. His relatives alone were inconsolable; for they could not succeed to his estate. Three-fourths of his wealth was confiscated into the King's treasury, and the other fourth was given to the envious man.

Just as he was preparing for death, the King's parrot flew from its cage, and alighted on a rose bush in Zadig's garden. A peach had been driven there by the wind from a neighboring tree, and had fallen on a piece of the written leaf of the notebook to which it stuck. The bird carried off the peach and the paper and laid them on the King's knee. The King took up the paper with great eagerness and read the words, which formed no sense and seemed to be the endings of verses. He loved poetry; and there is always some mercy to be expected from a prince of that disposition. The adventure of the parrot set him thinking.

The Queen, who remembered what had been written on the piece of Zadig's notebook, caused it be brought. They compared the two pieces together and found them to tally exactly. They then read the verses as Zadig had written them.

> Tyrants are prone to flagrant Crimes;
> To Clemency his Crown he owes;
> To Concord and to peaceful Times,
> Love only is the worst of Foes.

The King gave immediate orders that Zadig should be brought before him, and that his two friends and the lady should be set at liberty. Zadig fell prostrate on the ground before the King and Queen; humbly begged their pardon for having made such bad verses, and spoke with so much

propriety, wit, and good sense, that their Majesties desired
they might see him again. He did himself that honor, and
insinuated himself still further into their good graces. They
gave him all the wealth of the envious man; but Zadig restored
him back the whole of it; and this instance of generosity gave
no other pleasure to the envious man than that of having
preserved his estate. The King's esteem for Zadig increased
every day. He admitted him into all his parties of pleasure and
consulted him in all affairs of state. From that time the Queen
began to regard him with a tenderness that might one day
prove dangerous to herself, to the King her august consort,
to Zadig, and to the kingdom in general. Zadig now began
to think that happiness was not so unattainable as he had
formerly imagined.

CHAPTER V

THE GENEROUS

THE time was now arrived for celebrating a grand festival,
which returned every five years. It was a custom in Babylon
solemnly to declare, at the end of every five years, which of
the citizens had performed the most generous action. The
grandees and the magi were the judges. The first satrap, who
was charged with the government of the city, published the
most noble actions that had passed under his administration.
The competition was decided by votes, and the King pronounced the sentence. People came to this ceremony from the
ends of the earth. The conqueror received from the monarch's
hands a golden cup adorned with precious stones, his Majesty
at the same time making him this compliment:

"Receive this reward of your generosity, and may the gods grant me many subjects like you."

This memorable day being come, the King appeared on his throne, surrounded by the grandees, the magi, and the deputies of all the nations that came to these games, where glory was acquired not by the swiftness of horses, nor by strength of body, but by virtue. The first satrap recited, with an audible voice, such actions as might entitle the authors of them to this invaluable prize. He did not mention the greatness of soul with which Zadig had restored the envious man his fortune, because it was not judged to be an action worthy of disputing the prize.

He first presented a judge, who, having made a citizen lose a considerable cause by a mistake, for which, after all, he was not accountable, had given him the whole of his own estate, which was just equal to what the other had lost.

He next produced a young man, who, being desperately in love with a lady whom he was going to marry, had yielded her up to his friend, whose passion for her had almost brought him to the brink of the grave, and at the same time had given him the lady's fortune.

He afterward produced a soldier, who in the Hyrcanian war had given a still more noble instance of generosity. A party of the enemy, having seized his mistress, he was fighting in her defense. At that very instant he was informed that another party, at the distance of a few paces, were carrying off his mother; he therefore left his mistress with tears in his eyes and flew to the assistance of his mother. At last, he returned to the dear object of his love and found her expiring. He was just going to plunge his sword in his own bosom; but his mother remonstrating against such a desperate deed, and telling him that he was the only support of her life, he had the courage to endure to live.

The judges were inclined to give the prize to the soldier.
But the King took up the discourse and said:

"The action of the soldier and that of the other two are
doubtless very great, but they have nothing surprising in them.
Yesterday Zadig performed an action that filled me with wonder. I had a few days before disgraced Coreb, my minister and
favorite. I complained of him in the most violent and bitter
terms; all my courtiers assured me that I was too gentle, and
seemed to vie with each other in speaking ill of Coreb. I asked
Zadig what he thought of him, and he had the courage to com-
mend him. I have read in our histories of many people who
have atoned for an error by the surrender of their fortune, who
have resigned a mistress, or preferred a mother to the object
of their affection; but never before did I hear of a courtier
who spoke favorably of a disgraced minister that labored
under the displeasure of his sovereign. I give to each of those
whose generous actions have been now recited twenty thousand pieces of gold; but the cup I give to Zadig."

"May it please your Majesty," said Zadig, "you alone deserve
the cup; you have performed an action of all others the most
uncommon and meritorious, since, notwithstanding your being
a powerful King, you were not offended at your slave, when
he presumed to oppose your passion."

The King and Zadig were equally the object of admiration.
The judge who had given his estate to his client; the lover who
had resigned his mistress to his friend; and the soldier, who
had preferred the safety of his mother to that of his mistress,
received the King's presents, and saw their names enrolled
in the catalogue of generous men. Zadig had the cup, and the
King acquired the reputation of a good prince, which he did
not long enjoy. The day was celebrated by feasts that lasted
longer than the law enjoined, and the memory of it is still
preserved in Asia. Zadig said:

"Now I am happy at last." But he was wrong.

CHAPTER VI

THE MINISTER

THE King had lost his first minister and chose Zadig to fill his place. All the ladies in Babylon applauded the choice; for since the foundation of the empire there had never been such a young minister. But all the courtiers were filled with jealousy and vexation. The envious man, in particular, was troubled with a spitting of blood, and a prodigious inflammation in his nose. Zadig having thanked the King and Queen for their goodness, went likewise to thank the parrot.

"Beautiful bird," he said, "it is you that has saved my life and made me first minister. The Queen's bitch and the King's horse did me a great deal of mischief, but you have done me much good. Upon such slender threads as these do the fates of mortals hang! But this happiness perhaps will vanish very soon."

"Soon," replied the parrot.

Zadig was somewhat startled at this word. But as he was a good natural philosopher and did not believe parrots to be prophets, he quickly recovered his spirits and resolved to execute his duty to the best of his power.

He made everyone feel the sacred authority of the laws, but no one felt the weight of his dignity. He never checked the deliberations of the divan*; and every vizier might give his opinion without the fear of incurring the minister's displeasure. When he gave judgment, it was not he that gave it, it was the

* Council.

law; the rigor of which, however, whenever it was too severe, he always took care to soften; and when laws were wanting, the equity of his decisions was such as might easily have made them pass for those of Zoroaster.

It is to him that the nations are indebted for this great principle, to wit, that it is better to run the risk of sparing the guilty than to condemn the innocent. He imagined that laws were made to secure the people from the suffering of injuries as well as to restrain them from committing crimes. His chief talent consisted in discovering the truth, which all men seek to obscure. This great talent he put into practice from the very beginning of his administration. A famous merchant of Babylon, who died in the Indies, had divided his estate equally between his two sons, after having disposed of their sister in marriage, and left a present of thirty thousand pieces of gold to that son who should be found to have loved him best. The eldest raised a tomb to his memory; the youngest increased his sister's portion by giving her a part of his inheritance. Everyone said that the eldest son loved his father best, and the youngest his sister; and that the thirty thousand pieces belonged to the eldest.

Zadig sent for both of them, the one after the other. To the elder he said:

"Your father is not dead; he is recovered of his last illness and is returning to Babylon."

"God be praised," replied the young man, "but his tomb cost me a considerable sum."

Zadig afterward said the same thing to the younger.

"God be praised," said he, "I will go and restore to my father all that I have; but I could wish that he would leave my sister what I have given her."

"You shall restore nothing," replied Zadig, "and you shall have the thirty thousand pieces, for you are the son who loves his father best."

A young lady possessed of a handsome fortune had given

a promise of marriage to two magi; and after having, for some months, received the instructions of both, she proved with child. They were both desirous of marrying her.

"I will take for my husband," said she, "the man who has put me in a condition to give a subject to the state."

"I am the man that has done the work," said the one.

"I am the man that has done it," said the other.

"Well," replied the lady, "I will acknowledge for the infant's father him that can give it the best education."

The lady was delivered of a son. The two magi contended who should bring him up, and the cause was carried before Zadig. Zadig summoned the two magi to attend him.

"What will you teach your pupil?" said he to the first.

"I will teach him," said the doctor, "the eight parts of speech, logic, astrology, demonology, what is meant by substance and accident, abstract and concrete, the doctrine of the monads, and the pre-established harmony."

"For my part," said the second, "I will endeavor to give him a sense of justice and to make him worthy the friendship of good men."

Zadig then cried:

"Whether you are his father or not, you shall marry his mother."

CHAPTER VII

THE DISPUTE AND THE AUDIENCES

In this manner he daily showed the subtlety of his mind and the goodness of his heart. The people at once admired and loved him. He passed for the happiest man in the world. The whole empire resounded with his name. All the ladies ogled him. All the men praised him for his justice. The learned regarded him as an oracle, and even the priests confessed that he knew more than the old Archmagus Yebor. They were now so far from prosecuting him on account of the griffins that they believed nothing but what he thought credible.

There had continued in Babylon, for the space of fifteen hundred years, a violent contention that had divided the empire into two sects. The one pretended that they ought to enter the temple of Mithras with the left foot foremost; the other held this custom in detestation and always entered with the right foot first. The people waited with great impatience for the day on which the solemn Feast of the Sacred Fire was to be celebrated, to see which sect Zadig would favor. All the world had their eyes fixed on his two feet, and the whole city was in the utmost suspense and perturbation. Zadig jumped into the temple with his feet joined together; and afterward proved, in an eloquent discourse, that the God of heaven and earth, who accepts not the persons of men, makes no distinction between the right and the left foot. The envious man and his wife alleged that his discourse was not figurative enough, and that he did not make the rocks and mountains dance with sufficient agility.

"He is dry," said they, "and void of genius: he does not make the sea fly and the stars fall, nor the sun melt like wax: he has not the true oriental style."

Zadig contented himself with having the style of reason. Everyone was on his side, not because he was on the right road, or followed the dictates of reason, or was a man of real merit, but because he was grand vizier.

He terminated with the same happy address the great controversy between the white and the black magi. The former maintained that it was the height of impiety to pray to God with the face turned toward the east in winter; the latter asserted that God abhorred the prayers of those who turned toward the west in summer. Zadig decreed that every man should be allowed to turn as he pleased.

He also found out the happy secret of finishing all affairs, whether of a private or public nature, in the morning. The rest of the day he employed in the enhancement of Babylon. He exhibited tragedies that drew tears from the eyes of the spectators, and comedies that shook their sides with laughter, a custom which had long been disused, and which his good taste now induced him to revive. He never affected to be more knowing than the artists themselves; he encouraged them by rewards and honors, and was never secretly jealous of their talents. In the evening the King was highly entertained with his conversation and the Queen still more.

"A great minister!" said the King.

"A charming minister!" said the Queen.

Both of them added that it would have been a great pity had such a man been hanged.

Never was man in power obliged to give so many audiences to the ladies. Most of them came to consult him about no business at all, that so they might have some business with him. The wife of the envious man was among the first. She swore to him by Mithras, by the Zend-Avesta, and by the Sacred Fire that she detested her husband's conduct. She then told him in confidence that he was a jealous brutal wretch, and gave him to understand that heaven punished him for his crimes, by refusing him the precious effects of the Sacred Fire, by which alone man can be rendered like the immortals. At last she concluded by dropping her garter. Zadig took it up with his usual politeness, but did not tie it about the lady's leg; and this slight fault, if it may be called a fault, was the cause of the most terrible misfortunes. Zadig never thought of it more, but the lady thought of it with great attention.

Never a day passed without several visits from the ladies. The secret annals of Babylon pretend that he once yielded to temptation, but that he was surprised to find that he enjoyed his mistress without pleasure and embraced her absent-mindedly. The lady to whom he gave, almost without being sensible of it, these marks of his favor, was a maid of honor to Queen Astarte. This tender Babylonian said to herself by way of comfort:

"This man must have his head filled with a prodigious heap of business, since even in making love he cannot avoid thinking on public affairs."

Zadig happened, at the very instant when most people say nothing at all, and others only pronounce a few sacred words, to cry out: "The Queen!" The Babylonian lady thought that he was at last happily come to himself, and that he said, "My queen." But Zadig, still absent-minded, pronounced the name of Astarte. The lady, who in this happy situation interpreted everything in her own favor, imagined that he meant to say, "You are more beautiful than Queen Astarte." After receiving some handsome presents, she left the seraglio of Zadig and went to relate her adventure to the envious woman, who was her intimate friend, and who was greatly piqued at the preference given to the other.

"He would not so much as deign," said she, "to tie this garter about my leg, and I am therefore resolved never to wear it more."

"Oh," said the happy lady to the envious one, "your garters are the same as the Queen's! Do you buy them from the same weaver?"

This hint set the envious lady thinking; she made no reply, but went to consult her envious husband.

Meanwhile Zadig perceived that his thoughts were always distracted, as well when he gave audience as when he sat in judgment. He did not know to what to attribute this absence of mind, and that was his only sorrow.

He had a dream, in which he imagined that he laid himself down upon a heap of dry herbs, among which there were many prickly ones that gave him great uneasiness, and that he afterward reposed himself on a soft bed of roses, from which there sprang a serpent that wounded him to the heart with its sharp and venomed tongue.

"Alas!" said he. "I have long lain on these dry and prickly herbs; I am now on the bed of roses; but who will be the serpent?"

CHAPTER VIII

JEALOUSY

ZADIG's calamities sprang even from his happiness and especially from his merit. Every day he conversed with the King and Astarte, his august consort. The charms of his conversation were greatly heightened by that desire of pleasing, which is to the mind what dress is to beauty. His youth and graceful appearance insensibly made an impression on Astarte, which she did not at first perceive. Her passion grew and flourished in the bosom of innocence. Without fear or scruple, she indulged the pleasing satisfaction of seeing and hearing a man who was so dear to her husband, and to the empire in general. She was continually praising him to the King. She talked of him to her women, who were always sure to improve on her praises. And thus everything contributed to thrust deeper into her heart a passion, of which she did not seem to be sensible. She made several presents to Zadig, which discovered a greater spirit of gallantry than she imagined. She intended to speak to him only as a queen satisfied with his services, and sometimes her expressions were those of a woman in love.

Astarte was much more beautiful than that Semira who had such a strong aversion to one-eyed men, or that other woman who had resolved to cut off her husband's nose. Her familiarity, her tender expressions, at which she began to blush, and her eyes, which, though she endeavored to divert them to other objects, were always fixed upon his, inspired Zadig with a passion that filled him with astonishment. He struggled hard. He called to his aid the precepts of philosophy, which had always stood him in good stead; but he derived only the light of knowledge and received no solace. Duty, gratitude, and violated majesty presented themselves to his mind as so many avenging gods. He struggled; he conquered; but this victory, which he was obliged to purchase afresh every moment, cost him many sighs and tears. He no longer dared to speak to the Queen with that sweet and charming familiarity which had been so agreeable to them both. His countenance was covered with a cloud. His conversation was constrained and incoherent. His eyes were fixed on the ground; and when, in spite of all his endeavors to the contrary, they encountered those of the Queen, they found them bathed in tears and darting arrows of flame. They seemed to say to each other:

"We adore each other and yet are afraid to love: we both burn with a fire which we condemn."

Zadig left the royal presence full of perplexity and despair, and having his heart oppressed with a burden which he was no longer able to bear. In the violence of his perturbation he involuntarily betrayed the secret to his friend Cador, in the same manner as a man who, having long supported the fits of a cruel disease, discovers his pain by a cry extorted from him by a more severe fit, and by the cold sweat that covers his brow.

"I have already discovered," said Cador, "the sentiments which you would fain conceal from yourself. The symptoms by which the passions show themselves are certain and infallible. Judge, my dear Zadig, since I have read your heart, whether the King will not discover something in it that may

give him offense. He has no other fault but that of being the
most jealous man in the world. You can resist the violence of
your passion with greater fortitude than the Queen, because
you are a philosopher, and because you are Zadig. Astarte is a
woman: she suffers her eyes to speak with so much the more
imprudence, as she does not as yet think herself guilty. Con-
scious of her own innocence, she unhappily neglects those
external appearances which are so necessary. I shall tremble
for her so long as she has nothing wherewithal to reproach
herself. Were you both of one mind, you might easily deceive
the whole world. A growing passion which we endeavor to
suppress discovers itself in spite of all our efforts to the contrary, but love when gratified is easily concealed."

Zadig trembled at the proposal of betraying the King, his
benefactor; and never was he more faithful to his prince
than when guilty of an involuntary crime against him. Meanwhile, the Queen mentioned the name of Zadig so frequently,
and with such a blushing and downcast look; she was sometimes so lively, and sometimes so embarrassed, when she
spoke to him in the King's presence, and was seized with
such a deep thoughtfulness at his going away that the King
began to be troubled. He believed all that he saw and imagined all that he did not see. He particularly remarked that
his wife's shoes were blue and that Zadig's shoes were blue,
that his wife's ribbons were yellow and that Zadig's bonnet
was yellow, and these were terrible symptoms to a prince
of so much delicacy. In his jealous mind suspicions were
turned into certainty.

All the slaves of kings and queens are so many spies over
their hearts. They soon observed that Astarte was tender
and that Moabdar was jealous. The envious man persuaded
his wife to send the King her garter, which resembled those
of the Queen; and to complete the misfortune, this garter
was blue. The monarch now thought of nothing but in what
manner he might best execute his vengeance. He one night

resolved to poison the Queen, and in the morning to put Zadig to death by the bowstring. The orders were given to a merciless eunuch, who commonly executed his acts of vengeance. There happened at that time to be in the King's chamber a little dwarf, who, though dumb, was not deaf. He was allowed to go wherever he pleased; and, as a domestic animal, was a witness of what passed in the most profound secrecy. This little mute was strongly attached to the Queen and to Zadig. With equal horror and surprise he heard the order given for their death. But how prevent the fatal sentence that in a few hours was to be carried into execution? He could not write, but he could paint, and excelled particularly in drawing a striking resemblance. He employed a part of the night in sketching out with his pencil what he meant to impart to the Queen. The piece represented the King in one corner, boiling with rage and giving orders to the eunuch; a blue bowstring and a bowl on a table, with blue garters and yellow ribbons; the Queen in the middle of the picture, expiring in the arms of her woman, and Zadig strangled at her feet. The horizon represented a rising sun, to express that this shocking execution was to be performed in the morning. As soon as he had finished the picture, he ran to one of Astarte's women, waked her and made her understand that she must immediately carry it to the Queen.

At midnight a messenger knocked at Zadig's door, awakened him and gave him a note from the Queen. He wondered whether it was a dream and opened the letter with a trembling hand. But how great was his surprise! And who can express the consternation and despair into which he was thrown upon reading these words:

"Fly, this instant, or you are a dead man. Fly Zadig, I conjure you by our mutual love and my yellow ribbons. I have not been guilty, but I find that I must die like a criminal."

Zadig was hardly able to speak. He sent for Cador, and,

without uttering a word, gave him the note. Cador forced him to obey and forthwith to take the road to Memphis.

"Should you dare," said he, "to go in search of the Queen, you will hasten her death. Should you speak to the King, you will infallibly ruin her. I will take upon me the charge of her destiny; follow your own. I will spread a report that you have taken the road to India. I will soon follow you, and inform you of all that shall have passed in Babylon."

At that instant, Cador caused two of the swiftest dromedaries to be brought to a private gate of the palace. Upon one of these he mounted Zadig, whom he was obliged to carry to the door, and who was ready to expire with grief. He was accompanied by a single domestic; and Cador, plunged in sorrow and astonishment, soon lost sight of his friend.

This illustrious fugitive arriving on the side of a hill, whence he could take a view of Babylon, turned his eyes toward the Queen's palace and fainted away at the sight; nor did he recover his senses but to shed a torrent of tears and to wish for death. At length, after his thoughts had been long engrossed in lamenting the unhappy fate of the loveliest woman and the greatest queen in the world, he for a moment turned his views on himself and cried:

"What then is human life? O virtue, how have you served me! Two women have basely deceived me; and now a third, who is innocent and more beautiful than both the others, is going to be put to death! Whatever good I have done has been to me a continual source of calamity and affliction; and I have only been raised to the height of grandeur, to be tumbled down the most horrid precipice of misfortune."

Filled with these gloomy reflections, his eyes overspread with the veil of grief, his countenance covered with the paleness of death, and his soul plunged in an abyss of the blackest despair, he continued his journey toward Egypt.

CHAPTER IX

THE WOMAN BEATEN

ZADIG directed his course by the stars. The constellation of Orion and the bright star of Sirius guided his steps toward the pole of Canopæa. He admired those vast globes of light, which appear to our eyes but as so many little sparks, while the earth, which in reality is only an imperceptible point in nature, appears to our fond imagination as something so grand and noble. He then represented to himself the human species as it really is, a parcel of insects devouring one another on a little atom of mud. This true image seemed to annihilate his misfortunes, by making him sensible of the nothingness of his own being and of that of Babylon. His soul launched out into infinity, and detached from the senses, contemplated the immutable order of the universe. But when afterward, returning to himself and entering into his own heart, he considered that Astarte had perhaps died for him, the universe vanished from his sight, and he beheld nothing in the whole compass of nature but Astarte dying and Zadig unhappy. While he thus alternately gave up his mind to this flux and reflux of sublime philosophy and intolerable grief, he advanced toward the frontiers of Egypt; and his faithful domestic was already in the first village, in search of a lodging. Meanwhile, as Zadig was walking toward the gardens that skirted the village, he saw, at a small distance from the highway, a woman bathed in tears and calling heaven and earth to her assistance, and a man in a furious passion, pursuing her. The man had already overtaken the woman, who

embraced his knees, notwithstanding which he loaded her
with blows and reproaches. Zadig judged by the frantic behavior of the Egyptian, and by the repeated pardons which
the lady asked him, that the one was jealous and the other
unfaithful. But when he surveyed the woman more narrowly
and found her to be a lady of exquisite beauty, and to have
some resemblance to the unhappy Astarte, he felt himself
inspired with compassion for her and horror toward the
Egyptian.

"Assist me," cried she to Zadig with the deepest sighs,
"deliver me from the hands of the most barbarous man in
the world; save my life."

Moved by these pitiful cries, Zadig ran and threw himself
between her and the barbarian. As he had some knowledge
of the Egyptian language, he addressed him in that tongue:

"If," said he, "you have any humanity, I conjure you to
pay some regard to her beauty and weakness. How can you
behave in this outrageous manner to one of the masterpieces
of nature, who lies at your feet and has no defense but her
tears?"

"Ah, ha!" replied the madman. "You are likewise in love
with her; I must be revenged on you too."

So saying, he left the lady, whom he had hitherto held
with his hand twisted in her hair, and taking his lance, attempted to stab the stranger. Zadig, whose blood was cool,
easily eluded the blow aimed by the frantic Egyptian. He
seized the lance near the iron with which it was armed. The
Egyptian strove to draw it back; Zadig to wrest it from the
Egyptian; and in the struggle it was broken in two. The Egyptian drew his sword; Zadig did the same. They attacked
each other. The former gave a hundred blows at random;
the latter warded them off with dexterity. The lady, seated
on a turf, readjusted her headdress and watched the combatants. The Egyptian excelled in strength; Zadig in address.
The one fought like a man whose arm was directed by his

judgment; the other like a madman, whose blind rage made him deal his blows at random. Zadig closed with him and disarmed him; and while the Egyptian, now become more furious, endeavored to throw himself upon him, he seized him, pressed him close and threw him down; and then holding his sword to his breast, offered him his life. The Egyptian, frantic with rage, drew his dagger and wounded Zadig at the very instant that the conqueror was granting him mercy. Zadig, outraged, plunged his sword in the bosom of the Egyptian, who, giving a horrible shriek, expired struggling. Zadig then approached the lady and said to her in a gentle tone:

"He forced me to kill him; I have avenged your cause; you are now delivered from the most violent man I ever saw. What further, madam, would you have me do for you?"

"Die, villain," replied she, "die. You have killed my lover. Oh, that I were able to tear out your heart!"

"Why truly, madam," said Zadig, "you had a strange kind of a man for a lover; he beat you with all his might and would have killed me, because you did entreat me to give you assistance."

"I wish he were beating me still," replied the lady, with tears and lamentation. "I well deserved it, for I had given him cause to be jealous. Would to heaven that he was now beating me and that you were in his place."

Zadig, struck with surprise and inflamed with a higher degree of resentment than he had ever felt before, said:

"Beautiful as you are, madam, you deserve that I should beat you in my turn, so perverse are you; but I shall not give myself the trouble."

So saying, he remounted his camel and advanced toward the town. He had proceeded but a few steps, when he turned back at the noise of four Babylonian couriers, who came riding at full gallop. One of them, upon seeing the woman, cried:

"It is the very same; she resembles the description that was given us."

They gave themselves no concern about the dead Egyptian, but instantly seized the lady. She called out to Zadig:

"Help me once more, generous stranger. I ask pardon for having complained of your conduct. Deliver me again, and I will be yours forever."

Zadig was no longer in the humor of fighting for her.

"Apply to another," said he; "you shall not again ensnare me by your wiles."

Besides, he was wounded; his blood was still flowing, and he himself had need of assistance. And the sight of four Babylonians, probably sent by King Moabdar, filled him with apprehension. He therefore hastened toward the village, unable to comprehend why four Babylonian couriers should come to seize this Egyptian woman, but still more astonished at the lady's behavior.

CHAPTER X

SLAVERY

As he entered the Egyptian village, he saw himself surrounded by the people. Everyone cried out:

"This is the man that carried off the beautiful Missouf and assassinated Cletosis."

"Gentlemen," said he, "God preserve me from carrying off your beautiful Missouf; she is too capricious for me. And with regard to Cletosis, I did not assassinate him; I only fought with him in my own defense. He endeavored to kill me, because I humbly interceded for the beautiful Missouf,

whom he beat most unmercifully. I am a stranger, come
to seek refuge in Egypt; and it is not likely that in coming to
implore your protection, I should begin by carrying off a
woman and assassinating a man."

The Egyptians were at that time just and humane. The
people conducted Zadig to the courthouse. They first of all
ordered his wound to be dressed and then examined him
and his servant apart, in order to discover the truth. They
found that Zadig was not an assassin; but as he was guilty
of having killed a man, the law condemned him to be a
slave. His two camels were sold for the benefit of the town; all
the gold he had brought with him was distributed among
the inhabitants; and his person, as well as that of the companion of his journey, was exposed to sale in the market
place. An Arabian merchant, named Setoc, made the purchase; but as the servant was fitter for labor than the master,
he was sold at a higher price. There was no comparison between the two men. Thus Zadig became a slave subordinate
to his own servant. They were linked together by a chain
fastened to their feet, and in this condition they followed
the Arabian merchant to his house. By the way Zadig comforted his servant, and exhorted him to patience; but he
could not help making, according to his usual custom, some
reflections on human life.

"I see," said he, "that the unhappiness of my fate has an
influence on you. Hitherto everything has turned out for me
in a most unaccountable manner. I have been condemned
to pay a fine for having seen the marks of a bitch's feet. I
thought that I should once have been impaled on account
of a griffin. I have been sent to execution for having made
some verses in praise of the King. I have been upon the
point of being strangled because the Queen had yellow ribbons; and now I am a slave with you because a brutal wretch
beat his mistress. Come, let us keep a good heart; all this
perhaps will have an end. The Arabian merchants must

necessarily have slaves; and why not me as well as another, since, as well as another, I am a man? This merchant will not be cruel; he must treat his slaves well, if he expects any advantage from them."

But while he spoke thus, his heart was entirely engrossed by the fate of the Queen of Babylon.

Two days after, the merchant Setoc set out for Arabia Deserta, with his slaves and his camels. His tribe dwelled near the desert of Horeb. The journey was long and painful. Setoc set a much greater value on the servant than the master, because the former was more expert in loading the camels; and all the little marks of distinction were shown to him. A camel having died within two days' journey of Horeb, his burden was divided and laid on the backs of the servants; and Zadig had his share among the rest. Setoc laughed to see all his slaves walking with their bodies inclined. Zadig took the liberty to explain to him the cause and inform him of the laws of balance. The merchant was astonished and began to regard him with other eyes. Zadig, finding he had raised his curiosity, increased it still further by acquainting him with many things that related to his commerce: the specific gravity of metals and commodities under an equal bulk, the properties of several useful animals, and the means of rendering those useful that are not naturally so. At last Setoc began to consider Zadig as a sage and preferred him to his companion, whom he had formerly so much esteemed. He treated him well and had no cause to repent of his kindness.

As soon as Setoc arrived among his own tribe, he demanded the payment of five hundred ounces of silver, which he had lent to a Jew in the presence of two witnesses; but as the witnesses were dead, and the debt could not be proved, the Hebrew appropriated the merchant's money to himself and piously thanked God for putting it in his power to cheat an

Arabian. Setoc imparted this troublesome affair to Zadig, who was now become his adviser.

"In what place," said Zadig, "did you lend the five hundred ounces to this infidel?"

"Upon a large stone," replied the merchant, "that lies near Mount Horeb."

"What is the character of your debtor?" said Zadig.

"That of a knave," returned Setoc.

"But I ask you whether he is hasty or phlegmatic, cautious or imprudent."

"He is, of all bad payers," said Setoc, "the most hasty fellow I ever knew."

"Well," resumed Zadig, "allow me to plead your cause."

In effect, Zadig having summoned the Jew to the tribunal, addressed the judge in the following terms:

"Pillow of the throne of equity, I come to demand of this man, in the name of my master, five hundred ounces of silver, which he refuses to repay."

"Have you any witnesses?" said the judge.

"No, they are dead; but there remains a large stone upon which the money was counted; and if it please your grandeur to order the stone to be sought for, I hope that it will bear witness. The Hebrew and I will tarry here till the stone arrives. I will send for it at my master's expense."

"With all my heart," replied the judge and immediately applied himself to the discussion of other affairs.

When the court was going to break up, the judge said to Zadig:

"Well, friend, is your stone not come yet?"

The Hebrew replied with a smile:

"Your grandeur may stay here till the morrow and after all not see the stone. It is more than six miles from hence, and it would require fifteen men to move it."

"Well," cried Zadig, "did not I say that the stone would

bear witness? Since this man knows where it is, he thereby confesses that it was upon it that the money was counted."

The Hebrew was disconcerted and was soon after obliged to confess the truth. The judge ordered him to be fastened to the stone, without meat or drink, till he should restore the five hundred ounces, which were soon after paid.

The slave Zadig and the stone were held in great repute in Arabia.

CHAPTER XI

THE FUNERAL PILE

SETOC was so delighted that he made his slave his intimate friend. He had now conceived as great an esteem for him as ever the King of Babylon had done; and Zadig was glad that Setoc had no wife. He discovered in his master a good natural disposition, much probity of heart, and a great share of good sense; but he was sorry to see that, according to the ancient custom of Arabia, he adored the host of heaven; that is, the sun, moon, and stars. He sometimes spoke to him on this subject with great prudence and discretion. At last he told him that these bodies were like all other bodies in the universe and no more deserving of our homage than a tree or a rock.

"But," said Setoc, "they are eternal beings, and it is from them we derive all we enjoy. They animate nature; they regulate the seasons; and, besides, are removed at such an immense distance from us, that we cannot help revering them."

"You receive more advantage," replied Zadig, "from the waters of the Red Sea, which carry your merchandise to the

Indies. Why may not it be as ancient as the stars? And if you adore what is placed at a distance from you, you should adore the land of the Gangarides, which lies at the extremity of the earth."

"No," said Setoc, "the brightness of the stars commands our adoration."

At night Zadig lighted up a great number of candles in the tent where he was to sup with Setoc; and the moment his patron appeared, he fell on his knees before these lighted tapers, and said:

"Eternal and shining luminaries! Be you always propitious to me."

Having thus said, he sat down at the table, without taking the least notice of Setoc.

"What are you doing?" said Setoc to him in amazement.

"I act like you," replied Zadig. "I adore these candles and neglect their master and mine."

Setoc comprehended the profound sense of this apologue. The wisdom of his slave sank deep into his soul; he no longer offered incense to the creatures, but adored the Eternal Being who made them.

There prevailed at that time in Arabia a shocking custom, sprung originally from Scythia, and which, being established in the Indies by the authority of the Brahmans, threatened to overrun all the East. When a married man died and his beloved wife aspired to the character of a saint, she burned herself publicly on the body of her husband. This was a solemn feast and was called the Funeral Pile of Widowhood; and that tribe in which most women had been burned was the most respected. An Arabian of Setoc's tribe being dead, his widow, whose name was Almona, and who was very devout, published the day and hour when she intended to throw herself into the fire, amidst the sound of drums and trumpets. Zadig remonstrated against this horrible custom; he showed Setoc how inconsistent it was with the happiness of mankind to suffer young widows to burn themselves every other day, widows who were capable of giving children to the state, or at least of educating those they already had; and he convinced him that it was his duty to do all that lay in his power to abolish such a barbarous practice.

"The women," said Setoc, "have possessed the right of burning themselves for more than a thousand years; and who shall dare to abrogate a law which time has rendered sacred? Is there anything more respectable than ancient abuses?"

"Reason is more ancient," replied Zadig. "Meanwhile, speak to the chiefs of the tribes, and I will go to wait on the young widow."

Accordingly he was introduced to her; and, after having insinuated himself into her good graces by some compliments on her beauty and told her what a pity it was to commit so many charms to the flames, he at last praised her for her constancy and courage.

"You must surely have loved your husband," said he to her, "with the most passionate fondness."

"Who, I?" replied the lady. "I loved him not at all. He was a brutal, jealous, insupportable wretch; but I am firmly resolved to throw myself on his funeral pile."

"It would appear then," said Zadig, "that there must be a very delicious pleasure in being burned alive."

"Oh! It makes Nature shudder," replied the lady, "but that must be overlooked. I am a devotee; I should lose my reputation; and all the world would despise me, if I did not burn myself."

Having made her acknowledge that she was going to burn herself to gain the good opinion of others, and to gratify her own vanity, Zadig entertained her with a long discourse, calculated to make her a little in love with life, and even went so far as to inspire her with some degree of goodwill for the person who spoke to her. . . .

"And what will you do at last," said he, "if the vanity of burning yourself should not continue?"

"Alas!" said the lady. "I believe I should desire you to marry me."

Zadig's mind was too much engrossed with the idea of Astarte not to elude this declaration; but he instantly went to the chiefs of the tribes, told them what had passed and advised them to make a law, by which a widow should not be permitted to burn herself, till she had conversed privately with a young man for the space of an hour. Since that time not a single woman has burned herself in Arabia. They were indebted to Zadig alone for destroying in one day a cruel custom that had lasted for so many ages; and thus he became the benefactor of Arabia.

CHAPTER XII

THE SUPPER

SETOC, who could not separate himself from this man in whom dwelt wisdom, took him to the great fair of Bassora,° where the richest merchants on the earth resorted. Zadig was highly pleased to see so many men of different countries united in the same place. He considered the whole universe as one large family assembled at Bassora. The second day he sat at table with an Egyptian, an Indian, an inhabitant of Cathay, a Greek, a Celt, and several other strangers, who, in their frequent voyages to the Arabian Gulf, had learned

---

° Basra (Iraq).

enough Arabic to make themselves understood. The Egyptian seemed to be in a violent passion.

"What an abominable country is Bassora!" said he. "They refuse me a thousand ounces of gold on the best security in the world."

"How!" said Setoc. "On what security have they refused you this sum?"

"On the body of my aunt," replied the Egyptian. "She was the most notable woman in Egypt; she always accompanied me on my journeys; she died on the road! I have converted her into one of the finest mummies in the world; and, in my own country, I could have as much as I please by giving her as a pledge. It is very strange that they will not here lend me so much as a thousand ounces of gold on such a solid security."

Angry as he was, he was going to help himself to a bit of excellent boiled fowl, when the Indian, taking him by the hand, cried out in a sorrowful tone:

"Ah! What are you going to do?"

"To eat a bit of this fowl," replied the man who owned the mummy.

"Take care that you do not," replied the Indian. "It is possible that the soul of the deceased may have passed into this fowl; and you would not, surely, expose yourself to the danger of eating your aunt? To boil fowls is a manifest outrage on nature."

"What do you mean by your nature and your fowl?" replied the choleric Egyptian. "We adore a bull, and yet we eat heartily of beef."

"You adore a bull! Is it possible?" said the man from the Ganges.

"Nothing is more possible," returned the other. "We have done so for these hundred and thirty-five thousand years; and nobody among us has ever found fault with it."

"A hundred and thirty-five thousand years!" said the Indian. "This account is a little exaggerated; it is but eighty thousand years since India was first peopled, and we are surely more ancient than you. Brahma prohibited our eating of ox flesh before you thought of putting it on your spits or altars."

"This Brahma of yours," said the Egyptian, "is a pleasant sort of an animal truly to compare with our Apis. What great things has your Brahma performed?"

"It was he," replied the Brahmin, "that taught mankind to read and write, and to whom the world is indebted for the game of chess."

"You are mistaken," said a Chaldean who sat near him. "It is to the fish Oannes that we owe these great advantages; and it is just that we should render homage to none but him. All the world will tell you that he is a divine being, with a golden tail and a beautiful human head, and that for three hours every day he left the water to preach on dry land. He had several children who were kings, as everyone knows. I have a picture of him at home, which I worship with becoming reverence. We may eat as much beef as we please; but it is surely a great sin to dress fish for the table. Besides, you are both of an origin too recent and ignoble to dispute with me. The Egyptians reckon only a hundred and thirty-five thousand years, and the Indians but eighty thousand, while we have almanacs of four thousand ages. Believe me; renounce your follies; and I will give to each of you a beautiful picture of Oannes."

The man of Cathay* took up the discourse, and said:

"I have a great respect for the Egyptians, the Chaldeans, the Greeks, the Celtics, Brahma, the bull Apis, and the beautiful fish Oannes; but I could think that Li, or Tien,** as he is commonly called, is superior to all the bulls on the earth

* China.
** Voltaire uses Li or Tien indifferently, for God.

and all the fish in the sea. I shall say nothing of my native
country; it is as large as Egypt, Chaldea, and the Indies put
together. Neither shall I dispute about the antiquity of our
nation, because it is of little consequence whether we are
ancient or not; it is enough if we are happy; but, were it
necessary to speak of almanacs, I could say that all Asia takes
ours and that we had very good ones before arithmetic was
known in Chaldea."

"Ignorant men, as you all are," said the Greek, "do you
not know that Chaos is the father of all and that form and
matter have put the world into its present condition?"

The Greek spoke for a long time, but was at last interrupted by the Celt, who, having drunk pretty deeply while
the rest were disputing, imagined he was now more knowing
than all the others and said with an oath that there were
none but Teutat† and the mistletoe of the oak that were
worth the trouble of a dispute; that, for his own part, he had
always some mistletoe in his pocket; and that the Scythians,
his ancestors, were the only men of merit that had ever appeared in the world; that it was true they had sometimes
eaten human flesh, but that, notwithstanding that circumstance, his nation deserved to be held in great esteem; and
that, in fine, if anyone spoke ill of Teutat, he would teach
him better manners. The quarrel was now become warm, and
Setoc saw the table was going to be stained with blood.
Zadig, who had been silent during the whole dispute, arose
at last. He first addressed himself to the Celt, as the most
furious of all the disputants. He told him that he had reason
on his side and begged a few mistletoes. He then praised the
Greek for his eloquence and softened all their exasperated
spirits. He said but little to the man of Cathay, because he
had been the most reasonable of them all. At last he said:

---

† God of the ancient Gauls.

"You were going, my friends, to quarrel about nothing, for you are all of one mind."

At this word they all cried out together.

"Is it not true," said he to the Celt, "that you adore not this mistletoe, but him that made both the mistletoe and the oak?"

"Most undoubtedly," replied the Celt.

"And you, Mr. Egyptian, do you not revere, in a certain bull, him who gave the bulls?"

"Yes," said the Egyptian.

"The fish Oannes," continued he, "must yield to him who made the sea and the fishes."

"True," said the Chaldean.

"The Indian and the Chinaman," added he, "acknowledge, like you, a first principle. I did not fully comprehend the admirable things that were said by the Greek; but I am sure he will admit a superior being, on whom form and matter depend."

The Greek, whom they all admired, said that Zadig had exactly taken his meaning.

"You are all then," replied Zadig, "of one opinion and have no cause to quarrel."

All the company embraced him.

Setoc, after having sold his commodities at a very high price, returned to his own tribe with his friend Zadig; and the latter learned, upon his arrival, that he had been tried in his absence and was now going to be burned by a slow fire.

CHAPTER XIII

THE RENDEZVOUS

DURING his journey to Bassora, the priests of the stars had resolved to punish him. The precious stones and ornaments of the young widows whom they sent to the funeral pile belonged to them by right; and the least they could now do was to burn Zadig for the ill office he had done them. Accordingly they accused him of entertaining erroneous sentiments of the heavenly host. They gave testimony against him and swore that they had heard him say that the stars did not set in the sea. This horrid blasphemy made the judges tremble. They were ready to tear their garments upon hearing these impious words, and they would certainly have torn them had Zadig had wherewithal to pay them for new ones. But, in the excess of their zeal and indignation, they contented themselves with condemning him to be burned by a slow fire.

Setoc, filled with despair at this unhappy event, employed all his influence to save his friend, but in vain; he was soon obliged to hold his peace. The young widow Almona, who had now conceived a great fondness for life, for which she was obliged to Zadig, resolved to deliver him from the funeral pile, of the abuse of which he had fully convinced her. She revolved the scheme in her own mind, without imparting it to any person whatever. Zadig was to be executed the next day. If she could save him at all, she must do it that very night, and the method taken by this charitable and prudent lady was as follows.

She perfumed herself, she heightened her beauty by the richest and gayest apparel, and she went to demand a private audience of the chief priest of the stars. As soon as she was introduced to the venerable old man, she addressed him in these terms:

"Eldest son of the Great Bear, brother of the Bull, and cousin of the Great Dog" (such were the titles of this pontiff), "I come to confide in you my scruples. I am much afraid that I have committed a heinous crime in not burning myself on the funeral pile of my dear husband; for, indeed, what had I worth preserving? Perishable flesh, you see, that is already entirely withered."

So saying, she drew up her long sleeves of silk and showed her naked arms, which were of an elegant shape and a dazzling whiteness.

"You see," said she, "that these are of little worth."

The priest found in his heart that they were worth a great deal; his eyes said so, and his mouth confirmed it. He swore that he had never in his life seen such beautiful arms.

"Alas!" said the widow, "my arms, perhaps, are not so bad as the rest; but you will confess that my bosom is not worthy of the least regard."

She then revealed the most charming bosom that Nature had ever formed. Compared with it, a rosebud on an apple of ivory would have appeared like madder on the box tree, and the whiteness of new-washed lambs would have seemed of a dusky yellow. Her bosom; her large black eyes, languishing with the gentle luster of a tender fire; her cheeks animated with the finest purple, mixed with the whiteness of the purest milk; her nose, which had no resemblance to the tower of Mount Lebanon; her lips, like two borders of coral, inclosing the finest pearls in the Arabian Sea—all conspired to make the old man believe that he was but twenty years of age. Stammering, he made a tender avowal. Almona, seeing him enflamed, entreated him to pardon Zadig.

"Alas!" said he. "My charming lady, should I grant you his pardon, it would be of no service, as it must necessarily be signed by three others, my brethren."

"Sign it, nevertheless," said Almona.

"With all my heart," said the priest, "on condition that your favors shall be the price of my ready compliance."

"You do me too much honor," said Almona. "Be pleased only to come to my chamber after sunset, and when the bright star of Sheat shall appear in the horizon, you will find me on a rose-colored sofa, and you may then use your servant as you are able."

So saying, she departed with the signature and left the old man full of love and distrust of his own abilities. He employed the rest of the day in bathing; he drank a liquor composed of the cinnamon of Ceylon, and of the precious spices of Tidor and Ternate; and waited with impatience till the star Sheat should make its appearance.

Meanwhile, Almona went to the second pontiff. He assured her that the sun, the moon, and all the luminaries of heaven, were but will-o'-the-wisps in comparison with her charms. She asked the same favor of him, and he proposed to grant it on the same terms. She suffered herself to be overcome and appointed the second pontiff to meet her at the rising of the star Algenib. From there she went to the third and fourth priests, each time taking a signature and making an assignation from star to star. She then sent a message to the judges, entreating them to come to her house on an affair of great importance. They obeyed her summons. She showed them the four names and told them at what price the priests had sold the pardon of Zadig. Each of them arrived at the hour appointed. Each was surprised at finding his brethren there, but still more at seeing the judges, before whom their shame was now manifest. Zadig was saved, and Setoc was so charmed with the ingenuity and address of Almona that he made her his wife.

CHAPTER XIV

THE DANCE

SETOC had to visit the island of Serendib* on business, but the first month of marriage, which is, as everyone knows, the honeymoon, made him incapable either of leaving his wife or of imagining that he ever could leave her; so he begged his friend Zadig to make the journey for him.

"Alas," said Zadig, "must I set an even greater distance between the beautiful Astarte and myself? But to serve my benefactor is a duty."

He consented, wept and took his departure.

He had not long been in the island of Serendib before he was looked upon as a person of extraordinary character. He became arbiter of all the disputes that arose between merchants, the friend of sages and the adviser of that small number of people who accept advice. The King desired to see and hear him; he soon learned Zadig's worth; he grew to have confidence in him and made him his friend. The King's friendship and esteem for him caused a feeling of apprehension in Zadig. Day and night he was filled with memories of the unhappiness which Moabdar's favor had brought upon him.

"The King takes pleasure in me," he would say. "Shall I not be ruined?"

Yet he could not free himself of his Majesty's marks of affection; for it must be admitted that Nabussan, King of

* Ceylon.

178

Serendib, son of Nussanab, son of Nabassun, son of Sanbunas,
was one of the noblest princes in Asia, and when one spoke
with him, it was difficult not to love him.

This great prince was constantly fawned upon, cheated
and robbed. He was a prey to all who would plunder his
treasury. The receiver-general of the island of Serendib set
this example as a matter of course, and the others followed
it faithfully. The King knew of it; he had changed his
treasurer frequently, but he had been unable to alter the
established custom of dividing the King's revenues into un-
equal parts, of which the smaller was always rendered to his
Majesty and the larger to the ministers.

King Nabussan confided his distress to the wise Zadig.

"You who know so many excellent things," he said, "could
you not invent a means of finding me a treasurer who would
not rob me?"

"Certainly," replied Zadig. "I know an infallible way of
finding a man with clean hands."

The King, overjoyed, embraced him and asked how it
could be put into effect.

"You have only," replied Zadig, "to make all who present
themselves for the office of treasurer dance, and the one who
dances most lightly will indubitably be the most honest man."

"You are jesting," said the King. "That is a fine way of
choosing the receiver of my monies. What? You claim that
the man who cuts the best caper will be the most honest and
cleverest financier?"

"I do not claim that he will be the cleverest," replied Zadig,
"but I assure you that he will infallibly be the most honest."

Zadig spoke with such confidence that the King thought he
had some supernatural secret for divining financiers.

"I dislike the supernatural," said Zadig. "I have never
found any enjoyment among people and books with a tendency to the prodigious. If your Majesty will grant me

leave to make the trial I suggest, you will be quite convinced that my secret is the most simple and easiest affair."

Nabussan, King of Serendib, was much more astounded at hearing that the secret was simple than if it had been presented to him as a miracle.

"Very well," he said, "do as you propose."

"Leave me to carry it out," said Zadig, "and you will gain more than you think by this trial."

That very day, he had it publicly announced that all who sought the office of lord high receiver of the revenues of his gracious Majesty Nabussan, son of Nussanab, should present themselves in garments of light silk on the first day of the moon of the Crocodile, in the King's anteroom. They presented themselves to the number of sixty-four. Violinists had been summoned into a room nearby. All was prepared for the dance. But the door of the room was closed, and to enter it, they had to pass along a rather dark little gallery. A hussar came to fetch and introduce each candidate, one after another, by means of this passage, where he was left alone for a few minutes. The King, who had been informed beforehand, had spread out all his treasure in the gallery. When all the claimants had arrived in the chamber, his Majesty commanded that they should dance. Never did men dance more heavily and with less grace. All held their heads down, their backs bent, their hands glued to their sides.

"What scoundrels," said Zadig in a whisper.

Only one of them performed his steps with agility, his head high, his glance bold, his arms outstretched, his body upright, his legs straight.

"Ah, an honest man, a fine fellow," said Zadig.

The King embraced the excellent dancer and declared him treasurer, and all the rest were chastised and fined with the greatest justice in the world, for each, during the time that he had been in the gallery, had filled his pockets and could scarcely walk. The King was distressed at human nature, since among sixty-four dancers there were sixty-three thieves. The dark gallery was named the "Passage of Temptation." In Persia, those sixty-three gentlemen would have been impaled. In other countries, a court of justice would have been inaugurated which would have demanded as restitution three times as much money as was stolen. In another kingdom, they would have been fully justified and the agile dancer dishonored. In Serendib, they were condemned merely to make a contribution to the public treasury, for Nabussan was very indulgent.

He was also ready to recognize merit. He gave Zadig a sum of money considerably larger than any treasurer had ever stolen from the king his master.

Zadig employed it to send couriers to Babylon, who were to inform him of the fate of Astarte. His voice trembled as he gave the command, the blood ebbed back to his heart, his eyes were veiled with darkness and his soul was ready to leave him. The courier departed, Zadig saw him set out on his way, re-entered the presence of the King, and seeing no one, thought he was in his own room and uttered the word "love."

"Ah, love," said the King. "That is exactly the question. You have divined the root of my sorrow. How great a man you are. I hope you will teach me how to recognize a wife who is completely trustworthy, even as you have found me an honest treasurer."

Zadig, recovering his senses, promised to serve him in love as in finance, although the matter appeared to him even more difficult.

CHAPTER XV

THE BLUE EYES

"The body and heart . . ." said the King to Zadig.

At these words, the Babylonian could not forbear from interrupting his Majesty.

"How glad I am," he said, "that you did not say 'The heart and soul'; for in conversation at Babylon one hears nought but these words. There are no books to be seen save those which deal with the heart and the soul, composed by men who possess neither the one nor the other. But pardon me, sire, pray proceed."

Nabussan continued thus:

"The body and heart are in me destined to love. The former of these two masters has every opportunity of satisfaction. I have in my palace one hundred women at my will, all beautiful, obliging, willing to please, voluptuous even, or pretending to be so when they are with me. But my heart is very far from being in so happy a position. I have proved only too well that they shower caresses upon the King of Serendib, but have only too little thought for Nabussan. It is not that I believe my wives to be faithless, but I would wish to find a soul which would be my own. For such a treasure, I would give the hundred beauties whose charms I do possess. See if among the hundred sultanas you can find me one of whose love I may be assured."

Zadig replied as he had done in the matter of the financiers.

"Sire, give me leave to act; but grant first that I may

make use of the treasures you displayed in the Passage of
Temptation. I will render you a good account of them and
you will lose nothing by it."

The King gave him absolute control. He chose out, in
Serendib, thirty-three little hunchbacks, the ugliest he could
find, thirty-three of the handsomest pages, and thirty-three
of the most eloquent and vigorous priests. He gave them
absolute freedom to enter the chamber of the sultanas. Each
little hunchback had four thousand gold pieces to bestow,
and all the hunchbacks were successful the very first day.
The pages who had nothing but themselves to bestow
gained no conquest till the end of two or three days. The
priests had a little more trouble, but at last thirty-three pious
ladies yielded to them. The King saw, and marveled at all
these proofs of affection, through blinds which gave a view
into each chamber. Of his hundred wives, ninety-nine yielded
before his very eyes. There remained one, very young, very
new, whom his Majesty had never approached. One, two,
three hundred hunchbacks were sent to her, who offered
her up to twenty thousand gold pieces. She was incorruptible
and could not restrain her laughter at the idea that the
hunchbacks thought themselves more attractive by the possession of money. The two most goodly pages were presented
to her. She said that she found the King more handsome. The
most eloquent of the priests was let loose upon her, and then
the boldest. The first she found a blusterer, and as for the
second, she did not even deign to suspect him of merit.

"The heart accomplishes all," she said. "I will never yield
to a hunchback's gold, nor to the charms of a young man,
nor to the seductions of a priest. I shall love Nabussan,
son of Nussanab alone, and I shall wait until he deigns to love
me."

The King was beside himself with joy, amazement, and
tenderness. He took back all the money which had brought
about the success of the hunchbacks, and presented it to the

beautiful Falide, for such was the name of the maiden.
He gave her his heart, which she well deserved. Never was
the flower of youth so brilliant, never the charms of beauty so
enchanting. Historical veracity cannot allow me to suppress the fact that her curtseys lacked grace, but she danced
like the fairies, sang like the Sirens and talked liked the
Graces. She was as accomplished as she was virtuous.

Nabussan, knowing himself loved, adored her in turn. But
she had blue eyes, and this was the source of great unhappiness. An ancient law forbade kings to bestow their
affection upon one of these women, whom the Greeks have
since given the name βοῶπις. The chief priest five thousand years before that time had made this ordinance, and
it was in order to have for himself the mistress of the first
king of Serendib that the high priest had caused the denun-
ciation of blue eyes to pass into the laws of the land.

All ranks throughout the kingdom came to expostulate
with Nabussan. In public, men said that the last days of
the kingdom had come, horror was at its zenith and all nature
was threatened with sinister events; in one word, Nabussan,
son of Nussanab, loved two large blue eyes. The hunchbacks,
the financiers, the priests, and the brunettes filled the realm
with their lamentations.

Barbaric tribes dwelling to the north of Serendib took
advantage of this general discontent. They invaded the
territory of the good King Nabussan. He demanded subsidies
from his subjects. The priests who owned half the revenue
of the state were content to lift their hands to Heaven and
refused to put them into their coffers to help the King. They
uttered beautiful prayers to the strains of music and left
the state a prey to the barbarians.

"O my dear Zadig, can you save me yet again from this
most dreadful situation?" cried Nabussan in grief.

"Willingly," replied Zadig. "You will have as much money
from the priests as you wish. Only abandon the defense of

those territories in which their castles are situated and defend only your own."

Nabussan did not fail to carry this into effect. The priests came and flung themselves at the King's feet and begged his aid. The King answered them with beautiful strains of music accompanied by the singing of prayers to Heaven for the preservation of their lands. At last, the priests gave him money and the King concluded the war successfully. Thus Zadig, by his wise and fitting counsel and by his great services, was drawn into an irreconcilable hostility with the most powerful men in the state. The priests and the women with brown eyes vowed to bring about his downfall. The financiers and the hunchbacks gave him no respite. They even succeeded in making the good Nabussan suspect him. "Services rendered oft remain in the anteroom; suspicions enter even to the closet," as Zoroaster says. Every day came fresh accusations; the first is parried, the second grazes, the third wounds, the fourth kills!

Zadig became alarmed, and having successfully completed his friend Setoc's business and dispatched his money to him safely, he thought only of leaving the island and resolved himself to go and seek news of Astarte.

"For," said he to himself, "if I stay in Serendib, the priests will have me impaled. But where? In Egypt I shall be enslaved; in Arabia, burned by all appearances; in Babylon, strangled. Yet I must learn the fate of Astarte. Let us go, and we shall see what my sad destiny still holds in store for me."

CHAPTER XVI

THE ROBBER

Arriving on the frontiers which divide Arabia Petræa from Syria, he passed by a pretty strong castle, from which a party of armed Arabians sallied forth. They instantly surrounded him and cried, "All you have belongs to us, and your person is the property of our master."

Zadig replied by drawing his sword; his servant, who was a man of courage, did the same. They killed the first Arabians that presumed to lay hands on them; and, though the number was redoubled, they were not dismayed, but resolved to perish in the conflict. Two men defended themselves against a multitude, and such a combat could not last long. The master of the castle, whose name was Arbogad, having observed from a window the prodigies of valor performed by Zadig, conceived a high esteem for this heroic stranger. He descended in haste, and went in person to call off his men and deliver the two travelers.

"All that passes over my lands," said he, "belongs to me, as well as what I find upon the lands of others; but you seem to be a man of such undaunted courage that I will exempt you from the common law."

He then conducted Zadig to his castle, ordering his men to treat him well; and in the evening Arbogad supped with him. The lord of the castle was one of those Arabians who are commonly called robbers, but he now and then performed some good actions amid a multitude of bad ones. He robbed with a furious rapacity and granted favors with great

generosity; intrepid in action; affable in company; a debauchee
at table, but gay in his debauchery; and particularly remarkable for his frank and open behavior. He was highly pleased
with Zadig, whose lively conversation lengthened the repast.
At last Arbogad said to him:

"I advise you to enroll yourself under me. You cannot do
better; this is not a bad trade; and you may one day become
what I am at present."

"May I take the liberty of asking you," said Zadig, "how
long you have followed this noble profession?"

"From my most tender youth," replied the lord. "I was
servant to a pretty good-natured Arabian, but could not
endure the hardships of my situation. I was vexed to find that
fate had given me no share of the earth, which equally
belongs to all men. I imparted the cause of my uneasiness to
an old Arabian, who said to me, 'My son, do not despair.
There was once a grain of sand that lamented that it was no
more than a neglected atom in the deserts. At the end of a
few years it became a diamond, and it is now the brightest
ornament in the crown of the King of the Indies.' This discourse made a deep impression on my mind; I was the
grain of sand, and I resolved to become the diamond. I began
by stealing two horses; I soon got a party of companions;
I put myself in a condition to rob small caravans; and thus,
by degrees, I destroyed the difference which had formerly
subsisted between me and other men. I had my share of
the good things of this world and was even recompensed
with interest. I was greatly respected and became the captain
of a band of robbers. I seized this castle by force. The
satrap of Syria had a mind to dispossess me of it, but I was
already too rich to have anything to fear. I gave the
satrap a handsome present, by which means I preserved my
castle and increased my possessions. He even appointed me
treasurer of the tributes which Arabia Petræa pays to the
King of kings. I perform my office of receiver, but dispense

with that of paymaster. The Grand Desterham of Babylon sent a petty satrap in the name of King Moabdar to have me strangled. This man arrived with his orders. I was apprised of all. I caused to be strangled in his presence the four persons he had brought with him to draw the noose, after which I asked him how much his commission of strangling me might be worth. He replied that his fees would amount to above three hundred pieces of gold. I then convinced him that he might gain more by staying with me. I made him an apprentice robber, and he is now one of my best and richest officers. If you will take my advice, your success may be equal to his; never was there a better season for plunder, since King Moabdar is killed and all Babylon thrown into confusion."

"Moabdar killed!" said Zadig. "And what is become of Queen Astarte?"

"I know not," replied Arbogad. "All I know is that Moabdar lost his senses, and was killed, that Babylon is a scene of disorder and bloodshed, that all the empire is laid waste; that there are some fine strokes to be struck yet; and that, for my own part, I have struck some that are admirable."

"But the Queen," said Zadig. "For heaven's sake, know you nothing of the Queen's fate?"

"Yes," replied he, "I have heard something of a prince of Hyrcania. If she was not killed in the tumult, she is probably his concubine, but I am more curious about booty than news. I have taken several women in my excursions, but I keep none of them: I sell them at a high price, when they are beautiful, without inquiring who they are. In commodities of this kind rank makes no difference, and a queen that is ugly will never find a merchant. Perhaps I may have sold Queen Astarte. Perhaps she is dead; but, be it as it may, it is of little consequence to me, and I should imagine of as little to you."

So saying, he drank a large draft, which threw all his

ideas into such confusion that Zadig could obtain no further
information.

Zadig remained for some time without speech, sense, or
motion. Arbogad continued drinking, told stories, constantly
repeated that he was the happiest man in the world and
exhorted Zadig to put himself in the same condition. At last
the soporiferous fumes of the wine lulled him into a gentle
repose. Zadig passed the night in the most violent perturbation.

"What!" said he. "Did the King lose his senses? And is he
killed? I cannot help lamenting his fate. The empire is rent
in pieces. And this robber is happy. O fortune! O destiny!
A robber is happy, and the most beautiful of Nature's works
has perhaps perished in a barbarous manner, or lives in a
state worse than death. O Astarte! What is become of you?"

At daybreak, he questioned all those he met in the castle;
but they were all busy, and he received no answer. During
the night they had made a new capture, and they were now
employed in dividing the spoil. All he could obtain in this
hurry and confusion was an opportunity of departing, which
he immediately embraced, plunged deeper than ever in the
most gloomy and mournful reflections.

Zadig proceeded on his journey with a mind full of disquiet
and perplexity and wholly employed on the unhappy Astarte,
on the King of Babylon, on his faithful friend Cador, on the
happy robber Arbogad, on that capricious woman whom the
Babylonians had seized on the frontiers of Egypt; in a word,
on all the misfortunes and disappointments he had hitherto
suffered.

CHAPTER XVII

THE FISHERMAN

AT a few leagues distance from Arbogad's castle, he came to the banks of a small river, still deploring his fate and considering himself as the most wretched of mankind. He saw a fisherman lying on the brink of the river, scarcely holding, in his weak and feeble hand, a net which he seemed ready to drop, and lifting up his eyes to Heaven.

"I am certainly," said the fisherman, "the most unhappy man in the world. I have been, as all the world admitted, the most famous dealer in cream cheese in Babylon and yet I am ruined. I had the most handsome wife that any man in my station could have, and by her I have been betrayed. I had still left a paltry house, and that I have seen pillaged and destroyed. At last I took refuge in this cottage, where I have no other resource than fishing, and yet I cannot catch a single fish. O my net! No more will I throw you into the water; I will throw myself in your place."

So saying he arose and advanced, in the attitude of a man ready to throw himself into the river and thus to finish his life.

"What!" said Zadig to himself. "Are there men as wretched as I?"

His eagerness to save the fisherman's life was as sudden as this reflection. He ran to him, stopped him and spoke to him with a tender and compassionate air. It is commonly supposed that we are less miserable when we have companions in our misery. This, according to Zoroaster, does not proceed from malice, but necessity. We feel ourselves insensibly drawn to an unhappy person as to one like ourselves. The joy of the happy would be an insult; but two men in distress are like two slender trees, which mutually supporting each other, fortify themselves against the storm.

"Why," said Zadig to the fisherman, "do you sink under your misfortunes?"

"Because," replied he, "I see no means of relief. I was the most considerable man in the village of Derlback, near Babylon, and with the assistance of my wife I made the best cream cheese in the empire. Queen Astarte and the famous minister Zadig were extremely fond of them. I had sent them six hundred cheeses, and one day went to the city to receive my money; but, on my arrival at Babylon, was informed that the Queen and Zadig had disappeared. I ran to the house of the Lord Zadig, whom I had never seen; but found there the interior officers of the Grand Desterham, who being furnished with a royal license were plundering it with great loyalty and order. From there I flew to the Queen's kitchen, some of the lords of which told me that the Queen was dead; some said she was in prison; and others pretended that she had made her escape; but they all agreed in assuring me that I would not be paid for my cheese. I went with my wife to the house of the Lord Orcan, who was one of my customers, and begged his protection in my present distress. He granted it to my wife, but refused it to me. She was whiter than the cream cheeses that began my misfortune, and the luster of the Tyrian purple was not more bright than the carnation which animated this whiteness. For this reason Orcan detained her and drove me from his house. In my despair I wrote a letter to my dear wife. She said to the bearer, 'Oh! Ah! Yes! I know the writer of this a little; I have heard his name mentioned. They say he makes excellent cream cheese. Desire him to send me some, and he shall be paid.'

"In my distress I resolved to apply to justice. I had still

six ounces of gold remaining. I was obliged to give two to the lawyer whom I consulted, two to the procurator who undertook my cause, and two to the secretary of the first judge. When all this was done, my business was not begun; and I had already expended more money than my cheese and my wife were worth. I returned to my own village with the intention of selling my house, in order to enable me to recover my wife.

"My house was well worth sixty ounces of gold; but as my neighbors saw that I was poor and obliged to sell it, the first to whom I applied offered me thirty ounces, the second twenty, and the third ten. Bad as these offers were, I was so blind that I was going to strike a bargain, when a prince of Hyrcania came to Babylon and ravaged all in his way. My house was first sacked and then burned.

"Having thus lost my money, my wife, and my house, I retired into this country, where you now see me. I have endeavored to gain a subsistence by fishing; but the fish make a mock of me as well as the men. I catch none, I die with hunger and had it not been for you, august comforter, I should have perished in the river."

The fisherman was not allowed to give this long account without interruption; at every moment Zadig in his great emotion would say:

"What! Know you nothing of the Queen's fate?"

"No, my lord," replied the fisherman, "but I know that neither the Queen nor Zadig have paid me for my cream cheeses, that I have lost my wife and am now reduced to despair."

"I flatter myself," said Zadig, "that you will not lose all your money. I have heard of this Zadig; he is an honest man; and if he returns to Babylon, as he expects, he will give you more than he owes you. But with regard to your wife, who is not so honest, I advise you not to seek to recover her. Believe me, go to Babylon. I shall be there before you, because I am on horseback and you are on foot. Apply to the illustrious Cador; tell him you have met his friend; wait for me at his house. Go, perhaps you will not always be unhappy."

"O mighty Ormuzd!" continued he. "You employ me to comfort this man. Whom will you employ to give me consolation?"

So saying, he gave the fisherman half the money he had brought from Arabia. The fisherman, struck with surprise, and ravished with joy, kissed the feet of the friend of Cador, and said:

"You are surely an angel sent from heaven to save me!"

Meanwhile Zadig continued to make fresh inquiries, and to shed tears.

"What my lord!" cried the fisherman. "Are you then so unhappy, you who bestow favors?"

"A hundred times more unhappy than you," replied Zadig.

"But how is this possible," said the good man, "that the giver can be more wretched than the receiver?"

"Because," replied Zadig, "your greatest misery arose from poverty, and mine is seated in the heart."

"Did Orcan take your wife from you?" said the fisherman.

This word recalled to Zadig's mind the whole of his adventures. He repeated the catalogue of his misfortunes, beginning with the Queen's bitch and ending with his arrival at the castle of the robber Arbogad.

"Ah!" said he to the fisherman. "Orcan deserves to be punished, but it is commonly such men as those that are the favorites of fortune. However, go to the house of the lord Cador and there wait my arrival."

They then parted: the fisherman walked, thanking Heaven for the happiness of his condition; and Zadig rode, accusing fortune for the hardness of his lot.

CHAPTER XVIII

THE BASILISK

ARRIVING in a beautiful meadow, he there saw several women, who were searching for something intently. He took the liberty to approach one of them and to ask if he might have the honor to assist them in the search.

"Take care that you do not," replied the Syrian. "What we are searching for can be touched only by women."

"Strange," said Zadig. "May I presume to ask you what it is that women only are permitted to touch?"

"It is a basilisk," said she.

"A basilisk, madam! And for what purpose, pray, do you seek for a basilisk?"

"It is for our lord and master Ogul, whose castle you see on the bank of that river, at the end of the meadow. We are his most humble slaves. The lord Ogul is sick. His physician has ordered him to eat a basilisk, stewed in rose water; and as it is a very rare animal, and can only be taken by women, the Ogul has promised to choose for his well-beloved wife the woman that shall bring him a basilisk. Let me go on in my search, for you see what I shall lose if my companions are before me."

Zadig left her and the other Syrians to search for their basilisk and continued to walk in the meadow. When coming to the brink of a small rivulet, he found another lady lying on the grass, but she was not searching for anything. Her person seemed to be majestic, but her face was covered with a veil. She was leaning over the rivulet, and profound sighs

proceeded from her mouth. In her hand she held a small rod
with which she was tracing characters on the fine sand that
lay between the turf and the brook. Zadig had the curiosity
to examine what this woman was writing. He drew near;
he saw the letter Z, then an A; he was astonished. Then
appeared a D; he started. But never was surprise equal to his,
when he saw the two last letters of his name. He stood for
some time immovable. At last breaking silence with a faltering
voice, he said:

"O generous lady! Pardon a stranger, an unfortunate man,
for presuming to ask you by what surprising adventure I here
find the name of Zadig traced out by your divine hand."

At this voice and these words, the lady lifted up the veil
with a trembling hand, looked at Zadig, uttered a cry of
tenderness, surprise, and joy, and sinking under the various
emotions which at once assaulted her soul, fell speechless
into his arms. It was Astarte herself; it was the Queen of
Babylon; it was she whom Zadig adored, and whom he had
reproached himself for adoring; it was she whose misfortunes
he had so deeply lamented, and for whose fate he had been
so anxiously concerned. He was for a moment deprived of the
use of his senses; then when he looked into Astarte's eyes,
which now began to open again with a languor mixed with
embarrassment and tenderness, he cried:

"O you immortal powers, who preside over the fates of
weak mortals, do you indeed restore Astarte to me? At what
a time, in what a place, and in what a condition do I again
behold her?"

He fell on his knees before Astarte and laid his face in
the dust of her feet. The Queen of Babylon raised him up
and made him sit by her side on the brink of the rivulet.
She frequently wiped her eyes, from which the tears continued to flow afresh. She twenty times resumed her discourse, which her sighs as often interrupted. She asked by
what strange accident they were brought together, and

suddenly prevented his answers by other questions. She began the account of her own misfortunes and desired to be told of those of Zadig. At last, both of them having a little composed the tumult of their souls, Zadig acquainted her in a few words by what adventure he was brought into that meadow.

"But, O unhappy and honorable Queen! By what means do I find you in this lonely place, clothed in the habit of a slave and accompanied by other female slaves, who are searching for a basilisk, which, by order of the physician, is to be stewed in rose water?"

"While they are searching for their basilisk," said the fair Astarte, "I will inform you of all I have suffered, for which Heaven has sufficiently recompensed me, by restoring you to my sight. You know that the King, my husband, was vexed to see you the most amiable of mankind and that for this reason he one night resolved to strangle you and poison me. You know how Heaven permitted my little mute to inform me of the orders of his sublime Majesty. Hardly had the faithful Cador obliged you to depart, in obedience to my command, when he ventured to enter my apartment at midnight by a secret passage. He carried me off and conducted me to the temple of Ormuzd, where the magus his brother shut me up in that huge statue, whose base reaches to the foundation of the temple, and whose top rises to the summit of the dome. I was there buried in a manner, but was served by the magus, and supplied with all the necessaries of life. At break of day his Majesty's apothecary entered my chamber with a potion composed of a mixture of henbane, opium, hemlock, black hellebore, and aconite; and another officer went to yours with a bowstring of blue silk. Neither of us was to be found. Cador, the better to deceive the King, pretended to come and accuse us both. He said that you had taken the road to the Indies, and I that to Memphis; on which the King's guards were immediately dispatched in pursuit of us both.

"The couriers who pursued me did not know me. I had hardly ever shown my face to any but you, and to you only in the presence and by the order of my husband. They conducted themselves in the pursuit by the description that had been given them of my person. On the frontiers of Egypt they met with a woman of the same stature as I and possessed perhaps of greater charms. She was weeping and wandering. They made no doubt but that this woman was the Queen of Babylon and accordingly brought her to Moabdar. Their mistake at first threw the King into a violent passion; but having viewed this woman more attentively, he found her extremely handsome and was comforted. She was called Missouf. I have since been informed, that this name in the Egyptian language signifies 'the capricious fair one.' She was so in reality; but she had as much cunning as caprice. She pleased Moabdar and gained such an ascendency over him as to make him choose her for his wife. Her character then began to appear in its true colors. She gave herself up, without scruple, to all the freaks of a wanton imagination. She would have obliged the chief of the magi, who was old and gouty, to dance before her; and on his refusal, she persecuted him with the most unrelenting cruelty. She ordered her master of the horse to make her a pie of sweetmeats. In vain did he represent that he was a pastry cook; he was obliged to make it, and lost his place, because it was baked a little too hard. The post of master of the horse she gave to her dwarf, and that of chancellor to her page. In this manner did she govern Babylon. Everybody regretted the loss of me. The King, who till the moment of his resolving to poison me and strangle you had been a tolerably good kind of man, seemed now to have drowned all his virtues in his immoderate fondness for this capricious fair one. He came to the temple on the great day of the feast held in honor of the Sacred Fire. I saw him implore the gods in behalf of Missouf, at the feet of the statue in which I was enclosed. I raised my voice; I cried out, 'The gods reject the prayers of a king who is now become a tyrant, and who attempted to murder a reasonable wife, in order to marry a woman remarkable for nothing but her folly and extravagance.'

"At these words Moabdar was confounded, and his head became disordered. The oracle I had pronounced and the tyranny of Missouf conspired to deprive him of his judgment, and in a few days his reason entirely forsook him.

"His madness, which seemed to be the judgment of Heaven, was the signal for a revolt. The people rose and ran to arms; and Babylon, which had been so long immersed in idleness and effeminacy, became the theater of a bloody civil war. I was taken from the heart of my statue and placed at the head of a party. Cador flew to Memphis to bring you back to Babylon. The Prince of Hyrcania, informed of these fatal events, returned with his army and made a third party in Chaldea. He attacked the King, who fled before him with his capricious Egyptian. Moabdar died pierced with wounds. Missouf fell into the hands of the conqueror. I myself had the misfortune to be taken by a party of Hyrcanians, who conducted me to their prince's tent, at the very moment that Missouf was brought before him. You will doubtless be pleased to hear that the prince thought me more beautiful than the Egyptian, but you will be sorry to be informed that he designed me for his seraglio. He told me, with a blunt and resolute air, that as soon as he had finished a military expedition, which he was just going to undertake, he would come to me. Judge how great must have been my grief. My ties with Moabdar were already dissolved; I might have been the wife of Zadig; and I was fallen into the hands of a barbarian. I answered him with all the pride which my high rank and noble sentiment could inspire. I had always heard it affirmed that Heaven stamped on persons of my condition a mark of grandeur, which, with a single word or glance, could reduce to the lowliness of the most profound respect, those rash and forward persons who presume to deviate from the rules of politeness. I spoke like a queen, but was treated like a maid-servant. The Hyrcanian, without even deigning to speak to me, told his black eunuch that I was impertinent but that he thought me handsome. He ordered him to take care of me and to put me under the regimen of favorites that, my complexion being improved, I might be the more worthy of his favors, when he should be at leisure to honor me with them. I told him that I would put an end to my life. He replied with a smile that women, he believed, were not so bloodthirsty, and that he was accustomed to such violent expressions; and then left me with the air of a man who had just put another parrot into his aviary. What a state for the first queen of the universe, and, I will say more, for a heart devoted to Zadig!"

At these words Zadig threw himself at her feet and bathed them with tears. Astarte raised him with great tenderness and thus continued her story.

"I now saw myself in the power of a barbarian and rival to the foolish woman with whom I was confined. She gave me an account of her adventures in Egypt. From the description she gave of your person, from the time, from the dromedary on which you were mounted and from every other circumstance, I inferred that Zadig was the man who had fought for her. I doubted not but that you were at Memphis and therefore resolved to repair thither. 'Beautiful Missouf,' said I, 'you are more handsome than I and will please the Prince of Hyrcania much better. Assist me in contriving the means of my escape. You will then reign alone. You will at once make me happy and rid yourself of a rival.' Missouf concerted with me the means of my flight, and I departed secretly with an Egyptian slave-woman.

"As I approached the frontiers of Arabia, a famous robber, named Arbogad, seized me and sold me to some merchants, who brought me to this castle, where the lord Ogul resides.

He brought me without knowing who I was. He is a voluptuary, ambitious of nothing but good living, and thinks that God sent him into the world for no other purpose than to sit at table. He is so extremely corpulent that he is always in danger of suffocation. His physician, who has but little credit with him when he has a good digestion, governs him with a despotic sway when he has eaten too much. He has persuaded him that a basilisk stewed in rose water will effect a complete cure. The lord Ogul has promised his hand to the female slave who brings him a basilisk. You see that I leave them to vie with each other in meriting this honor, and never was I less desirous of finding the basilisk than since Heaven has restored you to my sight."

This account was succeeded by a long conversation between Astarte and Zadig, consisting of everything that their long-suppressed sentiments, their great sufferings, and their mutual love could inspire in hearts most noble and tender; and the genii who preside over love carried their words to the sphere of Venus.

The women returned to Ogul without having found the basilisk. Zadig was introduced to this mighty lord and spoke to him in the following terms:

"May immortal health descend from Heaven to bless all your days! I am a physician. At the first report of your indisposition I flew to your castle and have now brought you a basilisk stewed in rose water. Not that I pretend to marry you. All I ask is the liberty of a Babylonian slave, who has been in your possession for a few days; and, if I should not be so happy as to cure you, magnificent lord Ogul, I consent to remain a slave in her place."

The proposal was accepted. Astarte set out for Babylon with Zadig's servant, promising to send couriers constantly to inform him of all that happened. Their parting was as tender as their meeting. The moments of reunion and of parting are the two greatest of life, as says the great book of Zend. Zadig loved the Queen with as much ardor as he professed, and the Queen loved Zadig more than she acknowledged.

Meanwhile Zadig spoke thus to Ogul:

"My lord, my basilisk is not to be eaten; all its virtue must enter through your pores. I have enclosed it in a little ball, blown up and covered with a fine skin. You must strike this ball with all your might, and I must strike it back for a considerable time; and by observing this regimen for a few days, you will see the effects of my art."

The first day Ogul was out of breath and thought he would have died with fatigue. The second, he was less fatigued and slept better. In eight days he recovered all the strength, all the health, all the agility and cheerfulness of his most agreeable years.

"You have played at ball, and have been temperate," said Zadig. "Know that there is no such thing in Nature as a basilisk; that temperance and exercise are the two great preservatives of health; and that the art of reconciling intemperance and health is as chimerical as the philosopher's stone, judicial astrology, or the theology of the magi."

Ogul's first physician, observing how dangerous this man might prove to the medical art, formed a design, in conjunction with the apothecary, to send Zadig to search for a basilisk in the other world. Thus, after having suffered such a long train of calamities on account of his good actions, he was now upon the point of losing his life for curing a gluttonous lord. He was invited to an excellent dinner and was to have been poisoned in the second course; but, during the first, he happily received a courier from the fair Astarte. He rose from the table and departed.

"When a man is beloved by a beautiful woman," says the great Zoroaster, "he has always the good fortune to extricate himself out of every kind of difficulty."

CHAPTER XIX

THE TOURNAMENT

THE Queen was received at Babylon with all those transports of joy which are ever felt on the return of a beautiful princess who has been involved in calamities. Babylon was now in greater tranquillity. The Prince of Hyrcania had been killed in battle. The victorious Babylonians declared that the Queen should marry the man whom they should choose for their sovereign. They were resolved that the first place in the world, that of being husband to Astarte and King of Babylon, should not depend on cabals and intrigues. They swore to acknowledge for King the man who possessed the greatest valor and the greatest wisdom. Accordingly, at the distance of a few leagues from the city, a spacious place was marked out for the lists surrounded with magnificent amphitheaters. There the combatants were to repair in complete armor. Each of them had a separate apartment behind the amphitheaters, where they were neither to be seen nor known by anyone. Each was to encounter four knights, and those that were so happy as to conquer four were then to engage with one another so that he who remained the last master of the field would be proclaimed conqueror at the games. Four days after, he was to return with the same arms and to explain the enigmas proposed by the magi. If he did not explain the enigmas, he was not King; and the running at the lances was to begin afresh, till a man should be found who was conqueror in both these combats; for they were absolutely determined to have a king possessed of the greatest wisdom and the most invincible courage. The Queen was all the while to be strictly guarded: she was only allowed to be present at the games, and even there she was to be covered with a veil; but was not permitted to speak to any of the competitors that they might neither receive favor, nor suffer injustice.

These particulars Astarte communicated to her lover, hoping that, in order to obtain her, he would show himself possessed of greater courage and wisdom than any other person. Zadig arrived on the banks of the Euphrates on the eve of this great day. He caused his device to be inscribed among those of the combatants, concealing his face and his name, as the law ordained; and then went to rest himself in the apartment that fell to him by lot. His friend Cador, who, after the fruitless search he had made for him in Egypt, had now returned to Babylon, sent to his tent a complete suit of armor, which was a present from the Queen; as also from himself the finest horse in Persia. Zadig perceived that these presents were sent by Astarte; and from this his courage and his love derived new strength and new hope.

The next day, the Queen, being seated under a canopy of jewels, and the amphitheaters filled with all the gentlemen and ladies of rank in Babylon, the combatants appeared in the arena. Each of them came and laid his device at the feet of the Grand Magus. They drew their devices by lot, and that of Zadig was the last. The first who advanced was a certain lord, named Itobad, very rich and very vain, but possessed of little courage, of less skill, and of hardly any judgment at all. His servants had persuaded him that such a man as he ought to be king. He had said in reply, "Such a man as I ought to reign," and thus they had armed him *cap-à-pie*. He wore an armor of gold enameled with green, feathers, and a lance adorned with green ribbons. It was instantly perceived by the manner in which Itobad managed his horse that it was not for such a man as he that Heaven reserved the scepter of Babylon. The first knight that ran

against him threw him out of his saddle; the second laid him
flat on his horse's buttocks, with his legs in the air, and his
arms extended. Itobad recovered himself, but with so bad a
grace, that the whole amphitheater burst out laughing. The
third knight disdained to make use of his lance; but making
a pass at him, took him by the right leg, and wheeling him
half-around, laid him prostrate on the sand. The squires of
the games ran to him laughing and replaced him in his saddle.
The fourth combatant took him by the left leg and tumbled
him down on the other side. He was conducted back with
scornful shouts to his tent, where, according to the law, he
was to pass the night; and as he limped along, with great
difficulty, he said, "What an experience for such a man as
I!"

The other knights acquitted themselves with greater ability
and success. Some of them conquered two combatants; a
few of them vanquished three; but none but Prince Otamus
conquered four. At last Zadig fought in his turn. He successively threw four knights off their saddles, with all the
grace imaginable. It then remained to be seen who should be
conqueror, Otamus or Zadig. The arms of the former were
gold and blue, with a plume of the same color; those of
Zadig were white. The wishes of all the spectators were
divided between the knight in blue and the knight in white.
The Queen, whose heart was in a violent palpitation, offered
prayers to Heaven for the success of the white color.

The two champions made their passes and vaults with so
much agility, they mutually gave and received such dexterous
blows with their lances and sat so firmly in their saddles that
everybody but the Queen wished there might be two kings
in Babylon. At length, their horses being tired, and their
lances broken, Zadig had recourse to this stratagem: he passed
behind the blue prince, sprang upon the buttocks of his
horse, seized him by the middle, threw him on the earth,
placed himself in the saddle, and wheeled around Otamus

as he lay extended on the ground. All the amphitheater cried out, "Victory to the white knight!" Otamus rose in a violent passion and drew his sword. Zadig leaped from his horse with his saber in his hand. Both of them were now on the ground, engaged in a new combat, where strength and agility triumphed by turns. The plumes of their helmets, the studs of their bracelets, and the rings of their armor, were driven to a great distance by the violence of a thousand furious blows. They struck with the point and the edge; to the right, to the left; on the head, on the breast; they retreated; they advanced; they measured swords; they closed; they seized each other; they bent like serpents; they attacked like lions; and the fire every moment flashed from their blows. At last Zadig, having recovered his spirits, stopped, made a feint, leaped upon Otamus, threw him on the ground and disarmed him, and Otamus cried out:

"It is you alone, O white knight, who should reign over Babylon!"

The Queen was now at the height of her joy. The knight in blue armor and the knight in white, were conducted each to his own apartment, as well as all the others, according to the intention of the law. Mutes came to wait upon them and to serve them at table. It may be easily supposed that the Queen's little mute waited upon Zadig. They were then left to themselves to sleep till next morning, at which time the conqueror was to bring his device to the Grand Magus, to compare it with that which he had left and make himself known.

Zadig, though deeply in love, was so much fatigued that he could not help sleeping. Itobad, who lay near him, never closed his eyes. He arose in the night, entered Zadig's apartment, took the white arms and the device and put his own green armor in their place. At break of day, he went boldly to the Grand Magus to declare that so great a man as he was conqueror. This was little expected; however, he was proclaimed while Zadig was still asleep. Astarte, surprised and filled with despair, returned to Babylon. The amphitheater was almost empty when Zadig awoke. He sought for his arms, but could find none but the green armor. With this he was obliged to cover himself, having nothing else near him. Astonished and enraged, he put it on in a furious passion and advanced in this guise.

The people that still remained in the amphitheater and the arena received him with hoots and hisses. They surrounded him and insulted him to his face. Never did man suffer such cruel mortifications. He lost his patience. With his saber he dispersed such of the populace as dared to affront him, but he knew not what course to take. He could not claim the white armor she had sent him, without exposing her; and thus, while she was plunged in grief, he was filled with fury and distraction. He walked on the banks of the Euphrates, fully persuaded that his star had destined him to inevitable misery and revolving in his mind all his misfortunes, from the adventure of the woman who hated one-eyed men, to that of his armor.

"This," said he, "is the consequence of my having slept too long. Had I slept less, I should now have been King of Babylon and in possession of Astarte. Knowledge, virtue, and courage have hitherto served only to make me miserable."

He then let fall some secret murmurings against Providence and was tempted to believe that the world was governed by a cruel destiny, which oppressed the good and prospered knights in green armor. One of his greatest mortifications was his being obliged to wear that green armor which had exposed him to such contumelious treatment. A merchant happening to pass by, he sold it to him for a trifle and bought a gown and a long bonnet. In this garb he proceeded along the banks of the Euphrates, filled with despair and secretly accusing Providence, which thus continued to persecute him.

CHAPTER XX

THE HERMIT

WHILE he was thus sauntering, he met a hermit, whose white and venerable beard hung down to his girdle. He held a book in his hand, which he read with great attention. Zadig stopped and made him a profound obeisance. The hermit returned the compliment with such a noble and engaging air that Zadig had the curiosity to enter into conversation with him. He asked him what book it was that he had been reading.

"It is the book of destinies," said the hermit. "Would you choose to look into it?"

He put the book into the hands of Zadig, who, thoroughly versed as he was in several languages, could not decipher a single character of it. This only redoubled his curiosity.

"You seem," said this good father, "to be in great distress."

"Alas!" replied Zadig. "I have but too much reason."

"If you will permit me to accompany you," resumed the old man, "perhaps I may be of some service to you. I have often poured the balm of consolation into the heart of the unhappy."

Zadig felt himself inspired with respect for the hermit's mien, his beard, and his book. He found, in the course of the conversation, that he was possessed of superior degrees of knowledge. The hermit talked of fate, of justice, of morals, of the chief good, of human weakness, and of virtue and vice, with such a spirited and moving eloquence that Zadig felt himself drawn toward him by an irresistible charm. He

earnestly entreated the favor of his company till their return
to Babylon.

"I ask the same favor of you," said the old man. "Swear to
me by Ormuzd that whatever I do, you will not leave me for
some days."

Zadig swore, and they set out together.

In the evening, the two travelers arrived at a superb
castle. The hermit entreated a hospitable reception for himself
and the young man who accompanied him. The porter, whom
one might have easily mistaken for a great lord, introduced
them with a kind of disdainful civility. He presented them
to a principal domestic, who showed them his master's magnificent apartments. They were admitted to the lower end of the
table, without being honored with the least mark of regard by
the lord of the castle; but they were served, like the rest, with
delicacy and profusion. They were then presented with
water to wash their hands, in a golden basin adorned with
emeralds and rubies. At last they were conducted to bed
in a beautiful apartment; and, in the morning, a domestic
brought each of them a piece of gold, after which they took
their leave and departed.

"The master of the house," said Zadig, as they were pro-
ceeding on the journey, "appears to be a generous man,
though somewhat too proud: he nobly performs the duties of
hospitality."

At that instant he observed that a kind of large pocket,
which the hermit had, was filled and distended. And upon
looking more narrowly, he found that it contained the golden
basin adorned with precious stones, which the hermit had
stolen. He dared not then take any notice of it, but he was
filled with a strange surprise.

About noon, the hermit came to the door of a paltry house,
inhabited by a rich miser, and begged the favor of a
hospitable reception for a few hours. An old servant, in
a tattered garb, received them with a blunt and rude air and

led them into the stable, where he gave them some rotten olives, mouldy bread, and sour beer. The hermit ate and drank with as much seeming satisfaction as he had done the evening before; and then addressing himself to the old servant, who watched them both, to prevent their stealing anything, and rudely pressed them to depart, he gave him the two pieces of gold he had received in the morning and thanked him for his great civility.

"Pray," added he, "allow me to speak to your master."

The servant, filled with astonishment, introduced the two travelers.

"Magnificent lord!" said the hermit, "I cannot but return you my most humble thanks for the noble manner in which you have entertained us. Be pleased to accept of this golden basin as a mark of my gratitude."

The miser started and was ready to fall backward; but the hermit, without giving him time to recover from his surprise, instantly departed with his young fellow-traveler.

"Father," said Zadig, "what is the meaning of all this? You seem to me to be entirely different from other men. You steal a golden basin adorned with precious stones, from a lord who received you magnificently, and give it to a miser who treats you with indignity."

"Son," replied the old man, "this magnificent lord, who receives strangers only from vanity and ostentation, will hereby be rendered more wise; and the miser will learn to practice the duties of hospitality. Be surprised at nothing, but follow me."

Zadig knew not as yet whether he was in company with the most foolish or the most prudent of mankind; but the hermit spoke with such an ascendancy that Zadig, who was moreover bound by his oath, could not refuse to follow him.

In the evening, they arived at a house built with equal elegance and simplicity, where nothing savored either of prodigality or avarice. The master of it was a philosopher, who had retired from the world, and who cultivated virtue and wisdom in peace and yet did not lack humanity. He had chosen to build this country house in which he received strangers with a generosity free from ostentation. He went himself to meet the two travelers, whom he led into a commodious apartment, where he desired them to rest themselves a little. Soon after he came and invited them to a decent and well-ordered repast, during which he spoke with great judgment of the last revolutions in Babylon. He seemed to be strongly attached to the Queen and wished that Zadig had appeared in the lists to dispute the crown.

"But the people," added he, "do not deserve to have such a king as Zadig."

Zadig blushed and felt his griefs redoubled. They agreed, in the course of the conversation, that the things of this world were not always in accord with the wishes of the wise. The hermit still maintained that the ways of Providence were inscrutable and that men were in the wrong to judge of a whole, of which they understood but the smallest part.

They talked of the passions. "Ah," said Zadig, "how fatal are their effects!"

"They are the winds," replied the hermit, "that swell the sails of the ship. It is true, they sometimes sink her, but without them she could not sail at all. The bile makes us sick and choleric, but without the bile we could not live. Everything in this world is dangerous, and yet everything in it is necessary."

The conversation turned on pleasure, and the hermit proved that it was a present bestowed by the deity.

"For," said he, "man cannot give himself either sensations or ideas. He receives all, and pain and pleasure proceed from a foreign cause as well as his being."

Zadig was surprised to see a man, who had been guilty of such extravagant actions, capable of reasoning with so much judgment and propriety. At last, after a conversation equally

entertaining and instructive, the host led back his two guests
to their apartment, blessing Heaven for having sent him two
men possessed of so much wisdom and virtue. He offered them
money, with such an easy and noble air as could not possibly
give any offense. The hermit refused it and said that he must
now take his leave of him, as he proposed to set out for
Babylon before it was light. Their parting was tender. Zadig
especially felt himself filled with esteem and affection for a
man of such an amiable character.

When he and the hermit were alone in their apartment, they
spent a long time in praising their host. At break of day, the
old man awakened his companion.

"We must now depart," said he. "But while all the family
are still asleep, I will leave this man a mark of my esteem and
affection."

So saying, he took a candle and set fire to the house. Zadig,
struck with horror, cried aloud and endeavored to hinder him
from committing such a barbarous action; but the hermit drew
him away by force, and the house was soon in flames. The
hermit, who, with his companion, was already at a considerable distance, looked back to the conflagration with great
tranquillity.

"Thanks be to God," said he. "The house of my dear host is
entirely destroyed! Happy man!"

At these words Zadig was at once tempted to burst out
laughing, to reproach the reverend father, to beat him and to
run away. But he did none of these things; for still subdued by
the powerful ascendancy of the hermit, he followed him, in
spite of himself, to the last stage.

This was at the house of a charitable and virtuous widow,
who had a nephew fourteen years of age, full of charm, and
her only hope. She performed the honors of her house as well
as she could. The next day, she ordered her nephew to accompany the strangers to a bridge, which being lately broken
down, was become extremely dangerous in passing. The young

man walked before them with great alacrity. As they were crossing the bridge, the hermit said to the youth:

"Come, I must show my gratitude to your aunt."

He then took him by the hair and plunged him into the river. The boy sank, appeared again on the surface of the water and was swallowed up by the current.

"O monster! O you most wicked of mankind!" cried Zadig.

"You promised to behave with greater patience," said the hermit, interrupting him. "Know that under the ruins of the house which Providence has set on fire, the master has found an immense treasure. Know that this young man, whose life Providence has shortened, would have assassinated his aunt in the space of a year and you in that of two."

"Who told you so, barbarian?" cried Zadig. "And though you had read this event in your book of destinies, are you permitted to drown a youth who never did you any harm?"

While the Babylonian was thus exclaiming, he observed that the old man had no longer a beard and that his countenance assumed the features and complexion of youth. The hermit's habit disappeared, and four beautiful wings covered a majestic body resplendent with light.

"O sent of Heaven! O divine angel!" cried Zadig, humbly prostrating himself on the ground. "Have you then descended from the Empyrean, to teach a weak mortal to submit to the eternal decrees of Providence?"

"Men," said the angel Jesrad, "judge of all things without knowing anything; and, of all men, you best deserve to be enlightened."

Zadig begged to be permitted to speak.

"I distrust myself," said he, "but may I presume to ask a favor of you to clear up one doubt that still remains in my mind? Would it not have been better to have corrected this youth and made him virtuous than to have drowned him?"

"Had he been virtuous," replied Jesrad, "and enjoyed a longer life, it would have been his fate to be assassinated himself, together with the wife he would have married and the child he would have had by her."

"But why," said Zadig, "is it necessary that there should be crimes and misfortunes and that these misfortunes should fall on the good?"

"The wicked," replied Jesrad, "are always unhappy. They serve to prove and try the small number of the just that are scattered throughout the earth, and there is no evil that is not productive of some good."

"But," said Zadig, "suppose there were nothing but good and no evil at all."

"Then," replied Jesrad, "this earth would be another earth: the chain of events would be ranged in another order and directed by wisdom; but this other order, which would be perfect, can exist only in the eternal abode of the Supreme Being, to which no evil can approach. The Deity has created millions of worlds, among which there is not one that resembles another. This immense variety is the attribute of His immense power. There are not two leaves among the trees of the earth, nor two globes in the unlimited expanse of Heaven, that are exactly similar; and all that you see on the little atom in which you are born, ought to be in its proper time and place, according to the immutable decrees of Him who comprehends all. Men think that this child who has just perished is fallen into the water by chance, and that it is by the same chance that this house is burned. But there is no such thing as chance, all is either trial, or punishment, or reward, or foresight. Remember the fisherman, who thought himself the most wretched of mankind. Ormuzd sent you to change his fate. Cease then, frail mortal, to dispute against what you ought to adore."

"But . . ." said Zadig.

As he pronounced the word "but," the angel took his flight toward the tenth sphere. Zadig on his knees adored Providence and submitted. The angel cried to him from on high:

"Direct your course toward Babylon."

CHAPTER XXI

THE ENIGMAS

ZADIG, as it were entranced, and like a man about whose head the thunder had burst, walked at random. He entered Babylon on the very day when those who had fought at the tournaments were assembled in the grand vestibule of the palace, to explain the enigmas and to answer the questions of the Grand Magus. All the knights were already arrived, except the knight in green armor. As soon as Zadig appeared in the city, the people crowded round him; every eye was fixed on him, every mouth blessed him, and every heart wished him the empire. The envious man saw him pass; he trembled and turned aside; the people conducted him to the place where the assembly was held. The Queen, who was informed of his arrival, became a prey to the most violent agitations of hope and fear. She was devoured with apprehension. She could not comprehend why Zadig was without arms, nor why Itobad wore the white armor. A confused murmur arose at the sight of Zadig. They were equally surprised and charmed to see him, but none but the knights who had fought were permitted to appear in the assembly.

"I have fought as well as the other knights," said Zadig, "but another here wears my arms, and while I wait for the honor of proving the truth of my assertion I demand the liberty of presenting myself to explain the enigmas."

The question was put to the vote, and his reputation for probity was still so deeply impressed in their minds that they admitted him without scruple.

214

The first question proposed by the Grand Magus was:

"What of all things in the world is the longest and the shortest, the swiftest, and the slowest, the most divisible and the most extended, the most neglected and the most regretted, without which nothing can be done, which devours all that is little and gives life to all that is great?"

Itobad was to speak. He replied that so great a man as he did not understand enigmas, and that it was sufficient for him to have conquered by his strength and valor. Some said that the meaning of the enigma was fortune; some, the earth; and others, the light. Zadig said that it was time.

"Nothing," added he, "is longer, since it is the measure of eternity; nothing is shorter, since it is insufficient for the accomplishment of our projects; nothing more slow to him that expects, nothing more rapid to him that enjoys; in greatness it extends to infinity, in smallness it is infinitely divisible; all men neglect it, all regret the loss of it; nothing can be done without it; it consigns to oblivion whatever is unworthy of being transmitted to posterity, and it immortalizes such actions as are truly great."

The assembly acknowledged that Zadig was right.

The next question was: "What is the thing which we receive without thanks, which we enjoy without knowing how, which we give to others when we know not where we are, and which we lose without perceiving it?"

Everyone gave his own explanation. Zadig alone guessed that it was life and explained all the other enigmas with the same facility. Itobad always said that nothing was more easy and that he could have answered them with the same readiness, had he chosen to have given himself the trouble. Questions were then proposed on justice, on the sovereign good and on the art of government. Zadig's answers were judged to be the most solid.

"What a pity is it," said they, "that such a great genius should be so bad a knight!"

"Illustrious lords," said Zadig, "I have had the honor of con-
quering in the tournaments. It is to me that the white armor
belongs. The lord Itobad took possession of it during my sleep.
He probably thought that it would fit him better than the
green. I am now ready to prove in your presence, with my
gown and sword, against all that beautiful white armor which
he took from me, that it is I who have had the honor of con-
quering the brave Otamus."

Itobad accepted the challenge with the greatest confidence.
He never doubted but that, armed as he was with a helmet,
a cuirass, and brassarts, he would obtain an easy victory over a
champion in a cap and a nightgown. Zadig drew his sword,
saluting the Queen, who looked at him with a mixture of fear
and joy. Itobad drew his without saluting anyone. He rushed
upon Zadig, like a man who had nothing to fear; he was ready
to cleave him in two. Zadig knew how to ward off the blows,
opposing the strongest part of his sword to the weakest of that
of his adversary in such a manner that Itobad's sword was
broken. Upon which Zadig, seizing his enemy by the waist,
threw him on the ground; and fixing the point of his sword
at the extremity of his breastplate, he said:

"Suffer yourself to be disarmed, or you are a dead man."

Itobad, always surprised at the disgraces that happened to
such a man as he, was obliged to yield to Zadig, who took from
him with great composure his magnificent helmet, his superb
cuirass, his fine brassarts, his shining cuisses; clothed himself
with them and in this dress ran to throw himself at the feet of
Astarte. Cador easily proved that the armor belonged to Zadig.
He was acknowledged King by the unanimous consent of the
whole nation and especially by that of Astarte, who, after so
many calamities, now tasted the exquisite pleasure of seeing
her lover worthy, in the eyes of all the world, to be her husband. Itobad went home to be called lord in his own house.
Zadig was king, and was happy. He recollected what the angel
Jesrad had said to him. He even remembered the grain of sand

that became a diamond. The Queen and Zadig adored Providence. He left the capricious beauty Missouf to run through the world. He sent in search of the robber Arbogad, to whom he gave an honorable post in his army, promising to advance him to the highest dignities if he behaved like a true warrior, and threatening to hang him if he followed the profession of a robber.

Setoc, with the fair Almona, was called from the heart of Arabia and placed at the head of the commerce of Babylon. Cador was preferred and distinguished according to his great services. He was the friend of the King, and the King was then the only monarch on earth that had a friend. The little mute was not forgotten. A fine house was given to the fisherman, and Orcan was condemned to pay him a large sum of money and to restore him his wife; but the fisherman, who had now become wise, took only the money.

But neither could the beautiful Semira be comforted for having believed that Zadig would be blind of an eye, nor did Azora cease to lament her having attempted to cut off his nose. Their griefs, however, he softened by his presents. The envious man died of rage and shame. The empire enjoyed peace, glory, and plenty. This was the happiest age of the earth; it was governed by love and justice. The people blessed Zadig, and Zadig blessed Heaven.